COVER TO COVER

D. HALE RAMBO

THE PLANAR PAGES

Published by Fiercewood Press
ISBN: 978-1-960123-32-9 (eBook)

ISBN: 978-1-960123-28-2 (Hardback)

ISBN: 978-1-960123-29-9 (Paperback)

*

The Book of Larrakane Art by Rick Hertel

The Planar Page Logos by Grace Lewis

Cover Design by Fantastical Ink

Contents

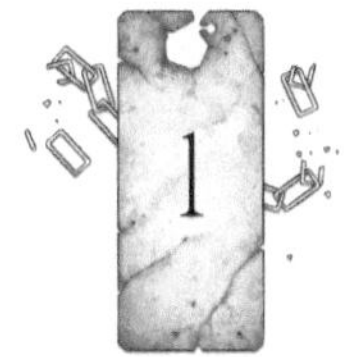

NIGHT DEEPENED, THE SHADOWS nearly engulfing Fiona as she ran down the shoddy paths from the Dani-damaged Rocky Bluff toward the docks below. Stumbling across the planks and through a smattering of buildings, she searched frantically for someone, anyone, who could help her. She was in luck: workers were preparing to head home in the last carriage of the night.

Between breathless words and the tremors emanating from the direction of the Bluff, she requisitioned one of the horses from the carriage. Using her name and saying that she was acquiring it for an emergency with the Travel Guild worked faster than she had imagined. If only she had tried that in better times. But she hadn't ever needed to. Not like now when her literal world was falling apart.

Fiona wished once again that there was a faster way to communicate across the Book than by sending a messenger via horseback. Hoofing it through the cobblestone streets, Fiona shouted, drawing the attention of couriers and opportunity seekers. She tossed them paper, sending them every which way throughout the city, like ants. To the Thread, her home, the church, and more, willing fervently that she was able to gather those who were left together at the Hinge. It was the only place she felt safe enough now without Mac or Nicolosia. Without them what were the Thread or the druids' grove but hollow places? Warm tears slipped down Fiona's face, throat tight and heavy, and she spurred the horse on through the blurry mismatched buildings of her home.

She threw the horse's reins to a surprised young woman at the bottom of the Hinge's marble steps and ran up them two at a time. The usually bustling entryway was almost at a standstill. Guild jackets slumped against the wall or sat heavily on benches, unable to move. Small portions of skin that she could see bore the telltale sign of rocky patches and water swirling on them that meant page turner sickness. Some had fallen unconscious in doorways or where they had stood, not outwardly changed from a quick glance. A few healthy jackets here and there were trying to put order to the chaos, getting the sick moved together and toward the infirmary.

Fiona scanned for familiar faces but, finding none, marched undisturbed toward the private wing of the Hinge and the Binder's office. Stopping and helping would do nothing for the larger problem, though that reasoning didn't ease the ache in her heart.

The wooden door to the Binder's office still held barely visible runes. How long until his removal affected Spine? Fiona threw open the door to find Marcia and Dodger side by side in silence at the Binder's desk. Like her, Dodger hadn't had a change of clothes since they hastily left Kerus and still wore his dirty tunic and leather sandals. Marcia seemed perfectly put together as always, like a noble with a host of servants to prepare her.

They didn't seem on the verge of page turner sickness. But the grim line on Marcia's face told Fiona her news wouldn't shock them.

Without words Fiona threw her arms around Dodger,

hugging him tight. She drew in a deep breath and pulled back before saying, "I have others coming. We don't have much time."

"Where did they go?" Marcia demanded. She mechanically smoothed out her tightly bunned hair. Her form flickered for a moment, but then she was a perfectly dressed, fair-toned human again, ruffled neckline and gray bodice dress all clean and in place.

"I'm not sure." Fiona sat heavily in a chair before them and stared at the Binder's desk and the space he once occupied. The large windows that showed a forest's edge dripped with melting frost. To imagine yesterday she was here thinking of trapping him... "Dani ripped open Spine to leave. It was...unnatural."

"We need to follow as soon as we can." Dodger grimaced. "We can't leave him outside of Spine. Who knows what that will do to him. Mac and Nic can help us find him, right?"

Fiona let her head fall into her hands, turning her face away from his hopeful stare. "Dani took them as well."

Marcia gasped. "All of the Seasons are gone? Then that means Spine is vulnerable."

"Yes, and with only a matter of days before it completely falls apart. Judging by the way the other pages..." Fiona choked up. "...the way the other pages broke." Her home was going to be destroyed. It seemed unfathomable. "How many jackets are down?" She looked to Dodger, but he seemed unable to speak.

Marcia cleared her throat. "All of the Gilded, besides me, and over two-thirds of our force. A lot of our available jackets are the ones who cycle in and out of Spine at pagemarks and the like."

"By Larrakane's grace, what are we going to do?" Dodger

said.

The door opened and Fiona shot out of her chair. Beyond the identically robed Fali and Priestess Raina were Gaili and Mistress Didia Humbledraft. Fiona could've crowed at seeing them upright and healthy. She clasped her arms around Gaili, not caring about wrinkling the bright-blue silk the fawn was wearing, "I'm so thankful you could get here so soon."

"It was a little easier with Mistress Humbledraft." Gaili nodded in the older woman's direction with a curious smile. "She insisted on coming with me, despite the danger, and gave very explicit directions to our driver."

"Yes, well, I don't know how much paper you gave those messengers, but I've never seen someone so happy to do a job in my life. Figured if it was as bad as a couple of weeks ago, you might need my experience again." Didia patted Fiona on the shoulder before squeezing her buxom form past Gaili. Instead of her customary dress like other humans from Rise, she looked like a weary forest traveler. Practical, sturdy black leather boots, a brown woolen tunic, and a deep-green cloak, ready for any sort of travel, swallowed her short form. Didia took Marcia's pale hand in her own and softly said, "Oh, dear."

Marcia swallowed and furtively looked away from the group.

"The Followers are doing just as badly as the jackets appear to be," Fali said, trunk closing the door. "A few had fallen ill in the last week. Before we knew it, most everyone was stuck in bed."

"She poisoned the new tea from the farming district," Fiona announced, making sure they all heard her. "The leaves and the water from the aqueducts that connect to the fountains of Hinge and the church were contaminated by black metal." It had clearly been the same sort of metal that was part of the diving rods from Clara and the airship that the Painted Edge had modified. "Did any of you drink it or water from there lately?"

They nodded in varying degrees, with only Gaili shaking her head.

Fiona rubbed her face. "So it's not all at once then."

"I would guess it's related to the amount you drink. The poison or catalyst acts quicker. But it was clearly a delayed effect," Gaili said.

"Some got sick over the last couple of days, but we thought them to be isolated cases." Marcia dropped Didia's hand and leaned heavily against the desk.

"If only we had known," Dodger said.

"We couldn't have," Marcia said through a tight mouth. "He didn't know, so why would we?"

"The Binder suspected though." Fiona started to pace. "He suspected it was one of the Leaves, while I thought it to be him or…" What was the point in trotting it out? "Regardless, Dani has been the leader. And far, far ahead of us. She says Spine will begin to crumble, starting in the Bluff." Fiona let out a heavy breath. "And I believe her." How were they to find a solution in such a short amount of time and with only a handful of them?

"Why trust her now?" Raina said. "Surely she's just lying so we spin our wheels here trying to stop it."

Fiona shook her head. "She cares about the page turners, the people, all of it. In her eyes, what she's doing is going to set everyone free from Larrakane. From being bound to Spine. From being turners at all." If anyone understood why that couldn't happen, it was Raina and Fali. She took a step toward Raina. "We need to talk to Larrakane. She's the only one who can point us in the right direction."

Raina licked her lips. "We can certainly try, but if the Seasons are gone, I'm not sure what she'll say." She squared her shoulders, sliding her sable hair to the side. "But I'll try."

"You may use the Binder's shrine, in here." Marcia strode to one of the few paintings on the wall, a scenic view of a crystal-blue coastline, and pushed it to the side. Reaching her hand in the wall, she seemed to twist something. A doorway on the opposite side of the office slid open, revealing a small room.

The walls held nothing save for a small profile portrait of a black-furred smilodon dressed in a silvery-white toga. Was this how the Binder saw Larrakane? Odd. Fiona expected something more in line with the fae themselves.

A short table, almost touching the floor, with a ring of candles took up the center. Wide dark cushions lay bereft in front of it. A few crates stacked at one end of the room suggested there may have once been more than what was seen. The smell of ash and fresh incense lingered in the chilly air trapped within the room.

The group gathered around the sparsely decorated shrine. Priestess Raina sat, staring straight ahead at the portrait, before lighting candles east to west.

Fiona watched plaintively and silently. Of all of them, Raina had the best chance at creating a hurried connection to the deity.

The Priestess tilted her head down, eyes closed. Her chest rose once and then stopped.

Fiona frowned. "Is that what it's always like?"

Marcia nodded. "I've only seen the Binder do it once or twice but—"

Raina gasped, drawing a ragged breath, and fell back against the floor.

Fiona crouched, grabbing her hand to help her back up. It wasn't a good sign that she was returned to them so quickly. "Take it easy."

The Priestess struggled. "I can't. She's not." Raina rubbed her flushed face. She looked so young in this state, as if the layers of prestige and responsibility had been ripped away. "There seems to be a block of some kind. I couldn't get through to her."

Grasping on to her arm, Fiona helped Raina to her feet. Silence permeated the small space. Blank and concerned faces stared at Fiona. Without the Seasons or Larrakane to guide them, they were at a loss. Well, her faith in the powers that be were always slim. Fiona pursed her lips. "Then we'll have to determine our direction for ourselves."

Raina wiped her hands together, seemingly more composed. She glanced to the other faces about the room. "I think it's time we had this conversation a little more privately."

"We're *all* here to help." Mistress Humbledraft adjusted the glasses on her stern face. "There was a time you would've asked for it, Raina, instead of pushing it away."

"I'm not at liberty to divulge information anymore, Didia." Priestess Raina's posture stiffened. "Or have you forgotten?"

"No, Didia's right," Fiona said, moving between them. "It's high time we make use of the knowledge we have. Together."

"We are bound to her, and that comes before everything," Raina whispered hotly.

How to make the Priestess change her mind and let the others in? Fiona couldn't do any of this alone and she needed the remaining Leaves of Spine with her. If they opposed her, it would waste time. "Larrakane's secrets mean nothing if we can't even save ourselves. And in the end, we *are* her Priestess. Or do you no longer believe in your own words?"

Priestess Raina's mouth opened; her eyes widened before she nodded.

Fiona pushed ahead before anyone else could disagree with her: "We are short on time, on people, and even Larrakane can't help us. It's us or nothing." She took a deep breath. "Raina and Fali are protectors of Spine, as were the Circle of Seasons. They each had a task, given to them by Larrakane over the years. Raina and Fali took their posts from others and kept Larrakane's name alive and active. Mac took care of us turners, emotionally it seems. The Binder trained some into an army. The Elder druid aided the Guardians of the pages. And Dani made sure we could survive here, growing food where none could without her." She pushed errant curls back from her grimy face. "I tell you this to show that each of them has been an integral part of this city. Of us. Without the Seasons, Spine—a part of Larrakane herself—will break like the other pages. I know Dani, Autumn Monarch for the uninitiated, is getting her power from a *creature* who has threatened the Book before. And I know this because the Guardian of Rise and Larrakane told me."

Without preamble Fiona quickly told them about Richard, his role, and who he suggested he was guarding against. She tried not to use the words that had pained her when she wrote them in her notebook with him but instead insinuated the relationship. Though pressed, she wouldn't name the entity, being clear that she believed Larrakane when the deity said giving it a name would give it power. Though she tried to keep her voice from trembling, she wondered—not for the first time—if Richard was safe and when she would see him again.

As soon as they made a plan, she would write to him, warn him as best she could.

"You didn't mention Richard before," Raina said in a raised voice.

"Which is why I'm saying it now. Let's have no more secrets. They aren't helping. Knowing that this creature exists and what the Painted Edge have been doing means we know how Dani is trying to free everyone. She's trying to get this creature to overpower Larrakane so that she and the other Painted Edge can be unbound as page turners. If we know where the creature is, we can stop her."

"We should be going after the Seasons," Dodger said. "We need them."

Fiona rubbed the ends of her scarf. "We don't know where they are. I saw ice and stone when she tore the page, but that tells me nothing. There was howling, too, but from what...? I don't know what could make that sound. For all we know, she's hidden them somewhere in the depths of the dark edge."

"Perhaps that's where the entity is, too," Gaili piped up.

"What makes you think that?" Didia asked.

"Where else would something so powerful be locked away? And no one to encounter it?" Gaili said.

Page turners were always warned never to venture into the dark edge. Was it more for secrets than protection or a combination of both? "It's a possibility. But we've barely touched moving through the dark edge. And if we risk ourselves trying to get there and neither the Seasons nor this creature is there, who will go after Dani?" Fiona said.

"We can ask Stella," Marcia said quietly. She cleared her throat and looked around. "Secrets don't help, right? Well, secrets are sort of my thing. But..." She gazed at Dodger, holding his stare for a moment. "Things are changing anyways. Might as well go with it." She took his paw and held it before turning back to the group. "Stella has been talking to me. Through the dark edge. She's been…" She trailed off, trying to regain her composure.

Dodger pulled her hand to his chest and cupped it with his own. "Trust me," he said softly.

Marcia nodded and took a deep breath. "She's been asking me to get her out. I'm not able to respond. I've tried and tried. But if we can communicate with Stella, get her, then we can get more information. Of everyone, she probably knew Dani's full plan."

Communicating through the dark edge? How was Stella able to manage that? Fiona looked around, but everyone seemed to be watching her. Without knowing it she had been giving orders, and now they were looking for their next one. What else could they do? It was somewhere to start at least. And they could put what little reinforcements they had into action while they did it. "It's a plan. Marcia, you continue trying to contact Stella and—"

"You have to do it," Marcia said, breaking away from Dodger. "I've tried but I've never touched the dark edge. Perhaps it's my nature." She glanced back at Dodger, and her shoulders slumped as if just couldn't hold them up anymore. "Holding one shape for so long takes a strain on me, but I think my ability to be mutable won't willingly let me in. You have to do it. You're the only other person who knows her. And you've done it twice before."

But they had been accidents. Split-second decisions. Could she truly do it again? Fiona tugged on her scarf. "Fine, I will. While I do, you and Dodger get what reinforcements you can to check in on the Guardians. Be specific and be clear. If the Painted Edge get remaining pieces of the keystones, then I fear they'll have what they need to complete Dani's plan." To break the Book and free page turners, did she have to give the pieces to the creature? All the pages needed to be warned. Fiona whirled around to Fali. "You too. I need you to start telling those Followers who can leave Spine to get to the other pages and send word. If anyone runs into the Painted Edge, they must do whatever is necessary to stop them."

Raina strode forward. "I'll tell them."

Fiona shook her head. "We need you here. Because if something happens to me, you're going to have to take over. This is headquarters now, Priestess, for a variety of reasons, which I don't think I have to explain to you." Fiona stood taller. She knew Raina was keeping quiet, still not divulging everything she knew.

Raina blinked but dropped her arms. "This place is still warded."

Fiona nodded, but before she could say something else, Raina said, "You thought me a traitor just yesterday, Fiona. Sending my Followers on a wild-goose chase to those Kerus pyramids."

"It wasn't wild." It had been necessary. It could have been the Binder or Raina. She needed proof that it wasn't. Fiona didn't think the Priestess was a traitor any longer, but that didn't mean she was an open book.

"It certainly seemed so. There was nothing there besides an old lodging. Home to some lovebirds at one point, no doubt."

Fiona frowned thinking of Richard's stay in the Forlorn Tower. "How did they determine that? It could've been the Guardian."

"It was not." She stiffened. "You wasted my and my people's time when we could've been here, protecting Spine. Protecting the Seasons. I will not forgive you so easily for that."

For once, Fiona missed the cold air that used to permeate the room. Her skin heated at Raina's words. But she couldn't take it back and she couldn't beg for forgiveness. Not with Raina. She would take it as weakness and take over. "I had to do what I thought was best. There was a traitor, and it could've been any of you. You all have secrets." She raised her chin. "Or was your letter writing to Hawkport and your thirst for Forlorn Tower simply a coincidence?"

Raina's mouth gaped open and she stuttered, "I-I wanted to get that island under control for Larrakane. It was important, clearly."

"How did you even know about it?"

Raina glanced away. "It was in Eleanor's memories."

Fiona shook her head. "And yet you said nothing about it to the other Leaves. You acted solely on your own. Giving information to a worthless nobleman that the island was more important than even he knew. So no, Priestess, I'm not asking for your pardon. I'm asking for your cooperation. For the Book's sake."

Her cheeks reddened. "So be it."

For now, that was enough. Fiona glanced at Dodger. "The Hinge pagemark to Rise, where is it?"

"Down the hall. I'll take you." Dodger pulled his arms slowly away from Marcia. He kissed her cheek before striding to the office door.

"I'm coming too," Gaili said lightly. She grabbed her satchel in one swift movement. "No one should attempt that darkness alone."

Fiona warmed at the confident faun but shook her head. "I can't ask you to do that."

"You're not." The faun smiled before clopping out into the hallway.

Didia bounced into the chair next to a fuming Raina. She gave Fiona a thumbs-up behind the woman's back.

Smothering a curious remark, Fiona darted away before Raina noticed. She wasn't sure of Didia's relationship to the Priestess, but it seemed complicated at best. Perhaps she'd be able to keep her reasonable. The older turner certainly had a way with Marcia.

"Wait." Marcia hurriedly followed her out. She linked her arm in Fiona's and pulled her away from the others. She whispered, "Stella will only believe you talked to me if you can prove it. Take notice." She glanced up and down the hallway before sighing, as if she had sunk into a comfortable chair after a long day.

Her form rippled. Peach skin deepened into short copper fur, almost like a smilodon but not quite as groomed. The amber glow of the torches cascaded fractals of light from the sheen of her. Even though she shrank a few inches until she was at Fiona's waist, vivid, wide sapphire eyes never shifted from Fiona's. A string of unique geometrical silver tattoos, not unlike the Binder's, adorned each corner of her heart-shaped face. "Describe me. And tell her, 'There is no cold nor dark powerful enough that Alina wouldn't give everything to find your way. Even her shoes.' But only say my name once." She squeezed Fiona's arm before stepping away.

"Thank you," Fiona said quickly.

Marcia stopped, her softened face crinkled in confusion. "For what?"

"Trusting me."

With a slight smirk more reminiscent of Stella than she probably knew, Marcia said, "Same." She strode off into the building, her form rippling back into her gray bodice dress and human visage.

Through eerily silent echoing stone corridors with well-marked signs, Fiona and Gaili followed Dodger to a cordoned-off area. The wide-open space had a tall ceiling that went all the way up to the Hinge roof. Etched markings on the floor indicated the same floating island symbol that often graced the banners flying at Travel Guild booths to denote safe pagemarks to Rise. In a wardrobe near the entrance were Guild-stamped ornithopters and a big sack of coffee beans—quick to use as a bookmark to the human page should a turner forget their own personal one.

"I'm going to try and turn to Rise but, instead of completing it, stay in the turn. I think it'll give me the best chance of encountering the dark edge." Fiona tugged one of the shiny metal bottle-laden 'thopters off the shelf and began clipping it on her back. Better to have it and not need to use it than to fall from the sky if the page turn was successful.

Dodger grabbed the straps, easing it on her back. "But what if you get stuck in the dark edge?"

"We'll be here to pull her back," Gaili said lightly. She pulled another ornithopter from the shelf and began putting it on. "I'll stay just outside the ring, but be ready to grab Fi if something looks amiss."

"That's too risky." He rubbed his face. "Interfering with a turn could be just as dangerous as trying to stay in one too long. You know the training."

"What else can we do?" Gaili grasped Fiona's arm. "You

know she'd jump into the fire for us."

He sighed and pulled Fiona into a warm hug before she could respond. "Don't do anything that could get you lost please. And if you see this dangerous creature or something even worse, don't engage. Remember, you're not alone in this fight."

Gratitude, surprise, and warmth mixed and filled Fiona like one of Mac's beloved cocktails. "I don't think I deserve you two."

"Remember that when the tab comes up at the Thread." Dodger's whiskers twitched. "What else are close friends for, eh? The treacherous jobs."

"And a few helping hands now and again." Gaili gave her a bright golden grin. "We're right here."

"Thank you." Fiona brushed the wetness from her eyes. As often as she liked to feel resilient against all odds, she did have to admit they were stacking up quite a bit lately. But the dark edge wasn't insurmountable. Not with these two behind her. She squared her shoulders and strode into the marked ring. With a deep breath and long exhale, she dipped her fingers into the lace pocket of her scarf but changed her mind. It wouldn't do to use Richard's journal as a bookmark. It might be too strong a connection. Instead, she thought of her old wooden spoon and let her fingers linger on it, not removing it from her scarf. One breath in, one breath out.

With a focus on the familiarity of people, she connected first to the mortal chapter. She lingered there, feeling the edges of the thrum that connected her to so many lives. They had been trained not to linger in the turn, but here she was, once again, flaunting the rules. She had often wondered why page turners were taught the way they were, but time had carried on and she had forgotten the curiosity in many other, larger, curiosities that she came across over the years. Distracted, she let her thoughts linger only briefly on the floating islands and the smell of fresh-sheared wool of Rise. Fiona took a step forward, and before she could connect to the page itself, she thought of Stella. She thought of coldness and inky star-filled essences. She let her hand drop from the spoon and connected to the vast void of the dark edge.

LIGHTS, BRIGHT PINPOINTS LIKE stars, encompassed her. The darkness she had expected swung on the edge of her vision like a boat barely tethered to the dock. She closed her eyes from the blinding light, but it had no effect. Eyes back open then.

Fiona clutched her scarf, shivering in the cold. She took a deep breath. Then another, trying to quell her churning stomach. Another inhale and she looked around, more confidently now, for glimpses of where she was. There was no more ground beneath her nor ceiling above her. Floating, unmoored. She tried not to wince.

Distant voices began to whisper her name as the lights faded off and then on. Should she answer them or push them away? The familiarity of questioning made her pause, and in that pause the glowing dimmed. Some control then. Perhaps it wasn't confidence or surety that made the space easier but uncertainty.

Well, she was certainly uncertain.

Floating through the slow blinking lights, she turned. The stars turned around with her.

"Stella?" she called out. Expecting her voice to echo, Fiona was a bit unnerved when it fell abruptly. She rubbed her velvet-covered arms. They were warm. Then where was the coldness coming from? "Stella, I'm here. Marcia sent me. She can't come through."

Voices, unfamiliar and discordant, rang out. Some her name, others her words repeated back to her. The loudest came from above. She glanced up and found herself drifting in that direction as if she had laid back in the sea and was being washed farther out from shore. Fiona let her arms dangle beneath her as she ebbed among the stars. She could get lost here. It was a deep internal recognition. But she didn't feel as if she didn't belong. How to get Stella, however, was curious. Perhaps if she said her name thrice, like when alerting her sister, it would work for her. "Stella, where are you?"

A hand grabbed her, warm and tight, jerking her floating to a halt. "I thought you were never going to figure it out," Stella's familiar voice said beneath her.

Fiona tried to turn and face the hag, but the stars and Stella turned with her. "Well, I did eventually. Why can't I face you?"

"You want it too much." She dropped Fiona's hand and then appeared above her, looking down on her. A soft radiance encased her whole body, showing her naked hag form. Her copper fur was ruffled and tufts stuck up at odd angles. Narrow turquoise eyes assessed Fiona. "I find it's easier to go where you want to go by not wanting to go there."

"Sounds chaotic."

Stella snorted. "I didn't make this place." She crossed her arms. "Come to save me out of the goodness of your heart?"

The hag seemed off. Was this Stella? Or something, someone else? The best way to find out was to get her to react.

"No," Fiona said shortly.

For a brief moment her eyes widened. But then Stella's form rippled and she was back to seeming neutral, calm, and confident.

The sisters were so much alike. Fiona sighed at the realization. "Stella, you don't need to pretend. Marcia is a wreck with you being here. She hates that she can't respond to you. Get to you. You're not faring much better, are you?"

Stella rolled her eyes. "If you're not here to retrieve me, what do you want?"

"Spine is breaking. Dani is winning. But we need to know what her end game is. How does she get her freedom this way? Marcia is asking you through me. Please tell us."

"And how do I know she truly sent you?" Stella pulled away from Fiona, increasing the distance between them. The glow swirling around her brightened as the distance grew.

Where was she going? Fiona tried to move closer but instead found herself sinking farther away. She stopped and called out, "She has silver squares at the corner of her eyes. And like you, copper fur, though her eyes are a deeper blue than yours." Fiona hesitated. A name was a powerful thing. She would only be able to say it once. She cupped her hands around her mouth. "There is no cold nor dark powerful enough that Alina wouldn't give everything to find your way. Even her shoes."

Stella's form burst into radiant silvery light.

Fiona winced. "Stella!" But when she blinked, the darkness pervaded in again and Stella was nowhere to be seen.

Her softened voice rose behind Fiona. "Trust the oldest to remember the most."

Trying to focus on anything but wanting to see Stella's face, Fiona drifted unintentionally and found herself facing the hag. The glowing that had encased her body was gone again. Stella stared away from her into the darkness unmoving.

"Are you alright? What happened?" Fiona asked.

"It was nothing." She crossed her arms again and said brightly, "What are your questions?"

The hag was closed off once again. As much as she wanted to argue, Fiona had to focus on the bigger picture. "You know Dani best. Where is she going?"

Stella bit her lip and then swallowed hard. "If I tell you, will you find a way to bring me back?"

"I'll bring you back right now." She was all for conversing like civilized beings in the marble halls of the Hinge.

Stella said in a thick voice, "It won't work. Edge turners have already tried and—well, we only did that once to know it shouldn't be attempted again."

"I'm sorry."

"Should you be?" Stella nodded. "I suppose. But it's my own nature that keeps me here. Not letting me pass on or come back." She scrubbed a hand over her face. "I have not always been my best ally."

The whiplash of confidence to vulnerable honesty confused Fiona. Whatever was happening to Stella in the dark edge must have been worse than she was letting on.

"Of course, I will help you come back."

"Promise."

"Isn't there a saying about making promises with faekin and all that?"

Stella smiled, the first semblance of her old self. "Habits are hard to break." Her form glimmered, soft gray light encasing her once again. She tilted her head. "Do you still have my knife?"

Why would she be bringing the pearl-handled knife up now? Besides being able to cut through everything and disturbing future visions, it had not proved to do much of anything else under Gaili's administrations. She rubbed the velvet pocket of her scarf where she kept it. "I do."

"I can always count on you do-gooders to keep up your end of a bargain." She rubbed the back of her neck. "I promise I will tell you all that I know while I can if you help me leave the dark edge." Her nervous energy was palpable but there were no games, no barely contained smirk.

"I promise to help you leave the dark edge."

The hag locked cloudy eyes with her. "Tell my sister that Dani plans to release the Forgotten One." The glow around her shifted abruptly from soft gray to inky blue.

Fiona's skin tingled. "How is that possible?"

"Through cunning and cleverness, of course." Stella sighed as if inconvenienced but floated close to Fiona.

They were inches apart. The dripping blue light from Stella washed across Fiona and she shivered.

Stella lowered her voice, an edge of fear creeping into it. "We wanted to go home. But there will be *no home* if she succeeds. Do you understand? I can only say this once."

Fiona slowly nodded. "She needs pieces of the pages to do it?"

"Specific locks take specific tools." Stella stared at Fiona unblinking and whispered rapidly, "The chains that bind are also the chains that separate. The every essence of one is the essence of everyone."

"Why are you speaking in riddles?"

"There is no other way." Stella gave a shrug. Its affectation was smooth, but her contorted face spoke of frustration. The blue light began to grow brighter. "You must understand. You've been there yourself."

Of course. She was bonded to Daniele. She could only say so

much without breaking that bond. Well then, it would be up to Fiona and the others to solve the riddles to move forward. Fiona licked her lips at the growing brightness but remained close. "Did she have a plan to get all these tools?"

"Of course. Ask better questions," Stella commanded. The brightness increased.

Fiona closed her eyes to steel herself from the brilliance for a moment. What would help them most right now? "What pages hasn't she gotten what she needs from?"

"Good one. In theory, there are three. The only way is through, however."

In theory? Coldness seeped into Fiona but then dissipated quickly. She opened her eyes to see Stella, a blue beacon among a backdrop of white stars in the inky void drifting away from her. Was she trying to keep her light from Fiona?

Stella snapped her fingers, the sound echoing. "Focus. We only have a moment more."

"Is the Forgotten One in the dark edge?" Fiona called out. Her voice thudded abruptly, like dropping from the sky.

"Links that weaken strengthen edges." She pointed past Fiona before an explosion of light rippled from her.

Turning toward where Stella pointed, a looming figure in the inky distance filled her vision. Cold dripping, like a plunge in the Depths, rushed through Fiona's chest. With a soundless gasp she keeled over, rubbing her chest. Her arms. Her legs. The cold covered her entire body in moments and no amount of soothing could stamp it out.

She cried out and tried to move away from the figure. Her betraying body moved closer without her command. Couldn't get closer. Shouldn't. Fiona focused on the figure once more and her body drifted farther away. But the distance did nothing to ease the chill that washed through her. It barely distracted her from the brush of biting solid metal that rubbed against her hand. She jerked back, but the black curved chain that swung at her slithered around her legs and tightened.

Warm arms wrapped around Fiona, a fiercely gripping hug, and ripped her from the curve of the chain. And then there was light.

She blinked in the abrupt change from darkest night to bright gray glimmerings surrounding her.

They dimmed as familiar hands brushed her arms and shoulders, as if wiping snow off them. "You scamp. Always running off into adventure, aren't you?"

She looked up into the big, soft eyes of her father. He was a tall man, that she remembered. His dark-brown skin glowed with a hazy gray light. She had grown. How could he still be so tall to her?

He gently pulled her into a hug. "Didn't I say it wasn't your time in the dark yet? Why do you persist on coming here?"

"I thought—I mean, I needed to speak with someone," Fiona said uncertainly. "Why are you here?"

"I'm resting." He chuckled loudly. "That is, until your mother gets here. Can't leave her to travel by herself, you know. All that flying. She'd never make it to the other side."

Fiona shook her head, a heaviness settling in. "I'm sorry, Papa, I don't understand."

He rubbed her back comfortingly. "Never you mind. Go home. Be safe."

It sounded like the right thing to do. What was she doing running out in the snow anyways? She hated being cold. But there was something she needed, something she wanted to know before she left. Fiona's feeble fingers grasped the scarf about her neck. Its varying textures and lingering heat wrapped around her helped her focus. "Can you see the man? The Forgotten One?"

Her father frowned. "Stay away from him, Fiona. He's the kind of power that's nothing but trouble."

"We have to stop him." Fiona grabbed her father's hand and squeezed it. "Please."

His face softened and he sighed. He tugged on the edges of her scarf, a familiar pull. "Only for a moment. But then you go back inside with her, you hear?"

She nodded.

Deftly he pulled the scarf from her shoulders. A cold chill wafted over her as it hung on his forearm. He swept his hand toward the distance. In the dim darkness amid blinking stars, a broad purple-gray light churned, swirling and pushing against a writhing red-blue storm—two halves fighting across slivers of bright wobbling colors, like sorted skeins of embroidery thread. Squinting to get a better look, Fiona felt herself being pulled closer to the storm, but her father's hand quickly grasped her arm, holding her back.

Movement caught her eye as black metal chains whipped past her into the horizon. She ducked out of reflex and saw that many chains spiraled and pulled across the inky darkness. Some strained, taut. Others cracked or broke apart as flecks of metal shattered and faded out into the darkness and down into the filed colors. When she glanced back at the warring lights, unmistakable figures were centered in them. Larrakane, her tight curls flowing out behind her as she stood tall against a red-robed man. His reddish-gold beard was long and unkempt. Tendrils of flaming hair swirled wildly behind him as his focus remained on Larrakane. They seemed unmoving, unflinching in the torrent that surrounded them and pushed against one another. Fiona stared, trying to comprehend the scene in front of her. Was it her imagination or reality filtered through her eyes? But no, he looked so much like Richard. The resemblance was uncanny.

The red-robed man's attention snapped to her, his golden eyes meeting hers.

In his moment of distraction, cascading gray droplets flung out at him from Larrakane. The deity hadn't seemed to move, but the pained look on his face made it apparent she had made her mark.

Fiona's father reared back, groaning as well.

Fiona turned away from the warring duo and grabbed on to him. "No!"

He rubbed her shoulder, face grimacing. "It's alright. It was an accident."

Fiona clenched her fists, feeling like a little girl again full of anger and frustration. She whirled around to face the deity but her father stopped her.

"She's not a perfect power, that one, but she's got the right of it." He draped the scarf around Fiona's shoulders, and warmth settled across her again. Comfort and confidence in one soft brush of his hand across her back. "Now stay inside with her," he commanded.

With a gentle shove propelling her, Fiona stumbled a step. Then another before she tumbled to the rough stone floor of the Hinge. She took a shaky breath as furry paws grabbed her hands to help her up.

"I've got you," Dodger said.

"Take this." Gaili handed her a cool, heavy mug.

Fiona drank the water happily, only wishing it was

something stronger when she had finished. She rubbed her face, trying to parse all she had seen and heard, the heaviness in her head still lingering. Stella was right. They only had a moment. She had a lot to say and a short time to say it in.

ABLE-BODIED JACKETS HURRIEDLY SALUTED Dodger as they ran through the hallways. Gaili said she'd been in the dark edge for less than an hour. But the tiredness from the full day ate at the corners of her thoughts. She moved slower than her friends but waved away their concern. Once a plan was in place, she could rest her eyes for a few minutes.

Fali was no longer at the Binder's office, having rushed to the temple. Marcia stood beside the Binder's empty chair, deep in his books. The late-night sky didn't yet show embers of dawn. Didia and Raina jumped up from their seats upon seeing Fiona. Faces matched as furrowed brows assessed her.

In better times she might have asked Gaili if she looked as haggard as she felt, but she knew it to be true. "I saw the creature Larrakane is fighting against. And, somehow, I saw all the pages in the Book." Fiona sat heavily down in the softest chair she could find. Gaili handed her a cup of hot coffee and a hunk of sweet bread as if out of thin air. Fiona took it gratefully, giving a small smile to the golden faun. Her mind felt muddled. "There were some I didn't recognize."

"Say more," Didia said brightly. She rummaged through her bag and pulled out a small journal. "How many did you see?"

"I don't think this is the best way to go about this," Raina hissed.

"No?" Fiona rubbed her tense shoulder to keep from glaring at the woman. "Larrakane is fighting, and she is not winning. Whatever you know about these pages or chapters—" She stopped as a brushed tendril of memory reappeared. Queen Eleanor had mentioned something about not telling the others of an abstract in her memory. Something she truly didn't want Larrakane to share information about. *Abstract* was an odd categorization, but it linked to what Stella said: *In theory, there are three.* Did she mean in the abstract of the Book there were three pages? "The abstract. Raina, you have to tell us about it."

Raina took a breath and glanced around. "Not with everyone."

"Why do you persist in wasting time like this?" Marcia snapped, closing the leather book she was looking at. "We have to find the Binder and the other Seasons."

Fiona came to her feet, raising her hands to intercede. "Let's calm down. Everyone here is willing to do whatever it takes to stop Dani and this dangerous creature she's releasing."

"She's doing what?" Marcia's eyes widened.

"Madness," Raina exclaimed. "No, that can't be right. She knows what would happen."

"She must have some sort of pact with him. Something that releases her and all the other page turners when he's free." Fiona clasped her hands together and let out a deep breath. "There are pages she hasn't gotten what she needs from yet. Three, in theory. If we can get there first, we can stop Dani. Maybe we'll even find the Seasons. I don't think she wants to hurt them, just keep them out of the way until she's finished. If we can get them back, we can secure Spine."

"Tell us what you know, Raina," Didia said in a gentle tone.

Raina took a slight step back from the group. She stood up

taller though she still avoided their gazes. "I won't betray her. She needs our faith in her more now than ever."

Fiona could see the trembling in her hand, the way she kept smoothing her robe. If Raina told this secret of Larrakane's, then she was saying she didn't believe the deity could handle the situation anymore. But faith had to work both ways, at least, to Fiona. A mutually beneficial relationship.

"You aren't betraying her," Fiona said. "You aren't the one plotting against her, moving to usurp her. And she wouldn't have entrusted you with so much if she didn't believe that you would use that information wisely." Fiona leaned against the desk, watching the Priestess lower her guard. "Having faith in someone doesn't mean you only follow them. Sometimes you have to lead. Sometimes you have to walk side by side."

"You have us here with you," Didia said. She gave her a small, sad smile. "Remember Rule #3, Raina. It isn't all on you."

Tucking her dark hair behind her ear covered the biting of her lip as Raina seemed to war internally. But only for a moment. She crossed her arms. "Alright. May Larrakane forgive me, but alright." She moved in closer to the group. "There *are* three abstract pages. They aren't like the elemental or mortal chapters. There are no creatures in them at all, and they're...well, dangerous." Raina glanced back toward the hidden shrine. "You have to understand. These are Larrakane's realm. Not made for us. They're the last barrier to destruction, she said." Raina looked at Fiona. "In Queen Eleanor's memory, I mean."

"Do you have bookmarks?" Dodger said.

Raina shook her head. "How can you bookmark something you can't physically take back with you?"

"That's why Stella said the only way was through. We have

to go through each one to get to the other," Fiona said. But how to get into one in the first place?

"Bright colors, echoes, and the ticking of a clock," murmured Gaili.

Dodger wrinkled his brow. "What do you recognize?"

Gaili sat up straighter, rosy-pink curls bouncing. "When we were trying to find the plant page, Phyta, we saw the Book. The flipping of pages, I mean."

"Yes, there were all the ones we know and then a bright-colored page. That must be the first in the abstract." Marcia nodded.

"And then the page that sounded like, well, echoes of my thoughts," Gaili said, raising her cup to hide her blush. "Oh, but then there was the page that ticked. And then it tocked. It reminded me of one of Clara's clocks."

"That one must be the page of time," Didia said, scribbling furiously in her journal. "I've been trying to find it for a while now. Makes sense it'd be in the last place I looked."

Fiona raised an eyebrow. She knew Didia studied the belief that there were other pages unknown to all. The books Fiona had recovered for her last year and how quickly Didia got on with her librarian friend Hanno were a testament to that. But that she knew or had figured out another page existed was surprising. Fiona had to spend more time with her. If they had it.

"What can you share about it?" Fiona asked.

"Nothing enough to hook a hat on, but format has it there was a place to rewrite your life. Or see glimpses of your future. Thought it was one of those pre-Inking myths, but it kept coming up in various ways over my years of research."

"And you've been searching for it." Gaili leaned toward the

older lady.

Didia shrugged. "It's what I do. Once a spotter, always one."

"This is all well and good, but if we're going to get into these pages, we have to know how. Quickly," Marcia said.

"What about the roaring one?" Gaili counted quickly on her fingers. "After the plant page came loud beast sounds."

Fiona's head snapped up. "That's the sound I heard when Dani tore into Spine. She already knew how to get into the abstract."

"Maybe if we get there quickly, we can follow her through or find a weak spot into the bright page," Gaili said.

"Weak spot?" Dodger said.

She nodded, setting her cup down excitedly. "All pages have weak spots to their flanking pages. They are isolated usually, but we have some criteria for finding it."

"And with my experience we can discover it quickly," Didia piped in, rising slowly from her chair.

Raina tutted. "You can't possibly go at your age."

"What else am I doing? Retirement isn't all it's cracked up to be, you know. This might be my last chance." Didia smirked. "Besides, any new pages will need good eyes and a great spotter." She adjusted her glasses. "I'm two in one."

A brief moment of lightness washed over the group at Didia's playful tone. They had managed to find a bit of hope quicker than expected.

Fiona wasn't going to let it fade away. She jumped up and clapped her hands. "If we can find Dani before she gets out of the roaring page, then we may be able to recover the Seasons and get them back to Spine before it starts to break."

"I think that's a little too late," Dodger said, staring out the window.

The glass wall that showed a view of the forest's edge was melting. The forest view looked the same but sliced into the building was a wide strip unnatural to Spine. A rose-gold fog poured through the tear in the room like molten metal, washing over the table and desk at an odd angle. Hissing steam rushed in along behind the fog, and the group scrambled away.

Deafening melodic singing twisted its way into the room from somewhere far off in the dense mist.

"What is that?" Fiona shouted.

Dodger shook his head. "I don't know. I—"

"Cover your ears!" Marcia grabbed the leather book she had been reading off the desk and clapped her hands over her own ears. "Marcius, get the door. Everyone out."

The lighting deepened into rosy copper. The singing changed—a subtle shift of curiosity in the pitch.

For once Fiona followed orders from Marcia without a question. Dodger closed the door behind the group, the singing abruptly cut off.

"Was that—?" Gaili said, wide eyed, to Marcia.

The hag nodded and waved them to follow her. "Sirens. A sliver of Dew Island breaking into Spine. Of all the places." Marcia pushed open another solid-metal door, revealing a simple passageway of stone walls and darkened interior.

Fiona rubbed the edges of her scarf, head pounding. How could Spine already be breaking apart? And at the Hinge. "I thought this place was warded."

"Against certain people, yes. Against the Book falling apart, well..." Raina murmured.

Marcia shook her head. "Even the Binder couldn't have foreseen this."

"We need to get to the roaring page and traverse into the

abstract," Fiona said. "There has to be a way or a bookmark into it somewhere. Didia?"

The older woman's face was tight. "I don't have anything. But if there is a bookmark, the Hinge will be the place to find it. The Binder kept everything spotters found that didn't seem to belong."

Of course he did. And most likely put them somewhere safe. Would something be in the vault that he and Dani argued over? He had moved it from his office, so conceivably it was somewhere else in Hinge. Safe but secret. "Marcia—"

"I know, I know. Where's the vault? I had a feeling it would come to this." Marcia sighed and glanced back over her shoulder. "Yes, I know of it. No, I don't know where he moved it. Or at least, I don't yet." She waved down the darkened passage. "Follow me."

"He moved it but didn't tell the Gilded?" Fiona said, stepping in after her and Dodger.

"Too many thefts, one after another. Gilded didn't need to know about it truly. He only told us as a sign of trust."

Fiona glanced around but in the darkness she couldn't see a thing. This passage was clearly for faekin only. She grabbed Gaili's arm, letting the faun get in front and lead. A few more minutes deeper into the dark tunnel and then Marcia stopped.

"Are we really going to go in there?" Dodger whispered.

"His ledger says he moved it to a place best kept close," Marcia said. "I know of none other than this. Do you?" There was a glint of metal from her hand and then a wide door opened, dim light pooling into the passageway. Marcia stepped in without a word.

With unmasked eagerness Fiona followed in after her. Cold air brushed against her face, leaving it tingling. Frost coated the stone-bricked circular walls of a large room. Expensive woven blankets and furs draped across chairs and settees, creating cozy seating off to one side. Tapestries hung on the wall depicting torchlit landscapes and snow-covered valleys. Thick though they were, they gave no added warmth to the space. On another side of the room was a thin wooden dining table. Empty plates with half-eaten grapes and overturned mugs were strewn about the top.

A few closed doors dotted the circular walls. Marcia strode to one, barely glancing at a passing window that looked out into the sedate forest. She threw open the door.

"The Binder's home?" Gaili whispered, standing on the front of her hooves to peer around Fiona into the room.

"And mine. Mind you follow my orders exactly," Marcia called out from within the room. "Normally I'd throw you in turn stoppers for daring to enter here, but time is of the essence. You all may search out in the living areas. Marcius and I will focus on his bedroom."

From what Fiona could see, it was a clean, functional room with a simple wooden poster bed and a fireplace. The only real adornments to the bedroom were blankets. Lots and lots of blankets. Dodger scampered in and closed the door behind him softly.

Dire times indeed to be searching the Binder's personal space, but Raina and Fiona started first in what appeared to be a kitchen. Wooden plates, bowls, and empty vials suspiciously reminiscent of Gaili's own experiments were all she found in the cupboards. She ran her hands across the cold, rough, solid stone walls. Dani had been doing much of the same in his office before she and Fiona had been caught by the Binder. But there were no ingress or sly catches to be found.

The others seemed to fare no better in the living space. Didia pulled back tapestries, revealing nothing but clean stone. Gaili dived through stacks of quilts and the arrayed furs that rested across all the furniture. But beyond one or two curious trinkets Gaili could easily identify from the Court of Copper, there was nothing revealing the location of the vault.

"There's no hint nor hair of an entrance in his bedroom," Dodger said, wiping his paws discreetly on his tunic.

Fiona sighed. There were only so many other places to search before they had to come up with another plan. If not in his actual bedroom, perhaps the second-best place. "What about in yours?" she said to Marcia.

The hag shook her head, bun unmoving. "He certainly would've told me."

"Well, perhaps. If he thought he had time to." Dodger rocked on his feet, hands clasped behind his back. "Has he given you anything recently? Anything new?"

Marcia narrowed her gaze at him, but instead of saying no, she slapped a hand to her mouth. "Oh!" She sprang to a door farther away from the Binder's and slipped inside, barely wedging it open. Before anyone could follow after her, she ran back out holding a silver walking stick. "He did leave this with me when Marcius told him about Fiona going after Dani."

Fiona peered at the cane closely. "I know I haven't seen the Binder much in person, but he's never been without that."

"Trust me. He never is," Raina said with wide eyes at the instrument.

"Twist it in the middle," Didia said, making the motion with her hands. "It might open."

With a wince Marcia slowly did so, testing carefully to see which way might be best. With a tiny clink, the walking stick opened. She pulled it apart slowly as they all gathered around to see what was inside. A tightly rolled parchment fell to the marble floor. Handing the cane to Dodger, Marcia opened it up and read the words out loud before quieting down to read to herself.

Fiona's eyes skimmed the contents involuntarily, but as it was addressed to Marcia, she pulled herself away. The others followed suit, giving the hag a moment to herself.

Marcia sniffed before rolling the parchment back up. "He says that the vault will open up when we're in need." She glanced around, eyes wide and shiny. She swallowed. "This way." Clenching the paper in her hand and grabbing pieces of the silver stick from Dodger, she marched back into her room and to the fireplace. Though there was a small fire lit now, it gave off no heat. Simply a soft amber glow reminiscent of all Court of Copper lamps.

Marcia threw the paper into the flames. A blaze of sapphire flames licked the parchment, eating its way through the material rapidly before it and the flames vanished. In their place, around the edges of the fireplace were small depictions of mushrooms and wildflowers, carefully drawn. A fae circle. "I don't know when he put this here," Marcia whispered. She held on to the wall as if needing the support.

"He had quite a few alternate plans. And guesses about who might betray him," Fiona said quietly. "But never you, Marcia."

"It's clear that he trusted in you." Didia patted the woman's arm. "As he had the brains to do."

Marcia tugged at a tendril of her bun, pulling it loose. "Yes, well." She sighed and leaned into the fireplace. She placed her hand on the symbols of the fae circle nearest her. Whispering in the faekin language, she trailed her hands in a semicircle from west to east.

"'Harmony through symmetry; wonder through design,'" Gaili whispered the translation back toward Fiona.

Trust her friend to know her questions without asking. Fiona bit her lip. Harmony again. Was this woman the Binder was so fond of quoting someone else? Because it was certainly feeling like Larrakane. But that couldn't be. Could it?

A light-gray glow shimmered as the din of cold wind howled through the fireplace. Marcia tucked the silver walking stick under her arm and walked into the fireplace, disappearing in the gusts.

Dodger leapt after her without so much as a word. The group one by one hurried into the portal, lest they be separated for too long.

Fiona appeared in a small stone room with a solitary door painted on one side. It was not real, though the detail in the painting was quite elaborate. Frost-edged and ash-colored wooden slats took up the height of the wall. Iron bolts and a silvery iron band crossed the width of the door. A flock of white doves trailed across the door, wings in flight. Fiona stroked one of the wings. She simply had to be imagining the soft down.

"The door won't budge. I have no doubt it's warded," Marcia said, running her hands across the walls.

"It's not like him to only have one security aspect." Dodger, too, ran his hands across the painted door.

The room crowded as the others swanned in from midair. Raina, the last to arrive, appeared squished between Didia and Gaili.

Scrape.

Stone shifted. Dust trickled down as the ceiling jostled. The walls of the little room moved inward toward the group.

"Well, why in Larrakane's name would it do this?" Didia exclaimed.

"The room didn't shift till Priestess Raina came down," Gaili said. She winced. "Apologies, Priestess. I'm not blaming this on you."

Fiona shuffled closer together with the others. But perhaps it was Raina's fault? The Binder was as worried as she had been about Raina being the possible traitor. Perhaps she had still been on his list when he created the room. But there certainly hadn't been enough time to modify his traps once it was confirmed to instead be Dani.

"Anyone but him and his closest allies could be considered against the Book. With so many of us..." It would do no good to pile on to Raina. Fiona scuffed her booted feet across the floor. "Why isn't there a fae circle to take us back!?"

"Did his note to you say anything more about getting in?" Dodger asked.

Marcia shook her head. "It's clearly not understanding our need," Marcia muttered.

"What if, with him gone from Spine, the ward has changed?" Fiona said.

"I'm certain he never thought he'd be leaving," Didia said.

"Perhaps the ward needs the Binder's magic." Fiona waved toward the painted wall. "Try pressing his walking stick to the door."

Marcia did as suggested.

Whump.

Frosty crystals formed on the edges of where the slabs met and underneath their feet. Crinkling and crackling, it began to cover the floor beneath them rapidly.

"So not the right move then?" Didia hopped from foot to foot, holding on to Gaili's arms to keep balance.

"Well, what do we do now?" Raina said, exasperated.

Fiona rubbed the bridge of her nose trying to think. It didn't make sense. The Binder would've never given Marcia something she couldn't use. He was a planner. Even if he never expected to leave Spine, as a leader he had to have a clear contingency on the slim chance. But if it wasn't Marcia, what was his backup? "If the Binder gave you his cane, he must've known there was a chance it could fall into the Painted Edge's hands." And with her sister trapped in the dark edge, they may have leverage over Marcia. But even Marcia wouldn't fall to their whims. Not unless she lost everyone she cared about. "But they wouldn't be able to coerce both of you." Fiona pointed to Dodger.

"What in the name of Larrakane are you mumbling about?" Marcia said.

"Hold the cane with Dodger. Dodger, you focus on it, too," Fiona said.

"She usually has some sense," Dodger said to Marcia. He grabbed her hand holding the cane.

The stone walls ground to a stop.

Fiona huffed out a breath. "Now, press the cane to the door. Both of you."

Dodger did so haltingly, laying the cane over the flock of birds.

The door swung open.

Mouth open, Marcia glanced at Dodger.

He raised an eyebrow at her and then grinned. He pulled her into a hug. "He did say he could always count on us."

Rows and rows of tables and shelves stood organized

and aligned inside the vast torchlit room. Small strips of parchment with scrawled words sat beneath crates and boxes. Books, scrolls, and stacked parchments had no such designations but were set precisely on shelves. In the midst of the room was an unassuming fae circle much like the one they used previously.

Marcia sucked in a breath. "He combined everything. But it's still relatively laid out the same." She pointed around the room. "Research materials, memory books, artifacts of pages separated by chapter and then by page, dangerous items best not left to the public, and items of unknown origin." She strode to the last table. It had stands elevating items as if they were seated in a theater.

Didia's eyes widened behind her thick glasses, and she whispered, "Never thought I'd see the likes of it again." She grinned, bending to examine the items alongside Fiona.

Small labels adhered to each riser: glass orbs with swirling blue-white smoke that said *Serenity*, a bottle with a stopper that said simply *Death*, a silver brooch with emeralds set within a label that said *Confusion*, and an ordinary small round golden mirror that said *Memory*. One of the risers was empty but labeled *Fate*.

Fiona reached out toward the empty riser, the label plucking at something familiar, but a yowl, like a cat accidentally being stepped on, stilled her hand. She winced and clutched her ears as the sound continued.

"Fi, are you alright?" Gaili pulled her close, looking her over.

She winced, looking frantically around the room for the sound. It seemed to be coming from deeper in, past the labeled tables. Fiona strode that direction. The sound softened. She dropped her hands from her ears and stopped. She took a step back and the sound grew again, this time changing into a roar. The familiarity snapped her to attention, and she hurried forward toward the sound. It grew softer but never completely quieted as she began grappling with a heavy crate lid.

"What's going on? What do you hear?" Raina called out from the other side of the room.

"I don't know. It's bellowing. Same as earlier." Fiona stopped. "You all don't hear it?"

"No, Fi." Dodger said. He marched over, sliding between her and the crate. He deftly plucked the lid from the box and stared into the bundles of straw. "What are we looking for?"

"I don't know. It feels familiar though. Warm." Yes, that was it. It wasn't an angry sound like fighting beasts. More protective. She stopped and cocked her head, listening to the call. It seemed to be coming from only one crate. "That one."

Dodger hefted it up and stacked it on top of the pile. With a minor grunt he pulled the top off.

Taking up most of the crate was a curved horn instrument, like one might see carried into battle by the Roma soldiers of Siamor. But it was made of a lustrous forest green material instead of any animal. Fiona ran her hands gingerly down the length of the shell to the small copper mouthpiece at the end. The horn had an almost leathery texture to it, but it felt as solid and hard as Cobbles rock. The roaring stopped. "What is it?"

"I don't know, but this wasn't part of the original storage rooms." Marcia turned the crate around, looking for something. She tapped it.

There was a wrapped vine in the shape of an intricate knot. The symbol that was on the ground of the druids' camp. This was the druids'? Or Nicolosia's in particular.

Fiona frowned. "Why would the Binder have it here?"

"Safety perhaps. Probably talked it over with Nic," Marcia said.

"This is connected," Fiona said. She kept her hands on the horn, running the length of it. It was hard to pull away from the thing now that she had found it. "It was the same sound. As the roaring beasts."

"Why were you called to it?" Didia asked.

"You're Nic's protégé. What was theirs is now yours," Raina said quietly. "The Book has a way of knowing."

"Does that mean…" Gaili started.

Raina shook her head. "No, only that his connection to the Book is severed. For all we know he's been put in turn stoppers. It's never happened before."

Fiona stood up, swinging the horn under her arm. It was unexpectedly featherlight, and she stumbled back before righting herself. "We have to go."

"Where?" Dodger asked.

"Out in the open. I know what to do." She needed to be outside; she could feel it. She pushed through the small crowd and hurried toward the fae circle, standing in the middle of it. Nothing happened. "What were the words?"

Marcia joined her and gently said, "Harmony through symmetry. Wonder through design."

The fae circle glowed and once again they were in Marcia's quarters. Fiona didn't stop to see if the others would be coming after her. She ran through the Binder's quarters, ignoring everything of interest, and to the main door. It opened without issue, and she tumbled into a dark passageway. How could she get out? She needed to be near the forest. "Quickest way outside the building?" she called out behind her.

"It's through here," Dodger said, sliding past Fiona and

grabbing her hand. He pulled her farther into the blinding passage and then through a door that melded into the stone wall. Footsteps echoed behind them as the others ran to catch up to Fiona's quick pace. A short jog through an upward-sloping corridor and they were outside. But what an outside that greeted them!

The expected bright-blue sky was mottled with swatches of raging fire, blinding copper, and rainy gray clouds. They shifted in and out, as if the pages fluttered in a stiff breeze. Eyes turned toward the sky, the group found themselves pressing close together, mouths agape in horror and confusion.

"What are we going to do?" Gaili whispered.

"Wake up a friend." Fiona put the horn up to her mouth and blew.

THE SOUND FROM THE horn was overshadowed by the answering call from the forest. A deep, bellowing roar like an impatient answer hearkened back to the group. Though the trees swayed in front of them, the ground itself didn't shake. The mottled sky seemed to vibrate on its own to the noise from the horn. But surprisingly, the ground beneath didn't move an inch as the forest in front of them rose up and away from them.

Fiona gently released the horn, eyes trained on the moving forest. A pearly-white gap appeared beyond a thin border of trees as the forest peeled away from the edge of the land. Fiona ran toward it, the others shouting out behind her. But she wouldn't be stilled.

"Spine!" she called out as she neared the edge. All she could see was forest, but there was more here. If she could talk to the massive creature, they could ask it questions. "It's me, Fiona!"

The trees continued their descent away from the land. The pearlescent gap beyond the thin border widened as the Spine forest flew down, down away from her. She crouched beside a tree to tentatively touch the gap and laughed with relief at cool, firm glass beneath her hands. "It's solid!"

"But how far?" Gaili asked, excitedly clomping over.

"Don't test it, Fi," Dodger yelled behind her.

Fiona nodded and rose from the ground. She shaded her

eyes, peering down at the creature. In more distance than she thought the city had to give, the massive creature flew spiraling away from them. Pine-needle-colored wings of an unfathomable size stretched out, studded with the familiar trees and land she had traversed for so many years. It was like trying to see the end of an elemental page. A branch-spiked salamander-like tail arched out from its back. Fiona squinted, trying to determine the shape of its head, but it was getting harder to make out anything at this distance. What was Spine? And where in the dark edge were they going?

"It's all gone," Raina said softly as she stumbled out of the Hinge, joining the others.

"It's not broken. Simply more than meets the eye," Fiona said, wiping her hands on her wool stockings. "Spine was—is—cared for by the druids. I'm not quite sure what they are but Nic said I could always call out to Spine if I needed help."

"They're coming back!" Gaili said, staring.

Fiona ran back to the glassy barrier as the creature spiraled up. Its long snout and horned brow seemed fierce. Its sharp teeth were very apparent. Was it grinning? She certainly hoped it was that rather than an expression of intimidation.

The creature dived as if circumventing an unknown edge and landed farther away on the translucent floor. A fierce wind knocked the group backward as their wings stilled. Even from a distance, the creature towered over them. Higher than the tallest temple steeple in the Book. And as wide as well. "You have called. I have answered."

Surprised by the rumbling speech of the creature, Fiona simply nodded, staring up into their emerald eyes. She rubbed the edge of her scarf, thinking. This creature wasn't like Soots or Richard. Or even the Leaves. It had only communicated with feeling before. Would it remember her? She said loudly, "Nicolosia has been taken. I tried to stop it, but...I failed. Do you remember me?"

"Yes. You went for my friend. You are my friend."

"Do you have a name?"

"You know my name. Though I have others." The creature chuckled. "But you may also call me Mother Nature. The druids often did."

The druids had more of a sense of humor than Fiona had been led to believe. She moved a step closer. "Spine. Can you help us get to your page?"

The creature closed her scaly eyes, and a low rumbling sound emanated from her throat.

Though Fiona couldn't quite understand it, she felt a wave of apprehension emanating from Spine. So she could still communicate without words?

"I will take you. But we must stay together. Danger."

Fiona raised an eyebrow. Yes, if the page was full of creatures like Spine, *dangerous* might be an understatement.

Didia ducked her head and said respectfully, "May I ask, what should we call your kind?"

Spine raised her massive head higher. "We are dragons."

"Is there a leader we should speak to when we arrive?" Didia said, as if checking another question off her list.

"You already are," Spine rumbled out.

It followed to pattern. Larrakane seemed to force all the page leaders into this accord of hers to this sliver of city and creation of her page turner army. How in the dark edge did Nicolosia hide the knowledge of Spine from the others?

As if Raina was on the same train of thought, she said, "I am

Priestess Raina, a Leaf of Spine. We didn't know about you or we would've contacted you sooner."

The dragon chuckled again. "I know. I have kept watch in my slumber. Important to sleep and heal."

"Heal?" Fiona's eyes roved across the rippling body of the dragon, but all she saw was unending trees. "Heal from what?"

"The other dragons."

Fiona rubbed her forehead. Well, she had to ask, didn't she?

"Fi, we should go," Gaili said quietly.

She was right, they were wasting time with questions when they had little to spare. "Raina, will you work on getting people to safety as best you can? I'm sure there will be—or already is, truly—some panic about the forest disappearing. Best to get people in one area."

"I'll start sending word for people to gather at the Temple," Raina said. "Anyone who can go back to their page should. At the very least Rise?"

Fiona nodded. It had already been hit by the Painted Edge. Surely it was the safest page at the moment. As soon as they were stopped, she would write to Richard.

Dodger chucked his bandolier at Fiona. "You might need it more than me. Keep focused, Fi."

"As much as I can. I promise." She gave Dodger a quick, tight hug. Fiona leaned toward Marcia and said quietly, "I told your sister I'd help her get back. I promise I will. She was more than helpful. She's trying to keep a stiff upper lip."

Marcia squeezed Fiona's hand. "Thank you. If you see her again, tell her, her sisters...well, we love her." Head high, Marcia strode away, calling out for Guild jackets as she reentered the building. Dodger ran in after her.

Fiona sighed and glanced between Gaili and Didia. Neither

were going to listen to her about safety or anything high handed. She simply gestured toward Spine. "Shall we?"

"You may climb." Spine lowered her head and neck until they were on the ground beside the trio.

With a helping hand to Didia, they climbed upon the dragon's leathery neck. It was like walking between wood-spiked spires. The thicket of trees that started the forest on Spine's body were some distance away. "Where should we, er, hold on?"

"The hut on my crown. You will remember it."

Questions bubbled up in Fiona, but she only nodded and led the way through sparse shifted plants, her feet kicking up familiar dirt to the only structure in sight. She stopped. It was Nicolosia's hut. The one she had only been in once before. Not the home Nic kept in the clearing but the secretive one. The druid had been close to Spine even yesterday.

It *was* a little different than before. The thick tree trunks bursting from the ground had lowered some, and the clinging nettle roof had retreated, leaving it open to the sky. A nest for traveling, it seemed. Could the dragon shift the wooden structures on her body at will?

The bookshelves that sprouted from the wall now wrapped around the books and trinkets left in their care. The small desk with its innate swirls that spoke volumes of its Copper origin now had wrapped limbs securing it to the floor. Spine cared for the hut, keeping it secure for Nicolosia's return. A moment of sadness caught Fiona by surprise as her eyes watered up. She brushed the tears away with the back of her hand and ushered Didia and Gaili inside. Holding on to the walls felt more stable than being out in the open on the dragon's neck. "We're ready, Spine," Fiona called out toward the dragon's head.

"No need to yell. I am all you see." Spine cleared her throat. "Friends of old. You must stay in the city. I must open my Rock of the Nest."

Fiona started to question the dragon, but the song of answering calls and skittering wildlife drew her attention. Birds darted out from the trees, frogs croaked, hopping off into the small strip of forest left near the Hinge. Small foxes with bushy tails darted toward the city. The life of the forest left in one fell swoop. Fiona hadn't thought that far ahead about all the life that encompassed Spine. But the dragon had remembered.

Spine gently rose up and flew away from the Hinge. Like a chariot over smooth road, the dragon hastened away from the rectangular city.

"You can leave here?" Fiona held tight to the wall, a little disoriented. The other Leaves of Spine were bound like Guardians. Why did Larrakane give the dragon the ability to leave but not the others?

"If I am called by the Leaves, yes. One of my duties."

Her job among the others. "Do you need a bookmark?" Fiona said.

"You have it."

Fiona rubbed her hands on the horn and placed it on the floor. The hut shifted, encompassing it. Well, that certainly answered that question. "How long till we get to the pagemark?"

"Not long," Spine rumbled.

Fiona pulled out her journal. If she was going to write to Richard, this might be her only chance. Hunched over the desk, she pulled out her quill, dipped it in the ink from the stand, and scratched quickly across the pages. "Spine is breaking. I'm traveling to recover the Seasons. There's not enough time to go in to details but know that the Painted Edge have escalated things." Fiona bit her lip trying to determine what she could write that wouldn't panic Richard nor let his brother attack her. "They are breaking the chains that bind."

Worry ate at her as she watched the page, hoping he would be around to see her words and respond but doubting that he could. It wasn't as if she waited for him to write to her. She started to close the journal, but a striking slash appeared across the paper as if someone was trying to get her attention. A few seconds more and hastily written words appeared: "Not while I still stand, they won't."

Relief at his response mixed with a deep ache in her stomach at his words. She wasn't warning him so he could walk himself into the lion's den, lion though he was himself. She hurriedly wrote back, "You can't leave Rise again. Go into hiding with the druids. As long as you remain, you should be safe there. They already have what they need from Rise and Blaze, I think."

"No." Sloping large words and dripping ink splattered on the page. "No, they don't, and no, I won't. Druids and I are fighting. The royal guard has been called. But the Painted Edge is attacking the palace. I think—I worry that they want something else. My Words seem to have no meaning to them. More and more are warded against me. Even physically the druids and guards seem no match for the Painted Edge anymore. They are strengthened."

The familiar niggle in the back of Fiona's mind snapped into place. Stella had been trying to warn her about this. Oh, if only she could've spoken more plainly! Bracing for pain, she scribbled, "There is no more time for subtlety. The Painted

Edge are getting their increased power from your brother's chains." She gritted her teeth as a stabbing pain like the prick of a hundred sharpened quills tore into her chest. She waited for the pulse of cold that would signal the end of the wretchedness and the beginning of Larrakane's protection, but the pain continued, growing stronger. Fiona cried out and arched back away from the table. Distantly she heard Gaili and Didia calling her name.

A deep voice whispered in her mind, *"Come to me, Fiona Thorne."*

Flinching at the voice, Fiona clutched at her chest. Was this him? Had her words allowed him to get closer to her? She tugged at her doublet, ripping her scarf out from within, and held it close, thinking fervently of her father and his words of safety: *Stay inside with her.* Quickly she took a deep breath, and focused on what she had seen of Larrakane in the dark edge, fighting.

A drop. Another. Ripplings of cold slowly splashed upon her until it built into a rushing tidal wave. Coolness washed over her and numbed out the tormenting pain, soothing it. She lay back against the floor, panting, sweat dripping down her neck and curls clinging to her face.

"Fi, what happened!?" Gaili put a small flask to her lips.

Fiona drank a bit too deeply before sputtering at the strong liquor hidden within.

Didia patted her on the back. "Should've warned you. It's the good stuff."

"It's alright. I'm alright." Fiona rubbed her chest where Larrakane's mark ached faintly. It had taken longer for Larrakane's protection to take hold. And in the gap... No, she'd rather not think about it more, lest it should happen again. She scrambled up from the floor and to the journal, which still lay open on the desk.

"It is as I feared. But knowledge begets tactics. We will continue to fight. Fiona, I will not give in. I will not give up the hope you have given me. I'd rather Larrakane's plan than surrender to those who would unleash such disaster. But if it comes to that, know that I...that I care for you."

What was he talking about? What plan of Larrakane's? Between being attacked and being confused, she took no more time and wrote hastily, ink smearing her hand, "Richard, explain. I don't know when I can write back, but don't do anything regrettable, you blasted man."

"We are here," Spine announced.

Fiona, hugging the journal to her chest, hurried to the window. They were surrounded by a white void on all sides. Squinting, she could make out a sliver of darkness far up in the horizon that must've been the city. How big was this space that contained them? How much of herself did Larrakane give to create it?

With distracted thoughts Fiona almost didn't catch the beginning turn from stark white to a pink twilight sky. Beyond the clouds drifting across, there were no shapes in the distance, no smoke or beasts roiling through the vignette. Simply sky and a musty earthy smell that carpeted them on the other side of the scene. It was the largest page turn Fiona had ever seen. Even more so than when Forlorn Tower was stolen. She choked back her question of where in this Rock of the Nest they were going so as not to distract Spine.

Spine tucked her wings to her sides and dived into the page turn. Cold wind met them on the other side, smacking the trio in the hut. The nettle of the building rose up, closing over them. Protecting them. Fiona stood in the doorway, holding tightly to the frame, watching as the white void of the city, her home, flipped back and closed, leaving only endless sky and the howling of wind.

FIONA WAS SURPRISED THEY weren't in immediate danger. On the Bluff there had been wild flames, less burnt orange than that of Blaze, licking through the torn page when Dani left. But here there was only sunset and strong cooling gales. She ventured a guess: "Was that the only safe pagemark here?" Holding on to any shrubs she came across for balance, she walked slowly to the thick neck of the dragon.

"Yes." Spine's voice rumbled low. "But it seems it did not matter." Spine dived toward a valley. She landed among dried clumps of tangled grass and barren cracked brown soil. Her massive bulk took up most of the clearing. "Look toward the haze."

Masses of scattered, broken trees covered the land like timber piled against the backdrop of the bonfire sky. Indeed, some were already aflame as thick plumes of smoke rose, dotting the far distant landscape. Fiona squinted but couldn't tell exactly where the fires were coming from or whether someone was maintaining them. They seemed to be lingering ghosts among the fallen. There were so very many damaged trees. Evergreen, oak, pine collapsed into one another. They matched the innumerable variety on Spine herself. Had this been Spine's home? Something sharp tugged at the back of Fiona's mind, but she couldn't put her thoughts into words.

"It's so quiet," Gaili murmured coming up behind Fiona.

Ah, that was it. Stomach sinking, Fiona said softly, "I believe the Painted Edge have already gotten the keystone here."

"Yes." Spine's thickened voice struggled with the word.

"The Guardian for Rock of the Nest is another dragon?" Fiona asked.

"My clan guarded alongside them." Spine snorted, puffs of green clouds escaping like small tornadoes up into the space before them. She shifted her massive body impatiently. "What now?"

Didia assessed the small brassy compass she had adhered to the desk. She pulled a wood-and-copper spyglass up to her round glasses, the intricate carved design a telltale sign of faekin ingenuity, and squinted at the horizon. "We need to head east, Spine, as far as you can." She thumped the floor of the hut, indicating the direction she was pointing. "If this page is between the plant page and the abstract like you saw, dear Fiona, the next page will have to be in the east."

The boards of the floor receded, freeing the horn from its chamber. Fiona scooped it up and slipped it on her chest across the bandolier. She kept her hand on the floor momentarily, feeling the warmth of Spine. "I'm sorry."

"They will pay." Spine pushed herself off the ground, talons digging into the cracking soil, wrenching deep grooves. She launched into the air, wings stretched to skim the wind.

"Is there somewhere toward the east where there have been stories of interesting landscapes? Some unexplained or mythical phenomena?" Gaili said, sitting down at the small desk in the room.

There was silence for a moment, but curiosity emanated from the dragon. "There were always tales of a few odd places before Larrakane came. The Keeper would know more."

"A Keeper?" Didia snapped her spyglass into her belt loop. "What are they keeping?"

"Our records. Of course," Spine said.

Even the dragons had historians. Fiona sighed, the fast familiar ache in her heart bubbling up. She leaned against the window and opened Richard's journal again. He had written nothing new. She pressed her fingers to the parchment, taking its warmth as a sign that he was somehow alright, before closing it. They had to stop Dani before Rise and Richard were overrun. A balance of methodical research and gut experience between Gaili and Didia was all they had to rely on. "If only we had some information on exactly where Dani went. How far is this Keeper?"

"Not far." Spine tilted down as if riding the wind, before veering off toward the east. "He kept his den in our area to study a multitude of sights. If we describe what we are looking for, he will know about it."

But would the Painted Edge already know that? Dani didn't seem one to leave too many loose ends. If there was someone who knew about possible entrances to other pages, would they already be on the side of the Edge? Fiona rubbed her temple, easing away the worry. No sense dwelling on it until they knew for sure about this friend of Spine.

"Fi, I packed supplies from the storage room," Gaili said, fiddling with the shoulder bag. She handed Fiona a grappling gun, a flare, and a flask. "If we get split up for any reason, use the flare."

"And the flask? Is it to soothe my nerves?" How could they be soothed? Richard still hadn't written back yet and his words, *I'd rather Larrakane's plan than surrender*, tumbled freely around her head. What was he talking about?

"Either that or to barter with." Gaili grinned but her smile dropped as she studied Fiona's face. She raised her hand and said quickly, "It's cold coffee. So don't become too concerned I've lost all my sense." She handed a larger satchel out to Didia. "Dodger thought you'd want this for the journey."

Didia's eyes opened wide and she eagerly tore into the bag. "Spotter gear!" She held up a long leather-bound knife, unsheathing and resheathing it with ease before tossing it back into the bag. A skinny cylindrical case was full of map parchment, some filled and some empty, ready to be sketched on. Didia hurriedly pulled out a blank piece. "Seems a more complete kit now than when I traveled. The Binder must've known about the other pages somehow."

"Yes, I do think the Binder did." Fiona wasn't sure how, but he seemed prepared. Not just for dealing with Dani but to update the spotter's gear as if new pages were going to spring up. That was some foresight. Perhaps he understood all of Larrakane's plans in a way no one else did. But why trust him when the deity didn't seem to trust anyone else? Even the man she let keep the only power she had ever given humans?

"How did you meet Richard?" Gaili's quiet voice interrupted her thoughts. "It's just, you never mentioned him before. Not that you need to tell me about everything."

Fiona sighed. "The sad part is I did. I did tell you. And Henrietta. She even met him." She choked on the laughter that bubbled up at the absurd situation. "And then he made you all forget."

"How in the Book could he do that?" Gaili clasped her hand to her mouth. "No, Fi, you don't have to go into it. It seems to make you sad."

"Only because I wanted to share him. And because he thought he had to be alone to do his job correctly." She shook her head. "I of all people understand that notion. That idiotic notion."

"I imagine you still gave him an earful," Didia broke in grinning.

"Much in the same way Dodger gave me one when I was being a blotter. But he's a good man. Stubborn and much too smart. He's been on his own too long. And now…" Fiona stopped and rubbed the errant tears from her face. "Well, he's ridiculous, but if I know him, he's about to do something foolhardy and I think it's a bit my fault."

"I very much doubt it's your fault." Gaili grabbed her hand, squeezing it gently. "You inspire people to do what they must. If anything, what they've needed to do but didn't have the courage for."

"Hear! Hear!" Didia nodded. "If he's anything like my Bernard was, he'll surprise you by being safe and sound and after you at the most inconvenient time."

Warmed though still head heavy with pushed aside fears Fiona smiled, "He is a bit like that."

"I'm sorry I haven't met him yet. The way you smile. He seems so special." Gaili dropped her hand and threw her arms open. "I'm positive there will be a time in the future where we're all together. Have faith, Fi."

It felt a bit like asking her to hang the sun. But a small piece inside of her latched on to Gaili's words and she found herself nodding along. Hope. That's what it was. If she could give it, why couldn't she keep some for herself too?

They took turns keeping watch as each of them tried to rest while they could. For Fiona the hours of sleep were fitful but appreciated. The others seemed to let her sleep more than they did, and she gave her thanks heartily. Between the rest and the light provisions Didia had provided out of the packs, Fiona was beginning to feel a bit sharper.

With the spyglass in hand, watching for any sign of life in the black night sky as they flew over the cracked and broken world of dragons was less difficult than relying on eyes alone. The scenery below shifted to silhouettes and sketches of what was, or could be, against the dark. The stench of wet ash and smoke permeated the air around them. Without word but with a sorrow that Spine couldn't keep from the others, she took off higher into the air. The clouds became their cover and their allies, hiding the world below.

Fiona removed her slingshot from her scarf in case it was necessary. She hoped to Larrakane it wasn't, though she worried that even that hope was taxing on the deity. But still she gratefully secured it and a pouch of rocks to her belt.

"I was wondering..." Gaili began, watching Fiona with bright eyes. She motioned to the pouch. "If you wanted to try something a bit more, well, volatile."

"What have you cooked up now?" Fiona said with a smile. She had missed Gaili's company, having been running for what felt like weeks on end without her.

Gaili pulled a thick brown leather pouch from her rucksack. "A few new bits. I thought about all your troubles in Rise and Kerus and put together a couple of shots. Strictly for incapacitation, mind you. I only completed the third one before the messenger came."

Fiona took the pouch carefully. It was heavy with a leather loop to tie it around her belt. She opened it up to see three small glass beads. Red, blue, and gray. "You are the best, Gails.

Why, I never would've thought about something other than rocks!"

The faun blushed, golden cheeks turning a rosy copper. "I'm glad to still surprise you."

"Always." Fiona tucked the pouch into her belt, almost dropping it as she lurched forward. Spine seemed to be moving at great speed back down below the clouds. With no sounds emanating from the dragon, Fiona suspected she was trying to keep quiet as they approached their destination. Was it to hide from other dragons?

Didia pulled the spyglass to her eye, leaning halfway out the window, but she quickly shook her head and attached it back to her belt. "I suppose we're near the Keeper, but I can't see anything past Spine's trees."

Spine slowed, circling before landing in a meadow of tall grass, which came farther up the dragon's body than Fiona expected.

Blinking fireflies, like small birds, danced among the tips of the grass, lighting trails in their wake. The gurgling rush of a stream trekked through the meadow, though she couldn't see it. Distant hills and mountains said they had gone far from Spine's domain but there was more beyond.

"The Keeper stays in a meadow on the edge of the forest, but his den is sometimes hard to see. We should go on foot now." Spine trudged forward, the ground barely shaking with each of her steps, though unseen dry leaves rustled.

"Watch for anything not us," Fiona whispered to Gaili. Though Spine would be the true opponent in any fight they might have in the dragon page, Fiona wasn't yet going to let down her guard. Besides the sound of Spine's steps, it was eerily quiet. Shouldn't there have been some life this far away from the destruction they had witnessed?

A hill came into view, the smell of moss heavy in the air. But she couldn't tell anything beyond that with the moonless sky overhead. The hill was, however, smaller than Spine, and Fiona wondered if they were to clamber over it or go around it when Spine stopped and stretched her long neck low to the ground toward the hill.

"Keeper," Spine called once, letting the word linger.

Silence met them. It was a slim chance that the dragon would still be in this location after two hundred years. Fiona hadn't wanted to think about it earlier, but clearly much had changed.

Spine sniffed and drew closer to the hill. She sniffed again, long and deep. "Keeper."

"Spine, they must've moved on—" Fiona started.

"No." Spine shook her head. "The moss does not lie. But there are others."

"Others?" Didia whispered hotly. She strode out the door of the hut, marching toward the crown of Spine's head.

Fiona leapt up to keep after her. She hadn't expected Didia to be the one to keep her on her toes, but she shouldn't have assumed otherwise. "Do you mean other dragons?"

Spine snorted. "Only one. I cannot fit into the Keeper's home. You must go."

"You mean, other dragons aren't as large as you?" Gaili said with an awed voice.

"We are not the same," Spine said. She shook her head lightly and then angled so that they could climb down.

The fireflies glowed brighter as the women climbed down the muddy-brown scales of the dragon. One by one they jumped to the soft ground. The grass hid them completely but for Gaili's horns and rosy curls that brushed past the pointed tops of the blades. Fiona was thankful that at least they had some cover if there were others about.

Silently they walked to the hill. An arched entrance had been carved into the side, roots and rock jutting out at odd angles. Darkness beckoned them. Though the arch was about the size of the entrance to the Hinge, the sloping of the ceiling made the interior feel tight, and Fiona ducked instinctively at the oppressive cap as they trudged in.

Damp earth and the sweet smell of overripe berries clung to the air. Fiona swallowed, her mouth watering. The rumbling of her empty stomach echoed loudly to her ears. She winced. Perhaps Spine could say what food might be safe to eat here. If any at all.

They walked deeper and deeper into the darkened tunnel, feeling the walls to guide themselves. Here nothing moved in the stillness. With a quick hand squeeze between them to decide the matter, Gaili pulled out her lantern and lit it, showering their path forward in flickering smokeless flames.

Didia was the first to break the silence, snapping her fingers to get the others' attention. She waved them over and pointed to the ground below. Footsteps. Small like hers, but the boots were different. There were many of them, crisscrossing and backtracking as they made their way farther in. Small bits of reeds stuck to the ground in some imprints, like arrows pointing the way. Proof they were not the first to have gotten to the Keeper.

Quicker now they strode until they came upon a small chamber. Animal furs cloaked the floor. Mounds of stone piled near the walls, their job not readily apparent to Fiona. Much of them were rough, but a few smooth stones littered the edges of the pile. A trickle of water poured in freely through one wall into a wide gray stone basin where it pooled slowly. Between the basin and the entrance were clusters of melon-sized berries. Some intact, but most squashed across the floor as if they had been trampled on accidentally. Deep gouges in the ground from the room to the tunnel said that the Keeper had not left his home willingly.

Didia poked around the water basin and behind berries, a stack threatening to topple over her.

"What are you looking for?" Gaili said quietly.

"I was hoping for some unconscious fool to question," Didia said, carefully sifting through rocks. "If the Keeper is even half the size of Spine, it would take a lot of people to subdue him."

"Yes, but how long ago was he here?" Fiona tugged on her scarf, allowing a small relief of air to her neck. Dani had known that anyone following her might seek out this Keeper dragon first. Could they find where he was? "And is he staying away willingly?"

"The berries are still fresh." Gaili sniffed them. "They haven't gone mushy. If they have the same ripen-and-decay cycle as our fruit, I'd say a few days. A week at most."

"Perhaps there's something telling in those rooms." Didia waved toward arched open doorways that led away from this room. "I don't hear anything, but I'm no fool alone."

Flanked side by side, the three made their way into another spacious area. In the center of a large room—big enough to fit what Fiona felt was her entire downstairs—was a pond. Water lilies floated about, only shifted by some unseen burbling. Fiona's hair clung to her neck in the increased humidity.

The last chamber, though rudimentary, was clearly used. Bowls of thick pigment were lined up side by side in the center of the room. Paintings—at least, if they had been on canvas—were drawn on the walls from the floor to a rounded ceiling. Bursting suns in pale cream skies. Massive tidal waves pouring over lava. Streaks of bright light arced against blackened landscapes. Flowers that seemed to hypnotize those beneath them—all painted one after another. Nestled among them were dragons in various sizes. Smaller ones cozied up to larger ones as if viewing the spectacles from a distance.

Gaili held the lantern up and stared at the drawings, mouth open . "He has seen quite a bit."

"Yes," Fiona murmured behind her, squinting in the dim light. "But which is the one we're looking for?"

"This one has been painted over recently." Didia showed her purple-stained hand.

Beside the purple paint Fiona could just make out the edges of blue water with rounded rocks situated in an odd shape. Was it a crescent?

"That must be where the exit is," Gaili said.

"Or simply where they took the Keeper," Fiona said.

Didia wiped her hands on a rough cloth she had produced from her bag. "Why would they paint over it? They had to know it would be obvious."

"Not all people are as clever as you," Fiona said, though she narrowed her eyes more, studying it. It did seem rather obvious. But Dani couldn't control everyone in her organization. Stella was a clear enough example of that. "Let's confer with Spine. About the painting, and the reeds and smooth rocks. Perhaps she can shed some light."

"Fiona, if there are really this many instances of possible unexplained phenomena, we have to find the Keeper and narrow it down," Gaili said, still riveted by the paintings.

"I know," Fiona said quietly. But whether they found the Keeper or not, there were no guarantees it would get them closer to where they needed to be.

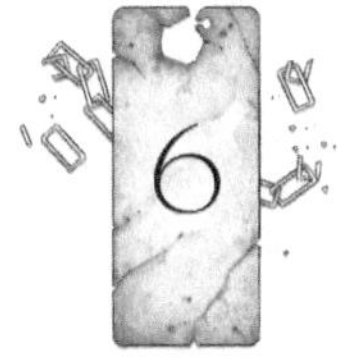

"WHAT DO YOU THINK, Spine?" Fiona settled back onto the crown of the dragon after outlining what they had found. She sat on the wooden floor of the small hut and crossed her legs. "Do the pieces fit together, or is there an odd one out?"

"Odd one out?" Spine said.

"Does one not belong?" Fiona said.

Spine was silent, though familiar curiosity emanated from her. "Your people are strange. Even in my slumber your choices filtered into my dreams." Spine shifted as if remembering something uncomfortable. "The paint might have been a rash moment. You tend to do rash things."

"No arguments there," Didia huffed, opening her bag.

"But the reeds and smooth stones are clear enough signs for a hunter. They are camped near the Great River. It is a large source of water. Your kind need that more often," Spine said.

Gaili took one of the food bars Didia offered and said, "Do you think they took the Keeper there?"

Spine grunted. "If they wanted to keep such a dragon hidden, they would do it where the ruins and the waters meet."

Fiona rubbed her face. "So we may have already passed them?"

"No, the first ruins," she grumbled, the vibration trembling through the floor. "Less talking. More flying."

Fiona didn't argue. Spine took off, only her eyes and Gaili's being able to see in the deep black. Though Fiona didn't particularly want to encounter another dragon, the less they saw of others, the sadder Fiona felt for Spine. How many had there been? Had they moved off, or were the unsaid words of sorrow she had felt the whole story? If there were some as massive as Spine but others much smaller, perhaps they had escaped the damage of the keystone being removed. But how long would the dragon page stay stable? Did it have more or less time than Spine?

After a while, Didia tugged on her arm, bringing Fiona out of her dark reverie. "I do believe we've found the camp." She gave the spyglass to Fiona.

In the distance the shadow of tents and a few scattered campfires flickered. "Gaili, can you see how many groupings?"

"Three." The faun peered through the passed spyglass. "They're a fair distance from the river, though, and deep in the thicket. I wonder why they aren't camping closer."

"If the fireflies are as big as birds, there's no telling how large the fish are," Didia said, wary. "A good rule of thumb is to stay out of the way of things that could you eat you quicker than you can run."

"Spine, can we stay up here unseen until we can ascertain whether the Keeper is there? If we have to go in, I'd rather know as much as possible before being spotted," Fiona said.

"We may be a tad too late for that," Didia said, squinting. "We're not the only ones in the sky."

Fiona's chest fluttered and she gripped the floor, jumping up. "Dragon or Painted Edge?"

"I'm not sure. Gaili?" Didia said, pointing out in the distance.

Gaili peered through the spyglass and made a small gasp. "A dragon. Why, it's massive!"

"What color?" Spine ground out.

"Oh, a sort of gray and red. Like a foggy sunrise." Gaili pulled down the spyglass. "There are people riding on top with torches!"

If there were people, they could only be the Painted Edge. That they had their own dragon had not been a card Fiona had been prepared for them to play. "Human, faekin, or beastfolk? Any details you can make out at all."

"Looks like a human and a faun," Gaili said, surprised. "I can't tell anything beyond the horns and the cloaks unfortunately."

"They are hunters but not good ones." Spine snorted loudly.

Didia held on to the hut as the dragon jolted forward. "Why is that?"

"They allowed themselves to be seen." She rose higher into a dense bank of clouds. Spine flew with an experienced air, seemingly heedless of the lack of view in their new surroundings.

"Is it looking for us?" Fiona asked.

"He has our scent," Spine rumbled. "Hold on." She flew up and behind the other dragon with a haste unexpected in so massive a creature.

The nettle of the building grew up and over the trio inside, closing off their view. Fiona understood it was to keep them hidden and safe, but she hated not knowing what was going on. She clung to the open doorframe. "The spyglass please."

Gaili handed it to her. "Be careful, Fi."

Fiona focused beyond Spine's head, trying to catch a glimpse of the dragon. Red-gray with an impassive rocky exterior faced off against them, snapping at Spine. From this closer proximity Fiona could see through the shadows of light thrown by their torches the surprise on the faces of the dragon's riders and the crossbows on their backs. She whipped the spyglass under her arm and reached out to tug the door shut.

The rocky dragon smashed into Spine, knocking them all off kilter. Fiona stumbled, holding on to the door. Hands grazed her jacket before slipping from her, and she was flung out into the open on the dragon's head. She scrambled across the leaf-covered ground on all fours to find something to hold on to. Not possible. She rolled against the brush, leaves scratching at her face. She yelled out toward the hut, "Stay inside and close the door!"

A crossbow bolt whizzed in the air past her and embedded itself in the dirt. Excellent, the riders had gotten their wits about them. Fiona looked desperately around for a shrub to get behind until she could make it back to the hut. From the corner of her eye she saw the rusty tail of the rocky dragon sweeping across the side of Spine. Granite met wood in a thunderous crash. Trees across Spine snapped and fell to the hard chop.

Spine grunted and pulled back, flying lower. Another crossbow bolt winged by Fiona, reminding her that she, too, was in a precarious situation. She swallowed hard, got to her feet, and dashed back toward the hut. Sheared rocks like sharp river stones belted across the landscape. Fiona covered her head but groaned as she kicked one and stumbled to the packed earth.

The onslaught ended as quickly as it had begun and she hazarded a glance to see the granite dragon roaring at them, mouth open. A volley of rocks shot forth from his mouth again. Fiona squeezed her eyes shut and cowered down, covering as much of her head as she could. But the motions of Spine rocked and tumbled her into the side of the hut. Crashing branches and wrenching trees filled Fiona's ears as Spine heaved herself toward the earth, some internal force propelling herself farther along. Where was she going?

Like a boulder being dropped in a pond, Spine dived into the massive murky river. Fiona's fingers clung to the wood of the hut, but the momentum was too great and she, too, splashed into the water. She kicked her legs, gasping for air as she surfaced. Glancing frantically around, she tried to assess the situation.

Spine was mostly underwater, though her head and the hut were above. Rocks continued to rain from the sky but slowed from the impact of the water before they sank. Fiona ducked back under the water, taking the lead from Spine that it was better cover than the open air. With a vigorous swim she reached the dragon's neck, her hands outstretched to feel her way without sight. When she poked her head out again, she heard Gaili's frantic voice among the backdrop of frothing water.

From the bank Gaili waved, golden hands flashing her lantern to light the darkness. She indicated for Fiona to follow before darting through swinging reeds behind giant boulders.

After another moment under the rough water, Fiona pulled herself up on the muddy shoreline. Cold and sodden to her undergarments, she jogged to the covered space.

Didia, sheltered by the dip between the two boulders, scribbled in a notebook as she peered out toward the lake. Gaili threw a blanket around Fiona's shoulder, tutting about getting her in front of a warm fire.

Fiona wiped the fishy water from her mouth. "Why didn't you stay in the hut?"

"Spine said it was too vulnerable," Gaili said.

"Look." Didia pointed toward the lake.

As if she had simply been playing hurt, Spine launched herself from the water and straight at the granite dragon. She roared, her wings flinging out toward the creature. Evergreen trees like massive arrows shot from her scales and pierced the granite dragon's crumbling underside.

"I do believe we were holding her back a bit," Fiona said, shaking her head. She unsnapped her wet doublet and began to wring it out as best she could.

"Seems we were. Though where are the riders?" Didia murmured, eyes squinting into the forest.

"Took you long enough to ask," a voice answered from behind the boulders.

Stepping around, flanking them with crossbows drawn, was a human man and a faun. Even in this warm area they seemed overdressed. The man wore stiff woolen breeches, thick stockings, and heavy boots. His wool doublet had certainly seen better days. The golden faun was even more warmly dressed. A fur-lined cloak was layered over much more expensive fabric and spotless attire. His black horns had wool caps covering the tips of each. As he raised his crossbow at them, Fiona saw a flash of a thick book clipped to his belt.

Excellent. She had let her guard down for one minute and now they had weapons pointed at them. What would Richard think about that? Fiona pushed aside the surprising thought and raised her hands. "You don't belong here. What brings you to the Great River?"

They both took a step closer to the small group, fencing

them in. Didia reached toward her glasses, but the man interrupted her. "Hands up and away from you."

Were they Edge members? If so, Fiona had a few ways to play this out. But if somehow they weren't, then she had no leverage. Only a lot more questions. "The Painted Edge has to threaten old ladies now?" she muttered.

"You had to know we'd watch out for you. It's your fault she's here." He shook his head as if disappointed. "You really do let curiosity get the better of you, Investigator. Glad we could count on it."

Her stomach dropped. The hidden painting truly had been too obvious in the Keeper's cave. "The lake clues were a trap?"

"She said it would draw you straight to us." The man smirked at the faun. "And you didn't think it would be so easy."

Roaring and the smashing cacophony of impassable walls striking into each other soared overhead. Everyone ducked instinctively.

The man shouted, "Move farther into the trees." He motioned with the crossbow at the women and herded them deeper into the thicket and out of sight of the dragons. "Once Feldspar is done with Spine, we'll take you back to camp."

Gaili gave a small gasp but pressed her lips together. Her eyes grew wide enough, however, to guess her thoughts. Fiona was of like mind. If the Edge members knew about Spine, that meant Dani had as well. Knew somehow they would wake the dragon to get into this page. She had much more information and planned avenues than they had even guessed. But could they get any clues out of these two before the dragons stopped fighting?

Fiona would distract them and, in that distraction, try for knowledge. It might also be enough to divert their crossbows.

"Feldspar is an interesting name. What kind of dragon is he?"

Silence lingered after her words. The human man scuffed the ground with his boot, ignoring her.

But the faun glanced between them both, a small exuberance rolling off him. As if he couldn't stop himself, he said quietly, "Mountainous."

"Do you think he's a real mountain?" Fiona said to Gaili. "Or simply rocky exterior?" She tilted her head as if curious but in the direction of the other faun, hoping Gaili understood her intentions.

"It would make sense," Gaili said, eyes glancing up at the dragons. "I wonder if he's the incarnation of a mountain spirit. But we would only be able to know based on seeing other dragons."

"You're on the right track. They aren't spirits as we are. Actual terrain come to life. It will make for a tremendous study." The faun took a step closer. "Each biome here contains a whole collection of creatures that thrive off the terrain, but the dragons seem infused with them."

"Infused," Gaili breathed, delighted. "Spine clearly came from the forest region, and Feldspar from the mountains. But what about smaller dragons? There must be only so many in a biome that could birth creatures of such immense size."

"The largest ones, like those two, are one of a kind, we think. In the whole of the eastern mountains, we've only seen Feldspar." The faun chuckled, lowering his crossbow. "Luckily, he was as intrigued by us as we were by him. But smaller dragons seem less unique."

Gaili scrunched her face. "Truly? I wonder the difference."

"It has to be the biome. Dragons prefer to stay in their terrain at all times. Now, I wondered if removing a dragon from their biome permanently would have an effect on them, but so far the study seems—"

"Quiet," the human said to the faun. "Before you say something you're not supposed to."

The faun, gulped, a little wide eyed, and took a step back.

The man must've been the brawn while the faun was the brains of this particular grouping. Fiona wished the fauns could've chattered away more, but still, it had been a helpful conversation. If they had come across Feldspar in his domain and he needed to remain there, that must be where they were holding the Keeper. Spine would know which mountains they meant; Fiona was sure of it.

The cold-weather clothing of the pair suggested it was high up, possibly toward a peak. But how to get away from them and help Spine so they could get out of here? The man and faun had weapons. She did not. Well, nothing that was useful in such short range. But they only seemed focused on capturing *her*. What did they know about Didia and Gaili? Perhaps she could use their ignorance of the two to her advantage.

"If you're only looking for me, perhaps you'll let the other two go. Or at least let this one sit down." She motioned to Didia. "She can't stand for long with those knees. Poor dear."

Didia, for her part, immediately swayed toward Fiona as if proving her point.

Fiona felt her belt lighten. She grabbed the woman's shoulders. Part distraction, part actual concern. "I'm sorry, here." And began helping Didia down to the ground against the trunk of a tree.

"Wait..." the faun started.

Gaili took a step forward, speaking rapidly in the faekin language about manners and elders. The look of disapproval toward the other faun was palatable.

The golden faun nodded without hesitation but moved his crossbow from Didia to Gaili.

Gaili licked her lips, widened eyes glancing at Fiona.

Fiona stepped away from Didia and the tree toward Gaili. What could she say that would keep their eyes on her? "I suppose that when you release Larrakane's enemy, you think you'll stop being page turners and get to go back home?"

The man darted a frown at the faun.

But the black-horned faekin didn't move his eyes off Fiona.

Another thunderous clap from the dragons overhead made them all shift uneasily.

The man rocked back slightly, raising the crossbow. "When the bonds to that cursed deity are broken, then we'll get to go wherever we want for as long as we want."

"You think someone else won't simply own you? Command you? Tell me, how long have you been page turners?" Did they go through Guild training or were they almost immediately roped into the Edge?

They said nothing.

Fiona pressed on: "A few years? Maybe less?"

The man swallowed.

It was much easier to read other humans than faekin, and she focused on him. She took another exaggerated, swaggering step toward Gaili. She hoped as long as they thought she was moving toward her friend they would be wary of what the two of them might do. "And how long have you been stuck in this page waiting for me to arrive?"

There was a small clink from the direction of Didia. Was she trying to figure out which to use? Fiona hastily said, "Are you starting to feel it yet? The shivering, the nausea of page turner sickness?"

"What are you talking about?" the faun said.

Fiona leaned forward and squinted, surveying them. "It's been about three days or so, hasn't it? And your body is starting to tense up. You feel the pull but you're resisting it. Parts of you have started to feel flushed and hot. The other parts a bit rough, am I right?" She glanced at Gaili. "What do you think comes first? Red-hot fire of Blaze? The swirling, frigid waters of Depths? Or the stones of Cobbles taking over?"

"Cobbles, no doubt. I've seen whole arms petrified from staying away too long." She shivered.

"They're simply messing with us," the faun said lightly. He leaned back and adjusted his crossbow.

The man nodded but wiped his brow with the sleeve of his doublet. "Stop talking."

If Dani had left orders for her to be captured, they wouldn't want to harm her. She needed to give Didia a window to act. If she kept going, they'd get frustrated at her. The man was nervous now and might accidentally shoot. The faun was the more insightful of the two. He needed to be distracted but not frustrated. Could she get information at the same time?

She leaned in. "Did you know that your boss captured the Circle of Seasons?"

The faun's brows furrowed, and he glanced at Gaili. "She didn't capture them. She's keeping them safe. When we go back to Copper, they'll have their rightful spots back."

Gaili shook her head. "It's not true. She fought with them. Took them from Spine. The Seasons cannot remain at odds. You know what will happen to Copper."

"Old sea nymph tales. That's all." His voice shook. "Besides, they're not separated. They're with her."

Fiona held back a sigh of relief. "At least she has some sense in that."

The man started to say something, but a small black bead shot toward his feet. A malodorous mist of indigo eclipsed him. The faun reached forward to push the human out of the way and the cloud swarmed around his features as well.

"Old lady, am I?" Didia shouted toward the men. She jumped up quicker than their captives would've supposed she'd been able and hurried away.

"Move back," Gaili yelled and tugged Fiona away from the cloud.

When the mist dispersed, the two Edge members were still as stone. Limestone, to be exact.

"Swell," Didia, said holding the leather pouch up toward Gaili. "Can I get more of those?"

Fiona fanned away from herself. "Yes, I'd like to put in an order myself."

"You'll be first on the list," Gaili said lightly. "Though I don't know how long this will last. First batch and all."

"Let's get back to the open where Spine can see us." Fiona led them away from the statued figures toward the lake. As they pushed past the trees they could see the two dragons still tussling in the sky. Forest against mountain, the two landscapes swirled around each other. How much longer could they go on?

"I wish there was something we could do to help," Gaili said, clutching the folds of her dirt-covered skirt. "They're so massive. Anything we have might not even be noticed by them."

Didia adjusted her glasses. "Maybe we can call out to

Feldspar. Divert him."

"I'm sure any distraction would be beneficial to Spine." Fiona nodded. "Didia, hide behind that boulder and keep a watch for our *stony* friends or any of their companions." Fiona brought the dragon horn up and blew it with as much force as she could muster. She cupped her hands to her mouth and yelled, "Feldspar!"

Gaili followed suit, adding in a few high-pitched whistles that made Fiona cover her ears. The two creatures came barreling closer, but it seemed that the distraction was more like a command. The granite dragon swooped away from Spine, diving toward Fiona and Gaili. They would be crushed if he landed on them, and Fiona wasn't sure that Dani's request for capture would be considered by the dragon. They ran, Gaili going one way and Fiona the other.

The granite dragon had a split second to make a decision and flew toward Fiona. Spine hastened to cut him off, and as she edged close she roared, exhaling a plume of green smoke toward the granite dragon. Then he choked, his own replying roar cut off, and seemed to lose all control. Spine rammed into Feldspar, pushing his collision course away from the trio of ladies.

Feldspar crashed to the ground, a mountain smashing from the sky down into the earth.

Spine circled above and then landed, forelegs sunk into the water of the lake. Her chest heaved as she lowered her head to the group. "Climb. Hurry."

The trio rushed toward the dragon and helped each other up onto her scales. Before they could reach the hut, Spine took off in the air and sped away from the noisy area.

"You're hurt," Gaili said. "How can we help?"

"I will be well. It is a small pain."

Fiona raised an eyebrow. "It is?"

"Compared to my last fight, yes." Spine snorted and emanated a feeling of satisfaction at whatever she was thinking of.

"Well, I certainly hope to hear about it. When this is all over." Fiona shook her head. What would be a hindrance to someone like Spine?

"You shall. Though that may be some time from now." Frustration vibrated off Spine in waves. "There was no dragon in that camp."

Lowering herself to the ground, Fiona rubbed the floor of the hut gently and said, "We gathered from the two Edge agents that Feldspar, the dragon you were fighting, is from the mountains. Possibly at the top where it's coldest. It seems to be where they are holding the Keeper. Do you know where exactly?"

Spine grunted. "He's from the Thundering Peaks." She hissed, "I have tasted his grit before."

"With speed then please." Fiona leaned back against the wall, closing her eyes for one blessed moment.

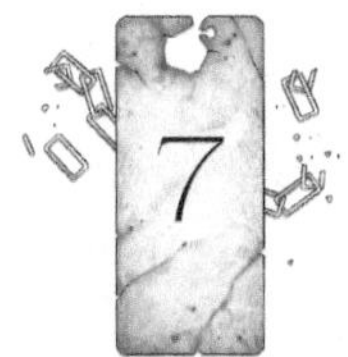

DOWN THE VAST RIVER and across the wide plains they fled. The sky thawed into warm, flushed pinks. Spine pointed out places she had once loved now gone, among the cloud-silhouetted sky. Dragons she knew now seemingly dispersed. She grew silent as they passed from the final deckled edge of a valley into the quiet grandeur of elevated snowcapped stone. Jagged peaks, more massive than the mountains of Restless Rise, spread out across the landscape. But they seemed haphazardly set within the range, as if placed there temporarily by a child during play. It was natural and yet disturbing.

No birds rose in the sky alongside them. No fluttering of wind. It was as if this was how the page replied to the destruction caused by the Painted Edge. A less combustible dying than Blaze had been, but dying nonetheless.

Fiona opened her journal to Richard, hoping against her own internal logic for some sort of message. But there never was one. She scrawled words of support, of impatience, but stopped before she let her worry turn to panic. He was not on his own. He had druids with him. Had the whole militia of Rise at his command. He would be fine.

Fiona ran her fingers over the smooth ink of Richard's last words. *I'd rather Larrakane's plan than surrender to those who would unleash such disaster. But if it comes to that, know that I...that I care for you.* As always, it seemed as if he was trying to say goodbye barely after saying hello.

But what of Larrakane? Fiona chewed on this, trying to understand what the deity might have as an escape plan to the whole of the abstract, the Guardians, and the keystones. Surely Larrakane wouldn't expect Richard to fight by himself?

Unless she was asking for more than that. It wasn't above the deity to use what tools she had to fight. She had created page turners for the express purpose of amassing an army. Guardians and the Leaves of Spine, too, yes. Why wouldn't she use Richard's very life if that meant his brother was defeated? Him with his goodbyes and the trappings he couldn't have. What could the deity be thinking! Asking him to sacrifice himself. Selfish, incomprehensible behavior. But Larrakane had shown in the dark edge that she would use any advantage to fight her enemy. Even if it meant hurting someone else.

"You see now why they all come to me." The deep voice of their enemy flitted through Fiona's thoughts.

She flinched, glancing at Gaili and Didia. They were deep in conversation about the slingshot projectiles Gaili had created and were paying no attention to her. Which also meant they weren't hearing him.

Fiona rubbed her chest, its normal warmth making her swallow hard. There was no dripping, icy coldness. No protection whatsoever. Did Larrakane abandon her?

"Are you still a useful tool?" the eerily familiar voice said.

She ignored it. It wouldn't do to give in to the creature. He was full of tricks. Getting into her head was simply another one of them. But the rebellious part of Fiona pushed back and she found herself thinking, *"I have never been a tool to anyone but myself. And I will not be one for you either. Get out of my head.*"

She waited.

There was silence.

But for how long?

No, she wouldn't let Larrakane use and discard Richard. She wouldn't let him sacrifice himself. She would do everything in her power to find an alternate way of defeating Dani and the Forgotten One so that Larrakane's final plan never had to come to fruition.

Flickering lights drew her attention as they flew deeper into the craggy cliffs of the mountains. In the shimmering surface of the snow, torches were quietly ablaze and set apart at the entrance to a narrow ravine. The sides were steep and emerald moss clung to the crags and roots.

"It is likely they have the Keeper there." Spine grunted. "For Feldspar nor I could fit within."

"And it would be a safe place for us squishy folk," Didia said.

"Well, let's fly closer and Spine can drop us off," Gaili said.

"Wait," Fiona said, squinting into the distance. "If we fly in with Spine, they'll notice it's not Feldspar. We don't want to give them time to react."

"How can we ambush them from here?" Gaili said.

"Spine could distract them." Didia twisted the spyglass as she peered out the now-open nettle roof. "Then we run in, take stock, and get the Keeper."

"It might have the same effect." Fiona rubbed the edges of her scarf. She started to pace the small hut. "Spine, move farther out and land somewhere behind cover."

Spine grumbled, "That is no small feat." However, she turned away from the sight of the ravine.

"If we don't want to use Spine as bait..." Didia started but then patted the wall. "Apologies, Spine. Then we need to repel down the walls of the cliff or sneak up through the ravine. I saw some, shall we say, dubious paths that could work." Didia opened her bag and pulled out thin leather gloves.

Fiona sighed. "I agree. I think it's the only unexpected way."

"Could we use ornithopters at all?" Gaili said.

"Not if we don't want to careen into the mountain. The space is too narrow and 'thopters need to be too precise," Fiona said. Flying over mountains and sightseeing were all good fun in Rise, but to try and go through such a tight passage…" She shuddered to think of the types of accidents that could happen.

"Don't worry, dears." Didia pulled on the leather gloves and strapped them over her delicate hands. "This isn't my first ravine. Nor my third mountain. Follow me." She pushed open the door and strode to Spine's crown.

With more quiet wonder than actual silence, Fiona and Gaili quickly followed after Didia and down Spine's lowered head. After confirming with Spine that Fiona would use the horn if they needed her, they pressed themselves to the granite walls of the mountain. Fiona wrinkled her nose at the mustiness of cold, wet rock. Dripping snow, melting in the sunlight, soaked through their garments little by little. She shivered with audible chattering of teeth.

"Put this on," Didia said, handing Fiona a thick woolen cloak from her bag. "It's standard issue although much better than the older ones. No, look at how Gaili's clasped hers."

Fiona snapped the cloak over her shoulders and followed Gaili's exact movements. Before she could complain of the heaviness of the garment not preventing further chill, she warmed instantly. "This is Travel Guild issued?"

"With a faekin touch. See." Gaili pulled the hood of the cloak over her head. Pressed against the rock, the cloak shifted between the light and the shadows as if she wasn't there. "Though they usually only give these to spotters, Dodger said."

"Well, we are the sterner stuff. Alright, dears." With no more than a crick of the finger, Didia began trudging her way gingerly across the thin, pebbly path.

Stepping lightly and keeping low, the women carefully moved, one after the other. Where Didia stopped, they stopped. When she took a quick step back, they too halted. Tension started to ebb away from Fiona's shoulders. She had never really known a spotter before, as most pages had been almost thoroughly mapped by the time she moved from skimmer guide to investigator. But following Didia's lead felt natural. It was a wonder the woman had retired at all.

The clean, cold scent of frost and vibrancy of intrusive vegetation restored some of Fiona's energy and optimism. By the time they came upon the entrance, a torrent of water smashing into rocks at the bottom of the ravine, she had even found her way to a plan. "I think it would be best if I went in first and announce myself as the distraction."

"Fi!" Gaili said before covering her mouth with a golden hand. "What if there are more Painted Edge than you can handle?"

"Well then, it will cause quite the commotion, won't it? Dani was—*is* prepared for me. But she couldn't have guessed that you two would have come with. It could've been anyone. All that to say, if I give you time to search, then it's danger well spent. And if they capture me, which they more than likely have been told to do, they might actually take me to the Keeper. And then you can follow in my trail."

"For a quick plan it does have legs, " Didia said. "And we don't know how long Feldspar will be out or if they are already close by."

Fiona handed the horn to Gaili. "This may not work for you, but at the very least it should be in your hands rather than the Edge's. When I think it's a good time for you two to come after, I'll shout."

"What if you're shouting because they make you shout?" Gaili said.

"If I'm shouting in pain, don't follow, but if I'm shouting in joy, do?" Fiona tried to keep the moment light, but it had no effect on the scowling faun. "I'll clearly call out in another language. I think fire would confuse them." Though Fiona was bad at Claire, Gaili would understand immediately.

Gaili sighed and nodded. "We'll follow slowly. But we're following."

Fiona squeezed her friend's shoulder before continuing on. The frothy water crashed against her boots, soaking Fiona's feet. It would be easier to walk in the middle of the ravine, away from the churning waterfall, but then she could also be spotted before she desired. She grimaced and ducked under the cascade. It pounded on her head and around her shoulders, as if it was alive with ill intention. But the cloak took the brunt of it, keeping her warm and dry. "There's little chance of this being returned to the Guild storage."

With her hands she felt her path forward, body heaved into the wall. She supposed there was some sort of entrance to a cavern within the rock as most people didn't prefer to camp in the middle of a cold, wet valley. Little by little she edged farther in. Under her feet, shale shifted with each step. She grasped tightly to any hand hold she could find, her fingers digging into slippery moss-covered rock. How much time had passed, step by haltering step? And where in the bloody dark edge was the entrance?

Clattering triggered a misstep as sudden rocks fell from above and pounded down onto her shoulders. Fiona sprung back away from the wall like a smilodon on a hot roof and into the narrow, unprotected middle of the ravine. She shaded her eyes, looking up to see no more rocks falling, but it was hard to see against the brightness of day. Disoriented, she glanced around, trying to determine if she should continue with her plan or search a different way.

Sweetness, like vine-ripened berries, wafted toward her. Vaguely familiar, but the scent quickly dissipated against the purging of the waterfall. She sniffed the air, glad to be alone for the moment thinking how absurd she must look. But no, there it was again. Faint. Fiona darted after it. Splashing through the rocky bottom, she came across a hulking boulder out of place against the steep wall. It was smooth, the water having worn at it for some time, but it didn't sit snuggly as if it had been here all its life. She trudged around it.

The sugary smell of berries was fresher here. Fiona ran her hand between the boulder and the sheered rock face, finding a small gap. She pushed, wedging her shoulder in, but the boulder didn't budge. So it wasn't simply for looks. Fiona glanced around, hoping her friends had seen her divert from the waterfall. If she was being watched, she couldn't tell. Be it them or the Painted Edge.

She slipped her hand inside the gap, looking for a latch or button. There was nothing. With a small sigh, Fiona slid her boot, then leg, then lithe body into the gap, pushing herself through. She thanked coffee for her lack of bulk and quickly dropped to the ground in the darkness.

Voices echoed farther into the cavern. Light—brighter than a torch, possibly a lantern—filled the space. On the wall there was a simple lever sticking out. Fiona grabbed it, pushing it down.

The boulder swung open easily as if it weighed no more than a feather. The crashing sound of the waterfall echoed in the cavern. Voices rose and footsteps quickened toward her.

Fiona squared her shoulders and stood tall facing the oncoming Painted Edge. "You have to tell me: What dessert are you cooking? It smells divine."

A tall black-furred smilodon got to her quickest. She crowded Fiona, one foot behind her to block any escape. "And who are you?"

Fiona raised an eyebrow but didn't move back. "Can't you tell? I'm Investigator Thorne."

"Brazen, coming in here directly," the panther said without moving. She narrowed her eyes. "Unless you think we haven't been told about you."

"I assume your venerable leader told you many things about me. But seeing as I'm in a hurry, you'll have to repeat what she said on the way." Fiona crossed her arms.

"On the way to where?" a puffing human woman blurted out. She bustled in, using her bulk and heavy black cloak to push the smilodon to the side. "You're not supposed to be here."

"Well, no one told me that. In fact I had it on pretty good authority this was your hideout near the entrance to the next page. Feldspar sends his regards."

The Painted Edge members glanced at each other, but the woman quickly shook her head. "I don't know what you're playing at, but it's not going to work. Antia, bring her in."

"I told you to stop telling me what to do," the smilodon hissed. But she grabbed the neck of Fiona's jacket and picked her up all the same.

"Where are you taking me?" Fiona called out in Claire.

Antia leaned away from her, whiskered face squished in pain. She shook Fiona hard. "Don't yell into my ear."

"Stop shaking and let me go," Fiona said. She hoped that Gaili was hearing this well enough and wished she could turn around to see if they were watching.

With sure steps the Painted Edge members carried her deeper through the narrow passage and into the cave. Dirt caked the floor, pooling into mud where water dripped from the ceiling. Beyond the stale air there was a scattering of wet moss here and there. A set of rudimentary stone table and chairs were connected to the wall, looking very much as if they had been made by the cave itself. Bedrolls, blankets, and other provisions were scattered about in the small space.

Fiona grabbed on to the stone table as Antia tried to drag her past it. They were moving much too quickly. "Let me sit at least!"

Antia dropped her roughly on top of the table. "Why is she so loud?"

"Am I?" Fiona yelled.

"I'm not sharing any space with her if she keeps this up." The smilodon glowered at both of them. "I don't care what our orders were. One noisy human is enough."

The woman pressed her lips together as if to stop a heavy retort. She sighed. "Fine. We'll put her in the cavern."

Before Fiona could respond to that loudly, Antia grabbed her doublet, dragging her from the table toward another small passage. This one was much shorter than the previous entrance. Crumbling rock had been evidently pushed to the side to make an entry hole into the mountain. It opened into a large chamber with arched ceilings, the space oddly reminiscent of a ballroom.

What was odder still was the small moss-covered hill taking up quite a bit of the cavern space. It seemed to swell and then deflate slowly. Extraordinary. It took a moment for Fiona's mind to catch up to what exactly she was seeing: the deep-slumbering mass of the Keeper.

Before she could begin to string together a full plan, another creature moved in her peripheral vision. What she had taken as crumbling rock before lumbered within the room. The muddy-brown earth elemental shifted the walls of the cavern with ease, forming a cage. Their hands smoothed the stone, and the rock of the mountain followed its direction. What was a rock golem from Cobbles doing in the page of dragons? Is this how they had gotten the Keeper in? Furthermore, how were they going to get him out?

The smilodon pulled Fiona farther into the cavern, dumping her inside the new cage. With barely a wave of limbs, the rock golem closed the cell, thin stony bars melding into place.

Fiona grabbed on to the cold stone and called out in Claire, "Keeper, wake up!"

The human smirked and replied in hisses of the smoky, spluttering language, "He will not anytime soon, Investigator. The cold mountain air doesn't agree with him."

Fiona didn't know if she was more upset by her flawless pronunciation or what she was implying. Perhaps what the Edge faun they had encountered with Feldspar said was true: the dragons were well in their own terrains. Perhaps this was part of the effect of removing them for so long. Even Spine had slept for two hundred years. Fiona paced the small cage and shouted in Claire, "You're fools to be unleashing such a dangerous force into the Book. Let me go so I can reason with your leader."

The human's smirk fell and she crossed her arms. "She has all the reason she needs. And why do you persist in butchering such a beautiful language?"

"I am not butchering it."

"You're certainly not doing it any favors."

Fiona glared at her but stilled her face when she saw a flash of a familiar golden hand in the entrance of the cavern. She coughed and said in the common language, "Now that you've gotten me, you can at least let the Keeper go."

She narrowed her eyes. "So that someone else from your little team can speak with him once he's home? I think not." She rolled her eyes, turning away from Fiona. "Antia, she's secured for now. Go make sure the gate is closed. If Feldspar really did speak with her, I suspect the others won't be coming back."

The smilodon glared but moved away from her stance against the wall with begrudging slowness.

Fiona knew she needed to keep the attention on her as long as possible so that Gaili and Didia could make a plan of action. "Oh, so you do work for her," Fiona called out bitingly. If this smilodon was anything like she seemed, she wouldn't be able to let that lie.

Unfortunately the human didn't see Fiona's plan quick enough. "Ignore her and go close the door!"

Between blinks, the smilodon was at the human's throat with her paw wrapped carefully around the pale flesh. "Tell me what to do again and she won't be the only human in a cage."

For her part, the human didn't flinch. "Either you watch her or you close the gate. Which job do you want?"

A clink of a small blue marble rolling through the cavern hole choked off Antia's reply. They both watched it before it burst into a tidal wave of warm turquoise water, sweeping them off their feet. With a pounding sound, like an elephas stampeding through a street, the Shimmering Depths pushed its way into the cavern.

Fiona grabbed on to the bars of the stony cage as the rippling water lifted her from the ground. Swiftly she pulled open her doublet and grabbed the murky green vial from the bandolier, drinking it in one gulp. Froth filled her mouth. She took one breath before diving under the water, purposefully swallowing it in gulps so that she could breathe it. Having taken care of her initial concern, Fiona held tightly to a bar, squinting in the clear water for sight of her friends.

She couldn't see much more than the bobbing heads of the Painted Edge members. Furiously, Antia and the woman swam toward the small door leading out of the cavern. The smilodon howled at the rock golem to help them. But the poor creature was pleadingly waving its stoic arms in the air, floating haphazardly toward the top of the cavern ceiling. As the water rose and the golem made contact with the stone, the ceiling shuddered. Rock peeled back, smoothing and melding away, to bright sky and cold tumbling snow.

Didia jerked on Fiona's hand, gaining her attention, and gave a thumbs-up. With one, two, three hits of a small copper tool, the stone spindles of Fiona's cage broke away from the floor. Between the two of them, Fiona managed to squeeze out, free at last.

They swam toward the grassy side of the still-sleeping Keeper. Gaili stood next to the creature's head, shouting at him under the water.

"What's wrong?" Fiona said.

"The water is helping him reacclimate but I don't think it's happening fast enough. I can't get him to stop being groggy."

"We need to get out before they close that hole and leave us on this side," Didia burbled.

Fiona snatched the horn from Gaili's belt and gave it a blow. No sound came out as water filled the instrument completely. "I have to get to the surface. We need Spine. She'll be able to carry him."

"Go!" Didia waved her on. "I'll stay with them."

With sure strokes Fiona swam up toward the light, cresting the surface of the water-filled cavern. As soon as she broke through she blew the horn. A loud, strangled roar echoed through the air, bouncing from rock face to rock face.

With a quick glance for the Painted Edge, Fiona swam toward the side, climbing up on the wet snowy ledge. Already the warm water of the Depths was turning the snow into slush. Humidity hung in the air. She shielded her eyes to the bright sun. Where was Spine? Why hadn't she replied?

Shadow encased Fiona and blocked out the sun as far as she could see: Spine!

"I cannot land for much would pierce me or be crushed. Where are they?" the dragon asked.

"In the cavern, it's filling with water and—"

Spine thrust the tip of her tail into the cavern, like a hook for a fish. With only a small grunt to give Fiona any sense of her ambitions, she pulled the grassy-winged Keeper from the water and high in the air. Gaili clung to his back, wide eyes watching Spine.

Fiona twisted the edges of her scarf until both Gaili and the dragon landed on Spine.

Didia bobbed up from the water, grinning. "They are never going to believe this at the Thread."

Fiona sighed with relief at the sight of her. She grabbed Didia's gloved hand, helping the older page turner up over the edge gingerly. Spine lowered her tail one more time. With a small boost and helping hands of Gaili, they were both safe, leaning against trees for support as Spine flew away.

Unable to stop herself, Fiona glanced back, searching. With open frustration, the Edge members watched them go. They were unarmed and without a dragon of their own. The rock golem was frantically trying to mold the stone of the burbling fountain hole without falling in.

The only place they would be able to return to quickly before they froze was Spine, the city. How long before Dani caught wind of their failure? Fiona hoped, with little optimism, it would be enough for her friends to get ahead.

INSTEAD OF FORCING THE ladies to walk all the way back to the hut on her crown Spine pulled together a large tree-lined glade for them to rest in. The Keeper slept on, unaware of the exact circumstances of their rescue.

"He will be out of it soon enough," Spine rumbled as she flew away from the cold mountain range.

Fiona wrung out her doublet, then spread it out among tree branches opened to the late-morning sun. She rubbed her tired arms, trying to put warmth back into them. While it was tempting to doze in this clearing, safe under the protective guard of Spine, she wouldn't chance it. Not until they talked to the Keeper. Instead she put her mind to something else. "Gaili, what did you do to that marble?"

The faun had no same compunctions as Fiona and was busy stretched out in the middle of the glade letting the sun's heat wash over her. Her voice rang clear: "I took Clara's work and tweaked it a bit."

"Tweaked it?" Fiona frowned. It wasn't like her not to expound on every part of the invention. "I'm sure you had the good sense to do much more than that."

"Well..." Gaili twisted her hands together. "Instead of it ripping open one page to another, I forced the interaction to open a small door. A tiny window really."

Didia chuckled. "That was a tiny window?"

"Well the Depths sort of decided to do its own thing. Sodden page. But it worked! I was just trying to wake up the Keeper."

"She thought with the terrain linkage, water would help the creature," Didia said, grinning.

"And if nothing else, it would be a distraction while we got the horn to you and you called Spine," Gaili finished.

"Marvelous." Fiona laughed. "Truly. You've learned more in the year we've been friends than I feel I've learned my whole lifetime. Opening the page a little."

"Sort of how your scarf works, I think."

Fiona stroked the wet scarf stretched across her body. She didn't dare let it hang out to dry, for it might get blown off in the wind. "Well, you keep that sort of information to yourself. If I learn everything there is about the thing, my curiosity might dwindle."

"Unlikely," came the rumbling voice of Spine. "Keeper, friend, please stop pretending to be asleep now. You are among friends."

A mousy voice replied questioningly. It was emanating from the hill of a dragon but in a vibrating language unknown to the group.

A reverberation of noises came from Spine, unheard by the ladies before. With little more than a whisper in between, the Keeper answered in kind. Rapidly the noises grew, with the Keeper becoming more animated. He sat up, his mossy body still somehow glistening even in the bright primal sun.

Wincing, Fiona moved away from the creatures and ducked her head toward Gaili's. "It seems they speak faster without prying ears."

Gaili laughed. "But think, Fi! Another language to learn."

"Oh, yes, that's exactly what I'm worried about." Fiona sighed. She didn't want to interrupt the dragons. Spine was so forlorn before this. and now she could talk to someone she used to know. How giddy that must feel. To be able to talk to someone who knew everything about you and not feel so alone anymore. It was how Richard said she made him feel. And how she had begun to feel about him. The thought warmed her. Quickly followed by the intrusive thought, the one she tried to push away, about how cold she would be if he was taken away. She didn't like to feel frightened. She always tried to conquer things that scared her. Nothing, she thought firmly, was completely out of her control.

The dragons slowed down their language. Spine turned, coasting in a different direction, judging by the new angle of the sun hitting Fiona.

She sat up on her elbows and cautioned a question: "Do you know where we should be going now, Spine?"

"The Dancing Lights of Augra," Spine said. "It is a small mystery in the southeastern range. But the Keeper says it has grown much larger over the centuries. The fae bargained for the information. He did not know it was also her who had him removed from his home."

Fiona hesitated before saying, "Please tell him I'm sorry for the trouble she caused. We are doing everything in our power to stop her."

"I will. I have told him not all of you squishy folks are the same. Unfortunately there is no real way to know danger from friend. But hopefully he will not have cause to put that into practice again."

"Is the Keeper coming with us?" Didia asked, waving at the mossy dragon.

"Only to see the phenomenon. It has been many years since he visited it. He will settle elsewhere until I return."

Fiona jumped up, dusting off her hands as her head began to ache. Yes, of course, why wouldn't Spine return home if she could? Perhaps that had been a deal she had with Larrakane. To return home after fulfilling her role as protector of Spine and sharing knowledge of the dragon page.

Still, to imagine Spine the city without Spine the dragon now seemed impossible. Fiona wiped away an errant tear and began piecing together her dried clothes to busy herself.

The day waned into afternoon. Streaks of clouds coursed through the sky in swirling trails. Spine used them to hide herself as much as she could while keeping up a fierce pace. Though she hadn't said it, the fear of being caught by Feldspar, or the Painted Edge, so close to their goal must've propelled her forward.

Without meaning to, Fiona slept. Exhaustion came for her and she couldn't fight it back. Only the shaking of Gaili's gentle hand on her shoulder woke her to the beginning of a dusky sky and the telltale sign that she had been out for more than a few hours.

The shadows of mountains deepened, and among them, swirls of glowing ruby and emerald lights danced from peak to peak. Arms and legs of the invisible performers touched down, shifting into cobalt and amethyst before leaping like gazelles back into the sky.

Without word Spine flew toward the shimmering curtains of jewel-tone colors. The Keeper departed them, preferring to use his own methods to look at the phenomena from a distance.

"Gaili, keep an eye out for anyone. I'd be hard pressed to

believe Dani would let us cross without issue," Fiona said.

Gaili nodded, peering through the spyglass at the landscape and air around them.

Didia scrawled furiously in her notebook. "There's a couple of plateaus between the forest and these mesmerizing lights that might make for a few pagemarks." She closed the book and tucked it into her sturdy garments. "Got a couple of stones and bark, should we need to come back here immediately."

"Good thinking," Fiona said with some regret she hadn't thought of it herself. She had gotten too wrapped in worry and too spooked by the Forgotten One to properly think about anything. She took the granite rock that Didia handed her and tucked it into her scarf. Did a new pocket already emerge for this place? Or would it once they left?

"Fi, this place has been utterly deserted. Look." Gaili handed the spyglass to her.

Large stone caves in the distance were empty and dark. She would've expected some flickering fires or candlelight. Hints of civilization. But there was none. "Spine, is it possible they moved while you were sleeping?"

"It is, though I suspect it is the lights," Spine said softly. "They were never this bright and moving when I flew these skies. They are beautiful."

"How do you think we go about swooping through a weak spot?" Fiona tossed the spyglass back to Gaili.

"Well, *weak* doesn't always mean *thin*. We'll have to push through, I imagine," Gaili said.

"Or break it down ourselves," Didia said. "Though if we're coming after the others, then perhaps Dani's done our work for us."

It was an odd thing to hope, but if it would make the journey through less difficult, Fiona would hope it. If the captured Seasons could pass through, so could they. "Alright then. Let's take it slowly and feel our way through. This isn't quite like flowers from Rise in a faekin pagemark."

"We should go ahead and crack some air," Didia said, rummaging through her backpack.

"Crack some air?" Fiona said.

"Never know if a place you're testing out will have a spot to breathe or not. Rule #5: Don't assume unless you're a blotter." Didia looked up at the unmoving Fiona and shook her head. "Those cartridges on your bandolier aren't just for show." She tapped the gray-blue bottle on Fiona's chest. "Air spores."

Before this mess with the Painted Edge, Fiona had always known which page she was turning to and could prepare for it. Or at least, only turned to safe pages or Spine if she needed to escape a situation. Now for the second time in her life she was jumping into a new page. One that was unknown and, possibly, unforgiving. She quickly grabbed the appointed gray-blue bottle; rice-sized black clumps barely moved inside. But following Didia's lead, she opened the bottle and popped them into her mouth. They crunched like crusty bread but tasted of nothing.

"Oh!" Gaili exclaimed. She rubbed her stomach, golden face changing from delight to concern. "Should it feel so heavy?"

"Until we need them, yes. You'll get used to the feeling soon." Didia capped her own bottle and placed it back in her sack. She frowned. "What about Spine?"

"I will survive," the dragon rumbled, somewhat impatiently. She sighed and fell into silence.

With a swift dive that startled the on-edge Fiona, they approached the swirling lights. Their brightness diffused the darkness around them. Fiona covered her eyes, but Didia handed her a pair of wraparound glasses, swapping out her own spectacles for the shielded ones as well.

"You turn the page toward a sun just once, you learn to carry everything," Didia said.

Fiona pushed off her immediate question and pressed the glasses to her face.

Dampness cloaked them as if trying to chill them to the very bone. The bright gems of light moved quicker. Rhythmically. Swaying curves enticing with the thread of danger in the unknown dangling before them. A tingling sensation crawled up Fiona's arms as they pressed toward the glow. Instead of the world continuing beyond with only the dark edge blighting the sky at night, a measure of darkness surrounded the swirling lights. Thick with nothingness.

A cold thread of terror wove through her as she focused on the lights. She stumbled back from them. *Flee.* Fiona gasped. Where could she hide to not be seen by the lights?

The shimmering curtain spun before them faster. Similar choking breaths and stutters came from Didia. The older woman turned away from the lights and ran toward the hut as fast as she could.

"Fiona, Didia, what's wrong?" Gaili said, reaching out toward them.

"We sh-shouldn't go in there," Fiona stammered out. She rubbed her chest as it grew tight at the thought of getting closer to the lights. What was there?

"We can't," Didia called out.

"I don't understand. I don't see anything to be scared of." Gaili looked back at the brilliant sky. "Spine! Can you push through with all of us?"

"I can't," Spine said, straining. "I can feel my wings as if pressed through a surface of water, free on the other side. But I can't move my body on."

"It has to be the lights. What they're made of," Gaili said and reached a hand through the brightness. "The other side is fluid. Cool and encompassing to the touch."

Fiona stayed far enough away that she wasn't near the gleaming colors but close enough to hear. What was wrong with her? She needed to get a grip on herself. Why was she so scared of this unknown? It wasn't like her. "What do you think it could be?"

"I don't know. It's certainly not a normal weather situation," Didia murmured, quite close behind her as if she was hiding. "I can't make myself move closer, but I feel a fool."

"Let me try to go all the way through," Gaili said. "I can report back what's on the other side. Maybe that will calm your fears."

Fiona shook her head. "I'm all for your experimentation, but we don't know what will happen if you go through. Or how time flows, or even if it does in the abstract pages."

"If we're separated now, we may be separated forever," Spine rumbled.

"If Dani could get through, then there's a fair chance I'll be fine. We are made of spirit," Gaili said as she pressed her hand through the barrier of colors again. It disappeared as if behind a velvet curtain. She smiled. "Besides the temperature change, it feels the same to me on both sides." She held out her other hand. "Let's see if I can help you through. Trust me, Fi." Gaili grabbed her hand and pulled her forward.

Fiona stumbled as she moved closer, clenching her scarf. Her heart raced as a surge of adrenaline flooded through her.

Why was she the one who had to do it all? What if she failed? She took a breath, but it was short. The rasping sound she made dragged at her ears. What if she could never go back home to Spine again? If Spine was gone, what would that make of her? Nothing.

A useless savior who couldn't save.

Gaili pulled her roughly back away from the lights. "Fi, look at me. Focus on me." Gaili rubbed Fiona's hands between her warm golden ones.

Feeling started to return, tingling through Fiona. She focused on her friend's bright-pink hair against the colorful display. When had she collapsed on the ground? She shivered and took a deep breath, gulping air. "Thank you. I don't know what came over me." She glanced back at the bright lights and tears pricked her eyes. She touched them, unsure of why they were there at all. What could possibly have made her react that way? "I don't think my fears are rational."

"Perhaps this is a test of some sort. Whatever is making us feel afraid," Didia said, still staring at the dancers. She took another step back. "I feel it keenly."

Why would Larrakane make such a test? One that would rob a person of their emotions like that? Or put them in such a panic to flee at the sight of this crossing. What could possibly be on the other side that warranted such anguish? Richard would have a guess. Fiona took another ragged breath. Richard would have a very good guess, but of course, he used the Word. The magic Larrakane wanted no human to have again. But it was magic the faekin already possessed. Maybe that was it. Maybe it was magic of some sort on the other side. Perhaps that was why Spine and Gaili weren't irrationally repulsed by it and could pass their hands through.

"I think it's us, Didia. We're human. I think we're why they can't go on. And why we fear it."

Didia adjusted her glasses, wide eyed at the threads in front of her. She nodded with little question and said, "Figures. Well, what should we do? Do we try to find another way?"

"I think," Fiona said, getting up and rubbing her hands on her doublet, "if I were Larrakane, I would want proof history wouldn't be repeated." But Larrakane didn't trust humans with the Word. So there was nothing, short of a miracle, the deity would possibly believe. Had Larrakane been scared when she made this? Was that why she had built in such an obstacle?

It was odd to think that a deity wasn't immune to fear. But Larrakane's fear, her wariness of repeating her mistakes was why they were in this situation to begin with. She had given *him* too much power. Let down her guard. But she overcorrected. By not trusting all the Leaves, she had created a weakness that the same creature could exploit. It was all counterproductive to what she wanted: for the Book to be safe.

"I want that too." Fiona's own soft voice surprised her. Yes, she wanted the Book to be secure, and she was willing to fight for it. She wouldn't let Larrakane's fear become her own. "Two steps, Fiona. Simply one after another." Slowly she edged toward the colors. No, she wouldn't turn and run, she told herself. She had faced other fears before. This manufactured feeling would not be the one that triumphed. Dizziness threatened to overtake her as her hand shook toward the light. Whimpering broke through her thoughts and she was startled when she realized it was her. She grimaced. Pushing herself forward into the lights, she muttered, "This is not your fear. Don't let it in." She would not let herself come this far and fail, turned away by nothing more than a manifestation of regret.

The shimmering colors dimmed. They were no less beautiful, but the fading melted away the urge to run. With a flutter, her chest throbbed. Her hand flew to Larrakane's mark. It was cold again. Fiona breathed a bit easier. She passed her hand through the barrier to feel the coolness on the other side. "I think that should do it." With quick breaths she explained to the others.

Didia inched up next to the glowing lights and held up her hand. Though she didn't say any words out loud, sweat beaded at her temple. She adjusted her glasses, swallowed, and passed her hand through as well. She nodded. "Well, let's get a move on before Larrakane changes her mind."

Fiona grinned and clasped Didia's hand. "Perhaps all together. To be safe." She put out her other hand to Gaili, who happily grabbed it. "Ready when you are, Spine."

Satisfaction with an edge of amusement emanated from the dragon. Silently she flew forward, through the ensemble of dancing lights and into the unknown.

BRIGHT WARMING LIGHT CASCADED through a long marble hall, fading into a darkened distance. Pillars every few feet dotted down the length. It reminded Fiona of the entrance to a grand gallery she once visited, tucked away in the Court of Copper.

But instead of resplendent gold ceilings, the sky above was a roiling sea of vivid colors that mirrored the whirling dancers in the dragon page. It was beautiful. But felt wrong to Fiona, having seen azure and copper skies all her life. As if pulled forward by some unseen hand, the shapeless swirls arced across the open ceiling of the hall before plunging into framed paintings of various shapes and sizes adorning the walls farther down. Like the pillars, there were new paintings only a few steps apart. A far as her eyes could see, in any case.

Glancing around, Fiona noticed that Spine had shrunk considerably. She arguably had enough room to walk behind them without knocking into the few statues here and there. "You're smaller, Spine."

Spine shuffled a little, pulling in her tree-dappled wings. She dipped her head, staring at the ground, and grumbled, "I don't like it."

When had they even dismounted from the dragon? Was it a trick of the magic? "It must be the page doing it." Fiona pushed down the odd mirth making her want to laugh. Was it the wonder of it all or something more?

Taking a step back, Fiona looked at where they had entered from the dragon page. There, a painting larger than herself hung on the wall. There were a plethora of humans with varying skin tones dancing among piles of colorfully wrapped gifts. While some were undeniably dressed in outdated fashion, others wore clothes the likes of which she had never seen before. No dancing swirls of color dived into this portrait.

Gaili gently grabbed Fiona's arm. "I've never seen something so mesmerizing. What do you think, Fi?"

"It certainly feels different. I didn't expect so much...grandeur." Fiona leaned closer, inspecting the painting. There wasn't a speck of dust on it. But a papery smell, like old books, tickled her nose. She took a hurried step back before she sneezed. She glanced around for Didia to make sure the older woman had come through in one piece and found her staring at the same painting with a strange drawn expression. "Mistress, what's wrong?"

"His face is so lifelike." Didia reached out her hand toward the dancing humans.

Fiona narrowed her eyes, on guard. "Who, Didia?"

"My husband, Bernard." She waved to the canvas, her face breaking out into a grin. "It's us in the orchard. Where we got married. Nothing but us, the birds, and the Elder druid." She sighed wistfully.

"That's not what I see." Gaili's eyebrows crinkled. "It's an oil painting of the seasons of the year, melding into each other from their four corners."

Fiona rubbed the edges of her scarf. "Interesting. Different entryway paintings, as if sensing something about each of us."

She quirked an eyebrow at the dragon. "Spine? What do you see?"

"Wild racing magic. Like a surging river." Spine tutted and curled her tail in toward herself. "It's everywhere. Step lightly." She shook her head roughly, tiny trees creaking as they rubbed against each other.

Didia pulled out her journal and began furiously writing in it. "This place is magic, real magic, and I want to remember all of it."

The sentiment was shared by Fiona, but Spine's warning had broken through her reverie. They needed to get a move on, see what they could discover, and get to Dani. "Spine is right, we need to be careful. Now does everyone see the colorful lights zigzagging about?"

The group nodded their heads and Fiona's shoulders relaxed.

"Then there does seem to be similarities in what we all see." Fiona pointed to a swirling amethyst statue. It wasn't a simple symmetrical spiraling shape. More undulating. Larger at the top and smaller at the bottom. Like a maelstrom in one of Mac's most famous drinks. "What about this statue?"

They all agreed that they could see the statue, settling Fiona's anxiety a bit. She hadn't counted on the new pages possibly being incomprehensible. She would need to think through everything she saw to truly understand them.

"Colorful lights and framed paintings. If we take the light to be magic, then what are the framed paintings?" Gaili murmured.

"Only one way to find out." Fiona nodded her head forward.

They took tentative steps down the hallway, footsteps echoing loudly in the quiet. Beyond the entryway the paintings were much smaller. The left side held a simple brown wood-framed view of an unfamiliar but lovely decorated parlor with varying mugs displayed on rows of shelves. A closed window above a plush settee looked out into a hazy purple sky.

The right of the hall held a white-framed painting of a study of some sort: dark leather chairs, black bookcases, and a flickering fire that cascaded light onto a stained glass window with the same purple view out of it, though darkened to an eggplant color. The scents of leather and oil mingled in the air as if it were wafting out of the painting. "Two different scenes. Two different places perhaps?"

"One feels like night and the other day." Gaili pulled out an empty vial from her bag and slowly pressed it against the wood, then the painting. Neither flexed nor gave way from the thin glass. Frowning, she tucked the glass back into her bag, "I wouldn't attempt to touch them just yet, but they do seem to be real paintings."

Eager to see more, Fiona continued down the hallway, boots thumping on the marble. Her eyes roved over the floor, walls, and ceiling, looking for the presence of other people. But all, outside the jewel-toned magic, remained still.

Another statue of the swirling amethyst vortex greeted them, this time a little larger than before. Beyond it began another set of paintings, now half as tall as Fiona herself. Beautiful brush strokes detailed vignettes into tidy rooms of dour stuffed-fabric furniture centered around short tables. Of oval rooms with empty wooden counters and a varying degree of scales that Fiona could only take as a workshop of some sort. One painting was even bent, showing what seemed to be a vacant street corner. The sign denoted some sort of Bread Street.

Dusty libraries, clean libraries, nursery rooms, antique stores, and more filled the canvases. The frames were just as diverse as the views: painted wood, plain wood, sculptured stone, gilded, marbled. No two were ever the same. But they all had one thing in common.

"It's so unexpected," Gaili said as they continued down the hall. "There are windows in every painting. But it's the same scene over and over beyond the window: a purple haze."

"But there's nothing to suggest where or when these places are," Fiona murmured, moving closer to one.

"Nothing beyond the styling of the room, no," Didia said, "and there's no one in them."

"They could all be the same place," Fiona said. It fit with what Richard had said, about Larrakane being an architect of sorts. If she made a dozen pages to fill her world, why not many more? But there was something off about the theory. For one, she had seen the whole Book in the dark edge and there weren't more than the twelve she had counted. And two, all the paintings were, well, not categorized in the least. "Do you feel like there's anything orderly about this place?"

Didia shook her head. Spine grunted, pulling her wings in again. She seemed to grow more uncomfortable by the minute.

Gaili smiled, her eyes bright. "It's flowy and more creative than orderly in my opinion. I quite like it."

"Yes, it doesn't quite feel like Larrakane." Fiona pressed her lips together, leaning into another painting. There were no signature strokes. No small initiates. Perhaps they were hidden within the flow of the paintings.

Didia stopped writing in her notebook. "Who would it be if not Larrakane?"

"*That* is a great question," Fiona said. Could it be the

Forgotten One? That didn't make any sense. Stella and Raina had acted as if these were still pages of the Book. Blocked ones guarding the entity. Not of his creation.

"We must keep moving." Spine gently pushed on Fiona's back with her snout. "It does not matter who or what this place is."

Fiona didn't necessarily agree. Dani had known and, if she was still here, would have the upper hand with that knowledge. But Fiona kept her comments to herself, for she didn't doubt that the magic was making Spine anxious on top of their mission. Fiona continued on, leaving the conversation behind for now.

Short marble steps led up to a raised portion of the hall. Flanking this change were marble pedestals. Each one held another amethyst cyclone. Tentatively, Fiona ran her finger across the statue. No dust. It was cold to the touch and solid. These weren't simply purple in color but also made of gemstone. Fiona glanced back to a painting, her mind clicking as slowly as her pocket watch. The purple haze and the purple swirling statues couldn't be a coincidence. They must be linked.

A glint from the turbulent magic above them lit upon a plaque on the pedestal. The symbols, however, were indecipherable.

"Gaili, can you translate this?"

The faun bent forward but shook her head. "I don't understand it at all. But there seems to be something behind here." Gaili pointed at the floor behind the pedestal.

"Oh?" Fiona bent to exam. There was a crack where plaster wall met cold floor. Though the museum had been virtually spotless up to this point, faint marks—scratches perhaps—dug into the floor at the wall. A secret door?

Fiona placed her finger over her mouth, motioning to the others to keep quiet. She pointed to the crack, then pulled out her slingshot. One could never be sure what they would find on the other side of a secret door. If they were lucky, it would be the Seasons. And if they weren't, they should be prepared. She gently pressed her hand on the wall behind the statue.

A click. Radiant gray light emanated from the slate floor of a passageway. Above, not too high from Gaili's taller head, the frescoed ceiling was edged in sculpted circles, intertwining with each other, the mural within them twinkling stars against a dark and inky backdrop. In the short distance was an open archway, but she couldn't see to whatever lay beyond it.

"Now why is this different?" Fiona murmured before walking through the gap. Though the air was warmer away from the grander hallway, Larrakane's mark fluttered like a cool breeze. Fiona halted for a moment but the sensation went away, and she continued on before anyone noticed, their shuffling and murmuring echoing behind her as they entered.

No portraits or paintings adorned these walls. But at the end of it all was a domed chamber. A few tapestries hung from the walls of a most unusual sort. One held a large visage of a brown-skinned woman, human, sitting with arms open as if she was expecting a hug. Fiona squinted as she stepped into the room. Was that her mother? She spluttered, "Umm, Didia. Gaili. Who do you see?"

"My mother," they both said simultaneously.

"Right." Fiona swallowed hard. She closed her eyes but there was no change to the figure upon reopening them. "So we all see our mothers?"

Spine sighed deeply. She could not fit in the domed room

and so stayed in the hall. "I see nothing of the sort. Perhaps it is for your minds and not mine."

That was in line with how Spine seemed to see most of the magic in the page. Fiona broke her gaze away from her mother's uncharacteristically gentle demeanor but noticed there was a smaller figure in the corner of the tapestry. A twinkling star, like one might find in the night sky, faded from white to gray to black as she looked upon it. There were more foreign symbols, like the plaque outside, at the top and bottom of the tapestry. But even with the context of the tapestry, Gaili could not puzzle out what they said.

The next tapestry depicted the same star as the first, but this time it took up most of the vignette. The star was dull, with no hints of twinkle about it. But the surprising element was a book below the figure. Splayed open. Pages mid-flutter. Gray motes floated down from the muted star to the book. As if it was filling it out from top to bottom. Indeed the bottom of the tapestry was somehow still unfinished as if it had been picked off the loom before it could be tied off.

The final tapestry displayed a triangle of figures: a twinkling star at the top, a swirling amethyst vortex at one corner, and a large fruit-bearing tree in the other. Before this was another stone plaque Fiona couldn't make out.

"Bold," Didia said, cleaning her glasses with a small cloth. "I didn't imagine her as someone who needed their own little shrine."

"You think one of these is Larrakane?" Gaili said with a wide-eyed stare.

"It must be," Fiona said. "The star at least. It's the one constant in all the tapestries. That book has twelve pages." She pointed to the middle hanging. If Larrakane was a star, was it the kind they thought of—pinpoints of brightness in the night sky? Or something else? Who was Larrakane really?

"There is nothing to show us the way out. We must continue on," Spine said, her voice rising.

Pushing down her inquisition, Fiona nodded. "I know but there's something I feel here." She rubbed her chest where Larrakane's mark throbbed, not uneasily. Was Larrakane trying to tell her something by the mark? Could she be communicating to her this way? Fiona moved back through the tapestries, one by one. When she came to the unfinished tapestry, her chest fluttered cool again. Without words she reached out, touching the threads of the unfinished tapestry.

Words, like a strained speech, flowed freely and loudly, into the chamber. The language was unknown. The tone, distant. Fiona clasped her ears, but it didn't block the noise. Another sound twined with the first, but this time it was voices. Millions of voices speaking one over another. Familiar voices of humans, faekin, beastfolk, plantfolk, and dragons alike. Questions. Shouts of anger. Prayers. Crying. "What is going on?" She glanced at the others to see how they fared but they watched her with confusion. Her vision began to darken.

Didia rushed to her side, catching her before she could fall to the ground. "Fiona, what are you hearing?"

Spine grumbled, "Rash decision as usual."

But Fiona paid them no mind. She was trying to understand what was happening. The voices of the Book she tried to push to the side. What was the speech flowing underneath it all? It was familiar.

"I hear something, someone. I think it may be Larrakane. But I can't understand what they're saying. I need to be able to translate it."

Gaili grimaced. "Languages are not your strong suit."

"I know but there has to be some way... See if you can hear it. Touch the tapestry." Fiona waved to the unfinished one.

"Or don't," Didia and Spine said.

Gaili looked between the two and then touched it tentatively. She shook her head. "Nothing. Maybe there's something here that can help you understand."

"See me. Help me," Larrakane's voice whispered, repeating itself without end.

"She's calling out for someone," Fiona said quietly. It was in a language not of the Book. But who could help the deity? And why could she hear it? Fiona dropped her hands, realizing the other voices had faded away. "The voices are gone."

Spine tapped her claws against the slate floor. "That was foolish. Who knows what could have happened to you."

Fiona's cheeks warmed at the dragon's tone. "I know. I do, but—"

"But nothing. Nicolosia would have never acted in this manner."

"But the druid would understand," Fiona said patiently. She took a steadying breath, reminding herself that she did not have to push back. But she found herself stepping forward toward the dragon regardless. "Do you not feel Larrakane's pull in this room? Does your connection with her not make you take notice?"

"I have no connection with Larrakane," Spine said uneasily. She shook her head. "My only connection is with you."

"Oh." She had supposed that all the leaders Larrakane had pulled to her safe haven for page turners were as connected to the deity as she was. Larrakane and Mac had certainly made it seem so. But in assuming Fiona had been wrong. And with that had not properly thought through what Spine's bond to herself must mean for the dragon. "The way you are connected to me, I am to Larrakane. I feel lost at times. Protected at others. But in this place I felt her stir. I'm sorry I didn't explain that." She placed a hand on Spine's neck and leaned in. "And I am sorry you're not connected to Nicolosia anymore. I know I'm not them. But there is method to my thoughts. And most of my actions." She gave a small smile. "I will be clearer in the future. And quicker."

The dragon blinked, large eyes staring into Fiona. She snorted, though not unfriendly, and said, "Thank you."

Fiona nodded, thankful that there was a better understanding between them. "If you want to lead the way, we're right behind you."

Spine agreed without grumbles.

Fiona gave the others reassuring glances as they filed out past her. She let out a deep sigh and gave the room one more lingering look before she had to leave it behind. She stifled a gasp as she realized she could read the words of the tapestries and plaques quite clearly.

All worlds must have their laws, the tapestry bearing the soothing visage of her mother stated.

The plaque simply said, *Celebrating Ascension.*

Tucking the information away, Fiona hurried after the others back into the hall. The hidden wall panel clicked back in place once they were all through. Fiona ran her fingers over the plaque under the amethyst swirl and read the inscription aloud: "I cannot yet save you, but your work lives on here." What had Larrakane said about her sisters before? They were gone, or shattered. Fiona stepped away from the pedestal, following Spine down the grand marble hall. "Not only can

I understand the plaque now, but I think I know what it represents."

"Truly?" Gaili's brow crinkled. "Did touching the tapestry do that?"

Fiona nodded. "Larrakane has family. Sisters. I believe this is the hall of one of them."

"The purple swirling thing?" Didia said.

"And the purple haze outside the windows. These paintings, or what we see"—she motioned to everyone but Spine—"must be hers. That's why they are so...unordered."

"I do not like to think there are more like Larrakane in our world," Spine said, staring ahead down the hall.

"I don't think there are," Fiona said quietly. "I believe they are... Well, what happens to a deity when they are no more?"

"Oh." Didia rubbed her heart. "Oh my."

"Yes," Fiona said simply. She didn't feel she needed to say more, judging by the looks on Gaili and Didia's face.

They continued on in silence, trying to keep to the quick pace Spine led them in. The paintings on either side of them began to dwindle in size and number. With the added context Fiona let herself idly wonder about what constituted work by a deity who controlled magic. And how had they handled so many worlds when Larrakane had only the twelve?

Finally they could see nothing but a dark fog ahead. The sea of magic stewed slower above them. The brightness of the jewel tones dimmed with each step.

"Why is it so much darker here?" Spine asked, wary.

"Perhaps because we're reaching the end," Gaili said brightly.

"But why would that also change the magic above?" Fiona said, taking quicker steps after Spine.

As they entered the darkened area they could see now what the fog had obscured. Nine framed pieces of parchment hung upon a massive plaster wall. They were stacked in rows of four and five. Side by side though several feet apart, equidistant, and identically framed in black obsidian.

Watercolor vignettes of the elemental and mortal pages in the Book.

Distinct slivers of the magic above zapped into the top four paintings, rippling through the landscape pictures of the elemental pages. The views within them shifted, very much alive.

"Well, I think we've found Larrakane's section," Fiona said. There were no more passageways or stairs. This was the end of the hall as far as she could see it.

"But is there any magic going to the mortal pages?" Didia squinted. "Hard to tell in all this darkness."

Fiona and Gaili took steps forward as if given permission to indulge themselves.

One picturesque scene of white clouds floating alongside earth eddies caught Fiona's attention immediately. A cascading waterfall flowed over the edge of the flying island and out of frame. But a thin, delicate black chain, like a Queen's necklace, weaved back and forth across the frame. It almost blended into the art under the dimness of the hall. No magic soared into this painting.

Gaili's golden hand fluttered to her mouth. "There's something wrong with this one."

Fiona tore herself away from the Rise art to examine the art Gaili stood in front of.

This piece held a watercolor of an open arched stained glass window in varying shades of amber and copper. The glass made a pretty picture of open hands revealing the twisted tree house of the Pavilion of Assembly in the Court of Copper. Seat of power for the Order of Seven who managed the faekin page. The likeness was uncanny, and Fiona had to remember that it was more than likely a living view.

Magic zapped into this piece from above, showering them with golden light for one brief moment. But instead of infusing the art, it rippled to the sides of the black frame. A strip of bronze filigree and beige lace nestled into the edges of the frame. Fiona took a step back, pulling Gaili with her. It was Dani's Seasonal Crown.

FIONA TENSED BUT TRIED to keep her tone calm. "I do believe that's Dani's collar."

"Truly?" Gaili's eyes widened. Swiftly she dug into her bag and pulled out a small magnifying glass. She took a step forward and examined the material. "It does have the same fabric as the crown. How she transmuted it to a cloak collar, though, is confusing. But what's it doing here?"

"Causing trouble," Spine grumbled. She snorted and lifted her head. "The magic flowing through to the copper one is pooling into the collar instead."

"Does that mean the Court of Copper is suffering?" Didia said, staying close to Spine.

"Probably so. If these watercolors are Larrakane's then, it's easy to see she's funneling her sister's magic from that storm up above into various pages." Fiona reached out her hand toward the black frame of the chained piece but dropped it before touching. "And how she did it through ours."

"It needs to be removed," Gaili said firmly.

"Wait." Fiona held up her hands, raised voice echoing out. "Dani wouldn't have modified the Copper picture if it didn't get her something. Remember, she wants to go back to Copper and take her place as one of its leaders. She wouldn't damage it too far." Fiona tugged her scarf, grimacing. "If the magic is funneling into the collar, then it might be funneling into Dani. She must have plans to come back and remove it."

"If we do it first, it might alert her," Spine said.

"It also might slow her down. Maybe even bring back the light here," Gaili said.

"But do we do this before we find the way out?" Spine said. "This is no weak spot to another page."

Didia walked up closer to the Rise painting, studying it. "Well, it's hard to tell what is real and what's not here."

"Everything is real, I believe," Gaili said. "We're seeing it in a way we can understand it but everything is actually *something* here." She dropped her magnifying glass back into the bag and sighed. "As for weak spots, well, we need to find where there's a blend of magic and echoes."

Didia placed her hand on the wall. She rapped it with her knuckle. The solid sound answered her in return. She nodded. "It would make sense it's in this direction. Opposite where we came from is logical, but this is a shared space between two powerful creatures. For all we know, it could be one of those paintings back there."

"For all we know, this is the reason there is no exit." Gaili flung her hand toward the Copper painting. "I think we should remove the collar. See if that helps. This darkness...it isn't right."

They could go in circles forever on what to do next. But Gaili was right. They needed to remove the obstruction from the painting and see if the change would make things better in this edge of the museum. Or worse. It was a chance they had to take.

"Alright. Stand back." Fiona slid out her crowbar from the leather pocket of her scarf and approached the painting.

Perhaps if she could wedge it between the lace and the frame, one tug would rip it out. But if she damaged the frame? No, she couldn't think in those terms. She simply had to do the best she could. She slid the end of the crowbar lightly between the two materials, resting it on the warm-painted watercolor.

No one breathed.

With a decisive tug she pulled back, snagging the collar at the end of the metal.

The crowbar sparked and turned into a carrot. Fiona dropped the fresh vegetable in surprise. "How in the Book did that happen?"

"She is Autumn," Gaili whispered. "The lace is still there."

Fiona took a step back, not bothering to retrieve the quickly decomposing carrot from the ground. "I'm very glad I didn't start with my hand."

"Let me try. I see nothing but magic." Spine pushed through the women, whipping around and swiping at the painting with the tip of her tail. A thin golden light pulsed from the painting, encasing the dragon's tail before fading away. Spine grunted. A heavy sound but she shook her head at Didia's unspoken questions. "Do not worry. It is nothing."

Darkness tightened around them as a crisp cooling breeze wafted through the hall. They coughed as dust rose around them, the memories of land and leaves dying over and over again.

Covering her mouth with her scarf, Fiona said, "This isn't working. What can we touch it with that won't change?

"I can do it." Gaili bit her lip. "I've touched it before, so theoretically, it should work."

Fiona knew her friend well enough now not tell her no. But she couldn't help but say, "What if it hurts you more because of it? Dani's power nearly suffocated Mac. It might not stop with your hand this time."

"It's a risk I'm willing to take, Fi. I've lived with it long enough to know what her power feels like." She lifted her head high and said firmly, "But if anything does happen, all my love to Henrietta and Matteo."

"Of course." Fiona squeezed her shoulder, than stepped in front of Didia, placing the older woman between herself and Spine in case things went awry.

Gaili reached out slowly, keeping the rest of her body as far back as possible with only the grace a faekin could have. Her golden fingers hesitated for only the briefest moment as she plucked at the tangled bronze lace and pulled.

Snap.

She flew backward, arcing into the air from the force of swirling colors rushing from the collar to the watercolor painting.

Spine leapt into the air, spreading her wings to catch Gaili against her chest with a small thud.

Her golden face was drawn and pale. Sweat dotted her brow, and she shivered once against the dragon. The bronze and lace collar dropped on the floor, forgotten as her friends rushed around her.

Fiona felt Gaili's chest, the thump of her heart encouragement that she was still with them. Fiona let out a ragged gasp of held breath before grabbing the faun's unaged hand and rubbing to warm it. "Gaili, can you hear me?"

Didia moved her hand above Gaili's mouth. "She's breathing. Slowly, but it's there."

Gaili's eyes fluttered open. "It's brighter."

Indeed the wisps of darkness had begun receding from

them, letting the jewel-tone light brighten the space. Grabbing her into a hug, Fiona laughed into her hair. "It is much brighter, yes. And you're well?"

The faun nodded and smiled sheepishly. "I'm going to have to study that sensation for a while. It was somewhat complex." She glanced at the burnt and ashen collar tangled beside her. "I suppose that's for the best."

Fiona shook her head at her friend but drew to attention as figures moved out of the corner of her eye. She hadn't realized how solitary the page of magic was until it was now filled with staring and chattering people in all the paintings outside of Larrakane's section. Those closest to them waved from the painting in greeting. The volume of so many people talking at once filled the hall with incessant noise that was hard to ignore.

"What is going on?" Fiona jumped up, wary that perhaps the paintings were more doorway than window.

"I think we fixed the page," Didia shouted.

"It doesn't feel fixed," Fiona muttered. All of the people looked human from what she could see. But they were more reminiscent of the entryway painting than Fiona and Didia's garden variety.

The massive wall with the nine black frames shifted easily in an orderly shuffle, making room for a door between the elemental and mortal side. It was a simple wooden thing, but the veins of the tree that it was made from were stark against the sandy color. A small black metal handle was the only indication that it could be used. Outside the door, running along the edges as a border in gold script was *A world begins and ends with love alone. — Kaira*

"What does it say?" Didia squinted.

"You can't read it?" Fiona said. But of course. They didn't have the same experience she did. She recounted what it said to them with a puzzled expression.

"What do you think it means?" Gaili said, leaning against the dragon.

"I think it means we can access the next wing of the museum, so to speak." Fiona helped Gaili up onto her hooves. She winced as the voices grew louder. "And perhaps sooner rather than later. It's getting hard to concentrate."

"My head is spinning," Didia groaned and slumped into Spine's side.

Spine slid her wing under the older woman, propelling her up and onto her back. "We must move."

Fiona took a deep breath and then pushed open the door. Her chest throbbed where Larrakane's mark inked her. It reminded her of Mac's warded door to her office. Perhaps there was more here than she previously thought in the way Larrakane had guarded these areas. Only certain people would be able to move on. Without whatever brute force Dani was using.

They stumbled through the opening door in hurried footfalls. Cloudy puffs of lilac and white intermingled around them, cascading suffused light as if they were lit by candle alone. They could see no farther than their own hands and the opening beside them.

Fiona turned around, curious about what the view was like from this side as the voices faded to a whisper. An archway led back to the page of magic instead of a door. It was deeply lavender with roiling and twisting swirls etched into every surface of the stone border surrounding it. Scripted above the arch in delicate lines was *Wonders never cease when mortals dream. — Alexandra.*

"If the page of magic belonged to one of her sisters, I do believe this new place is from the other," Fiona said quietly. Was this all Larrakane had left of her siblings while she was, herself, bound in chains? She cleared her throat trying to remove the sudden ache within. "I don't know anything about this other sister, but if the statement Larrakane remembers her by is love, I have hope this will be an easier place to navigate."

The clouds began to shift. Grew deeper. Turned to mist. Solidified into smoky columns. Broke apart. Drifted around them. Fiona had expected to find something more concrete here based on Gaili's definition of the echoing page that sounded like her mind. Though she hadn't heard her thoughts reflected back to her, she wondered if that was some sort of problem with being human. If this page, too, were part of the magic taken away from them.

The clouds weaved in and around them. Didia grabbed Fiona's hand and called down, "Rule #3: Best to hold on to each other. Never know when an environment will try to pull you apart."

Fiona grabbed Gaili's hand. She wished that Spine was back to her normal size, but there was no control of it in these abstract pages, it seemed. "Spine, perhaps you should hold on to Gaili somehow."

Spine nudged Gaili's back with her head. "This should work."

They moved slowly through the stirring feathered clouds. Fiona tapped with her feet, but no sound echoed back. They were walking on something, but it wasn't exactly a floor. More billowy puffs floated by them. Nothing kept shape for long.

How would they ever find their way through here? Better yet, how would they ever get to Dani and the Seasons in such a place?

The clouds shifted, parting back to show a sunlit beach up ahead. From the horizon amber pink light glowed, washing over the tan miles of sand. Crashing waves rolled on the shore dissolving into foam and pulling sand away from scuttling crabs.

"Well, that's a bit unusual." Didia pushed her sliding glasses. "Even for me."

"I've never seen a place like this before," Fiona murmured. While there were lakes and ponds throughout the Book to be sure, this place looked like a little bit of paradise.

"It's Sunset Bay." Gaili tugged on Fiona's hand. "I'm sure of it. The outskirts of the Summer fae's court."

"You mean Mac's?" Fiona quickened her steps, scanning the horizon. The clouds drifted by as her rugged boots hit sand. The smell of saltwater and baked air enveloped them. She tugged on her scarf, pulling it away from her heated neck. "How is this possible?"

"Perhaps the echoes were taking thoughts from my mind," Gaili said. "Perhaps this place is something like a mind reader."

If it were, it might only be showing them something linked to Mac. Not that the fae was actually here herself. "But you all see the same thing?"

"Sand, blue sky, hot sun." Didia fanned herself. "Yes, I see it.

"It is unusual but no doubt it exists." Spine thumped her tail in the sand, moving it about. "Feels very real. Gritty."

"Well, let's scout around. There may be miles to this beach."

Fiona started to pull away, but Didia called out to her.

"No, we need to stay together. I know you want to find them quickly. We all do. But if we separate, this place could just as easily change."

"Yes, you're right. I'm sorry." Fiona grabbed Gaili's hand again. It was hard to fight the anxiety that fed the urge to run as fast as she could until they found someone, anyone from the Seasons. She sighed and rubbed her forehead. "Well, Gaili, is there anything particular we should look out for first? From a past perspective?"

Staring out at the water, Gaili tugged on one of her pink curls. "Historically, the Summer fae's domain was the eastern edge of the continent. It was the hottest, of course. Although whether that was because of the Summer fae or the other way around has always been debated." Gaili pulled at her bodice. "Oh, I don't know, Fi. It's all such an old history. If this is a re-creation of that coast, there should be a pavilion or something set up for the Summer fae's court to rest and take counsel in."

"We'll look for tents and such." Fiona pulled them on.

They searched for what seemed to be over an hour. Up the beach, across the sand, behind dunes. Avoiding sand pits and what Fiona was sure was a small sand castle at one point. But they didn't find her.

"What if it's not a recreation of history? But of Mac in present day. What would you expect to find then?" Didia leaned against Spine, her chest rising rapidly with the exertion.

Fiona thought hard about that. Mac was doting to all who came in the bar. And always inventing things. She was warm, bold, and forward without putting anyone down. But she worked hard, very hard, every day. Her easygoing personality was hard earned, now that Fiona knew more about her past. She couldn't imagine the fae surrounded by attendants and overly attentive people. "Probably somewhere she can relax, take in the sight, and enjoy herself alone."

"There's a cove, over there." Spine pointed with her snout.

Didia squinted and mumbled, "But was it there before?"

"I don't believe we've been this way yet," Fiona said. It certainly looked different enough. But the spotter's questioning nature rivaled that of her own, and she took wary steps toward the rocky hideaway. Her steps increased, however, at the sight of the figure in the distance.

Lying in the sand, radiant golden skin a rival to only the sun above them, was Mac staring out to the sea before her. Her cream-and-indigo tattoos dappled in the light subtly spreading from her. Her ethereal azure robe flowed out behind her like the train of a queen, though her toes were dug deep down into the beach as playful as a child.

"Mac!" Gaili said brightly.

The fae turned to them with a happy smile. "Well, hello, children."

THOUGH HER SMILE WAS bold, it was not easy. Fiona stopped Gaili from running to the fae and whispered, "Mac has never called me a child in my life. Even when I was one."

Gaili frowned. "Do you think it's not her?"

"What are you whispering about? Like bees in a bonnet," Mac shouted. She jumped up, dusting sand from her matching azure-colored bodice and skirt. Ignoring the wind catching at her loose golden hair, she beckoned them over.

Had she been wearing those clothes before? Fiona tilted her head. "Possible, though she does seem to act like herself. Let's simply be cautious." She waved to Mac and shaded her eyes against the honeyed glow radiating from the aura of the fae. Fiona's shoulders relaxed and she couldn't hold back a grin as she quickened her steps. She could almost taste the sweetened cold ice she had in her youth sitting in the comforting warm heat of the Thread. Fiona sighed with pleasure as she reached her friend. "Are you alright?"

"Peached." Mac nodded. She wrapped her billowing robe around herself. "Come on, this strip of beach is perfect for sitting. Private and not a cloud in sight." She turned her golden face back to the sun and closed her eyes against it. "It's lovely here."

Something flashed in Fiona's mind, a query of concern. But

the warmth felt so good she, too, turned to the sun and closed her eyes. She hated being so cold all the time. It had been a dreary winter in Rise when she was inked. And she had met dreary people still throughout the first few days of being a page turner. The Hinge with its cold marble halls. The rough training grounds and endless rows of beds in the dormitory. It wasn't until she ran into Mac walking through the bustling marble corridors of the Hinge that she had felt an inkling of comfort. And she had to know where such a lady like that thrived.

For a moment she felt like she was back in the Hinge. Winding her way through the cold corridors out onto the open vestibule. Between the darkened sky and the fat raindrops was a beacon of amber light floating through the streets. Sky-blue trails she followed right up to the door of the Thread. Fiona pushed her way in to see a room full of warm-faced individuals. Though they all looked at her as she entered, no one shooed her away for being too young or acted as if she didn't belong.

She hurried to a corner and sat down, trying to make herself small and unforgettable. Fiona scanned the room looking for the ray of sunshine she had followed here. But it was hard to see over so many people. Humans mingled with smilodon. Elephas with fauns. A lone fairy flitted across the tavern to take a seat with an unusual grouping. In watching the others she didn't realize Mac had slid right next to her.

"What will you have?"

Fiona jumped. She looked up into the amber eyes of the fae and said breathlessly, "Umm, coffee. If you have it."

Mac looked her up and down. "Aren't you a bit young to drink that bitter stuff?"

"No," Fiona said, "I drink it all the time at home."

"I suppose you haven't had any since you were inked?" Mac said softly.

Fiona shook her head. She felt a little nervous, but there was something about the fae woman that didn't seem worrisome. She relaxed into the seat.

"Alright then. One coffee for you. My name's Mac." The fae stuck out her hand.

"None of the other faekin shake hands," Fiona said with curiosity. She took the hand and shook it.

Mac winked. "I'm not like other faekin." With that, she disappeared into the crush of Thread patrons.

Fiona let her head rest on the worn leather back of the chair, watching the others. She could learn so much about people, about the other pages just by sitting here. Her curiosity in the world around her might actually be sated in the Thread. She glanced at the stairs that led out of the tavern. Did those lead to bedrooms? Could she rent one? It would be better than the dormitory. She could stay here awhile, talk to people, get a feel for things before going back to training. It was hard, and here it didn't have to be.

Mac came back with her coffee and put the mug on the table.

Steam rose from the cup and the familiar smell had her taking a deep whiff. "It's perfect."

"I should hope so. If I can't brew a perfect cup of coffee, then I'm not really fulfilling my role." Mac smiled.

Fiona frowned. "What do you mean?"

Mac waved with a rag. "I'm a tender. The bar, the page turners, the drinks. It's what I do."

This seemed reasonable. The smell of the coffee invaded her nostrils, reminding her it was hers, and she took a long sip.

"So are you going to stay awhile?" Mac said.

Fiona hesitated. "I'd like that. If I can. At least for a little bit until I have to go back to training."

"Of course. Stay as long as you like." Mac rapped the table with her knuckles and went back to the bar.

Fiona closed her eyes, wrapping her hands around the mug. Of course, she should stay awhile.

There was a sharp tug on her arm, and the hot coffee sloshed across her hand and table. Her eyes flew open to see an older brown-skinned woman with big glasses staring at her.

"Who are you?" Fiona asked.

"Get up." The older woman tugged on her arm again with more strength than it looked as if she had. "Rule #7: Coincidences are best poked."

"What are you talking about?" Fiona said. She pulled away from the old woman. "I'm not following you."

"Fiona, snap out of it," the woman said.

"What's going on here?" Mac bustled over and crossed her arms. Her aura grew brighter. "You leave her be."

The older woman ignored the fae and grabbed Fiona's hand. "Think about it, Fiona. When we thought of the Seasons, we found the beach. When we couldn't find Mac, we thought of a place she would be, and lo and behold, there she was. And now you're suddenly in the Thread. Why do you think that is?"

Fiona stammered, "I saw her and I wanted to follow her. It's nice here. It's warm and has chairs."

"Release her immediately or you will regret it," Mac said, a radiance showing from her like no other.

"I can't pull you out if you don't want to come out," the older woman said, "but doesn't it seem too easy?"

Mac flicked her eyes between Fiona and the older woman. Her aura dimmed. "Relax. Stay here. You can always go back to turner training when you're ready."

The hubbub in the Thread seemed to increase. Patrons were talking louder, more animatedly to each other. The air heated up around them all. Fiona yawned and leaned deeper against the back of the chair. "It's the first place that's felt like home."

Mac put her arms around Fiona's shoulders and pulled her away from the grasp of the older woman. "It is your home, Fiona. It'll always be your home. You don't have to go back out there." She turned to the older woman. "But you have to leave."

The older woman adjusted her glasses and stood taller. "Make me."

Mac grabbed the older woman's shoulders, pushing her forward. The sea of patrons parted, clearing her hurried path. With a heavy push, Mac shunted the older woman out of the tavern.

Cold trickled in from the open door, making Fiona shiver. Her head snapped up as Mac approached.

"You truly made her leave."

"Of course. She doesn't belong here. Not like you and the others do." She waved her hand to the patrons.

Fiona stared into the crowd, her interest high again. No one was looking at her or Mac. They were talking among themselves as if nothing had happened. How odd. Page turners loved gossip. Why wouldn't they be talking about Mac throwing someone out of the Thread? That never happened.

That never happened.

Mac never threw someone out of the Thread.

It was the one place that could be home to all page turners, no matter who they were.

Fiona took a step back away from Mac. "I think I want to ask her some more questions."

Mac blocked her path. "There's no need for that. You can find all the answers you need here."

No, this didn't make sense. Mac would never encourage her not to seek out answers. She didn't try to keep her protected. Fiona needed to get away from here. She needed to get to the door. She put a hand on the spilled mug of coffee and handed it to the fae. "May I have another please?"

Mac smiled, wide and uneven. "Of course."

As soon as Mac turned back toward the bar, Fiona took off. She tried to push her way through the patrons, but they seemed to crowd around her more. They didn't grab her but took up more space, more sound. She wouldn't be able to push through, not even in whatever fake place this was. But she was smaller than normal. She dropped to the ground and rolled beneath the feet of an elephas blocking her path. Two more steps and she was at the door.

A golden tattooed hand grabbed her own. "If you go out there, I can't keep you safe."

"There's no point in being safe if it's not real," Fiona said. She jerked on the door, throwing it wide.

Coldness swept over her and she opened her eyes. Manacles of misting clouds swirled around her arms and legs. She tugged her hands free and they dissipated into smoky trails, reforming farther away.

Clouds weaved in and around the prone forms of Gaili and Mac. Fiona rushed to them, and as the clouds parted she saw Didia hunched over Gaili and whispering to her. Spine was nowhere to be seen.

"What happened?" Fiona said.

"As soon as you laid down with Mac on the beach I knew

something was wrong. I tried to keep to my rules, reciting them until I could understand what was at play here. Spine got distracted and flew off."

That didn't bode well at all. "I almost didn't get out."

Didia grimaced. "Glad you could though."

"I wouldn't have if it wasn't for you." Fiona sighed. She took Mac's hand but dropped it just as fast. It was blazing hot. "How did you go in and out of my dream?"

"It wasn't a dream. It was your mind. I found that holding your hand did the trick. Gaili tried it with you first, but she promptly laid down too." Didia shook her head. "I can't get into hers."

Fiona grabbed Gaili's hand and closed her eyes. She tried to keep a running list of the order of the pages in the Book, reciting it as Didia did her rules. But nothing happened. Fiona bit her lip. Hopefully it wasn't fae nature against human that prevented them. Maybe her connection with Mac would help? Picking up the Summer fae's hot hand again, she concentrated and found herself on a sunny beach.

Mac lay on her stomach facing the sea and away from Fiona. It was warm and inviting.

"No." She had to keep her wits about her this time. "Blaze before Depths. Depths before Mistral." She repeated herself until she felt she was firmly in hand. Once she did, she stood a distance away from the Summer fae and said loudly, "Mac, we have to go."

"Go? Why?" Mac didn't turn around but instead sighed, her eyes trained on the sunset across the blue waters. "It's quite lovely here."

"Because we're not really at your beach. We're in a page that plays with your mind. And you've been stuck here."

Mac waved her words away. "Impossible. I think I can tell the difference between a real beach and a fake one."

Fiona tilted her head, glancing around. What made this place such a draw for Mac? If the Thread had drawn Fiona as her home, was the beach doing the same for Mac? "You haven't been to the beach in two hundred years, have you?"

"I come here every day." Mac turned toward her finally, brow furrowed. "Are you sure you're fine, Fiona?"

"No. No, I'm not." Fiona sat, getting to her eye level, and said softly, "I've never been to your beach, Mac. I met you long after you were inked and had to come live on Spine. Remember Spine? It's under attack now, by Dani and the Painted Edge."

Mac rolled away from Fiona and sat up. "What? No, stop it."

"I need your help, to save the city of Spine and the Book. Page turners need you to leave your home and help us. I know it's hard, this is a place of comfort for you. And I'm sorry. But we're lost without you." She reached out and gently grasped Mac's hand. "*I'm* lost without you."

A gull cried in the distance and wind picked up bits of sand, drifting around the pair. Mac's golden eyes stared into hers as the sun began to set more rapidly behind her. She shuddered and sighed. "Fiona, what's going on? Where are we?"

The pink and amber sky melted away into gray shapeless clouds. Fiona wrapped her arms around Mac. "We're in one of the abstract pages. You were brought here, by Dani, and got stuck. But you're back now."

Mac rubbed her downy ear and looked around frantically. "Where's Nic and Arc? They were with me."

"I don't know. We've come across only you," Didia said, rising from the ground. "Glad to have you back, though, dear." She gripped Fiona's shoulder. "Gaili's still trapped."

"Mac, can you help her? I tried but I couldn't get through."

Mac tugged on her ear again before nodding. She looked over Gaili, holding her hand and then pulled her into a loose hug. She stroked her back gently and murmured softly in her ear.

Gaili's eyes popped open. "Oh! I was in the kitchen at home. You were there, Fiona. I thought so, at least." Her expression went blank as she realized she was in Mac's arms. "Did I fall?"

Mac gently released her. "Simply an old trick my mother used to do when I was having a bad dream. Though that wasn't any dream I've ever felt."

"It's odd that all our places would be so different in this trap. But I suppose they all had a common feel of comfort." Fiona rubbed the edge of her scarf, thinking of the quote on the archway they entered. Fiona realized the inscriptions were very apt for the pages they adorned. "Or love." She shook her head, clearing away her thoughts, and grabbed Mac's arm to help her up. "Do you know what page we're in? We need to find the others."

"The page of mind." Mac carefully rose from the clouds to stand. She stretched, though she grimaced in the effort. "It's an abstract page alright. One of Larrakane's connections to her sister's domain."

"Domain? As in not from around the pages?" Gaili said.

"Correct. The deity is from outside the pages." Mac groaned. "There's something wrong. I can't feel the Book."

"Dani severed your connection with metal shavings from black chains." Fiona swallowed hard at the mention of the chains. "*The black chains*, if you understand what I mean."

Mac's eyes widened. "She truly did it. And now we're all gone from Spine."

"It's breaking apart. If you return, can you stop it?" Fiona said.

"Each Leaf that returns will stem the tide. But we all have to go back." Mac pulled the folds of her azure gown tightly around her. "I find it hard to believe Dani thought of this escapade of hers being round trip."

"Do you know where she took the others?" Didia asked.

"No. I don't remember anything after Dani…" Mac rubbed her face, seeming much older than she had before. "I can't turn the page like this."

Gaili glanced at Fiona before leaning in and offering Mac her hand. "I'll take you home."

Fiona's chest tightened at her friend's words. She started to say that she would instead but stopped. As much as she hated it, Gaili was the best choice. With Spine flown off, Fiona would need Didia's counsel in the page. But Gaili wouldn't be able to simply turn back to them. Once she left, Fiona wouldn't see her till they got back to the city. Fiona rubbed the edge of her scarf. "Thank you, Gaili." Before the faun could reply, Fiona hugged her hard. "Please let the others know how we're faring."

"Of course, Fi. I have great confidence I'll see you soon." Gaili smiled wide, hugging her back. She took off her bag and handed it to Didia before hugging her. "Stay safe and keep an eye out for her. She gets into the most curious situations."

Mac grabbed on to Fiona's arm. "Dani bound herself to that creature. Do you understand me? Even if she wants to, even if she regrets what she's done, she can't go back on a binding like that."

"I understand." Fiona covered her friend's hand, the panic in her eyes raising her own apprehension. "She'll stop at nothing till she releases him."

"It's not just about releasing that *thing*. Larrakane has to be weakened. Without that, it's simply an even match. You have to find Archae and get him to Larrakane. He'll know what to do."

"Alright, Mac. Alright." Fiona rubbed her back gently before hugging her tightly. "We'll try to come home as soon as we can with the others. Be careful. I don't want to lose you two."

Gaili shook her head, bubblegum curls bouncing. "You won't."

Gaili took hold of Mac's waist and turned the page.

The clouds shifted as the world folded away in front of them. Through the opening was a mottled sky of bright-blue storms and crumbling rock. The city of Spine was struggling and had certainly seen better days.

The shapeless gray clouds perked up. Pushing against each other like impatient school children, they began to lunge through the opened vignette. Fiona tensed. "I think the abstract is trying to leave."

Hurriedly they strode forward into the city. The fold smoothed out with an audible *clack*. Fiona winced at the sound. The clouds hastily fanned away.

"We can keep hope we're not too far behind them," Didia said, holding out Gaili's pack.

Fiona nodded, shouldering her friend's bag. It would be rather good luck if Spine and the other Seasons weren't too far ahead. But luck wasn't a skill the investigator was used to leaning on.

12

"SPINE!" DIDIA AND FIONA called out in unison. The sound echoed. Off what, Fiona couldn't tell. The page of mind, as Mac had called it, seemed a little at odds with itself. Solid enough to traverse but so dense nothing could be seen beyond the next person. Until one fell into their own mind apparently.

Fiona rubbed the edges of her scarf and called out again, "Spine, where are you!?"

"What do you think about using that horn?" Didia motioned to the instrument on Fiona's hip. She raised an eyebrow. "Seems to work mighty well on the dragons."

"Yes, it does. But seeing as Spine could so easily slip through the barrier from the page of magic to the page of mind, there might be other dragons as well." Fiona tapped the horn. "The area beneath the colorful lights was quite barren, remember?"

Didia's jaw dropped and her eyes darted around. "Well, I never thought I'd see the day I didn't put two and two together faster than anyone else."

Fiona snorted. "Yes, well, what was it? Rule #7: Coincidences are best poked?"

The older woman adjusted her glasses and nodded. "Knew you were a quick learner when I met you." Didia sighed and waved out into the dim clouds. "We're getting nowhere here. We don't know how far we have to go, and we might run into someone who likes us a bit less than Spine or the fae do. We need a plan." Didia shrugged off her pack and dug in. She pulled out a folded Travel Guild ornithopter and handed it to Fiona. "Here, let's see if we can't get above the clouds and spot the dragon."

"How in the world did you—" Fiona stopped upon seeing Didia pull another ornithopter out of the bag. She couldn't help herself and said, "You have more tricks than you let on."

"Rule #8: Best way to keep a secret is to keep it to yourself." She winked and shrugged the ornithopter on, then reached out and helped Fiona put on hers.

Holding hands tightly, they pulled the rip cords and took off. The clouds rose with them, continuing to mask the distance. Perhaps there was something more to this page than simply putting you in your own mind. Perhaps it could continue reading it as well. Maybe it *was* trying to block their path.

"Follow my lead," Fiona said. She squeezed Didia's hand and barreled ahead.

The clouds followed, thinning into streams of smoke and fog to swirl around them.

Fiona leaned left, directing the ornithopter. The fog came with. She leaned right and backward, and the fog followed along. Thinking of going backward, she shot forward. The fog fell behind like a distracted puppy. So not all-knowing, this page of mind. Interesting. Like Larrakane herself.

"It's Spine!" Didia called out, pointing ahead. She tugged on Fiona's hand, directing the ornithopter down into bright green leafy trees. A bountiful forest lay below them, trees blossoming with buds, a feast for the eyes.

Fiona squinted trying to make out the arms or legs of the dragon, but she could see nothing but treetops and thick brambles. Perhaps if Spine encountered Nicolosia, she was now back to her normal size. Wind rustled through the leaves and the gentle buzz of insects greeted them pleasantly. The familiar sound mingled in the air with the jostling of nimble creatures running just out of sight. The heavy perfumed scent of jasmine and honeysuckle hung around, cocooning them in their sweetness.

Fiona jerked to a halt and pulled Didia back. "There's movement."

"Of course there's movement," Didia said with a frown. "She's a living creature."

"No, there's movement among the trees and in the branches."

And Spine had released all her forest friends before they had ever left the city.

Shadow arched over them, blocking out the familiar warm light. Thick leafy vines dropped from above, encasing them in a tangle together. The blades of their ornithopters abruptly stopped spinning, chugging against the rope of vegetation. Fiona pulled her cord, lest the ornithopter break. They were dangling above the forest, but what had caught them?

Nicolosia, pine-green hair blowing in wild stirs around their head, stood on the back of the dragon Spine above them. The druid looked as young and vibrant as they had in Queen Eleanor's shared memory. From their hands, the ends of the vines wrapped up their wrists and forearms, but it seemed no issue for the fae to be holding the ladies.

Spine swooped down closer. "Now you're ours."

"Nic, what are you doing?" Fiona called out. She could hear the waver in her own voice and swallowed, trying to gain control of herself. "We're here to help you."

"Help? No, you're here to hurt the Book. Otherwise you wouldn't have made it this far. And we can't allow anyone to do that."

The vines flexed and danced, intertwining into a tightened net that began rising up toward the duo.

Didia glanced frantically around. "Clearly Nic is in their mind, but Spine must be too. She's not recognizing us."

They needed to get out of this net before they could hope to do anything. Fiona reached her hand inside her scarf. "Keep them distracted."

"Nicolosia, what in the blessed Book are you doing?" Didia said with an unexpected amount of nag like a mother hen. "Don't you remember me? I still have the coffee set you gave me for my sixtieth birthday. With the flowering bulbs across the handle." She pulled a small porcelain cup out of her bag and waved it in the air through the netting. "Now would an enemy of yours have this?"

With small movements Fiona pulled the pearl-handled dagger from her scarf, palming it closely. She swallowed roughly with the remembrance of the last time she used it but crouched, wrapped her arm through the vines, and with one swift cut destroyed the bottom of the webbing.

A flash of a moment, like memory she had forgotten, washed over her. She was seated in a plush chair, cutting a blank piece of parchment with the dagger. And then it was gone. Fiona shook her head and dropped through the newly made hole after Didia. She pulled the rip cord on her ornithopter as soon as she was cleared from the vines. Tucking the knife back into her scarf, she flew, following Didia toward the illusionary forest below. Where was she going? How long did they have before the druid and the dragon caught up with them? Fiona hazarded a glance back.

Spine was hurtling toward them in an all-too-familiar and frightful manner. Her mouth was closed, but tendrils of green smoke emerged from her nostrils.

Nic stood upright without so much as clinging to anything on the dragon and called out, "I will protect the Book at all costs. You won't take our home so easily."

"I'm not trying to take your home at all," Fiona yelled back. "Well, I guess...but not in that sense."

"Fiona." Didia waved her farther above the forest.

Fiona increased her speed, pushing the concoction powering the ornithopter to its boiling point. She grabbed Didia's hand and they flew forward. "We can hide in the forest until we figure out how to clear their mind."

Didia shook her head. "Nic's domain? In their mindscape? Absolutely not. We'll be sitting rabbits." She tugged Fiona's hand and pulled to the right as a shower of pollen and tree fluff shot at them.

A few stuck to her and she started to sneeze. Quickly she brushed them off, not wanting to see the effects of having it on her too long. Fiona held her breath until they were out of the shower. "We can't outrun Spine forever. She's determined."

Didia pressed her glasses against her face. "Nic is too powerful to fight close together. The only reason we have even a chance is because they're bent on capturing us. Not harming us."

"We could try to lead them into a place that would stop them. Your mind perhaps? You seem to have the strongest defenses."

"My mind!" Didia spluttered. "But what if we get trapped there too?" She shook her head. "I can't, Fiona. If I see Bernard again, I'll be done for."

The ache in her voice made Fiona's heart burn. "Well then, a trap. Let's see if I can't make this mindscape do what I want for once." Dredging up a memory of briny water and twirling algae, Fiona focused on her first time in the Shimmering Depths.

The gray clouds oscillating from a distance rushed in, converting the vibrant forest landscape into rippling blue-green water. It surged up to meet them, lapping at their boots.

Fiona hurriedly grabbed Didia's cloak so as not to be parted from her. They yanked their 'thopter handles and plunged into the warm water.

"Don't breathe!" Didia instructed her before the water flowed over them. Didia waved her hands, then motioned to her stomach. She put her finger to her lips as if shushing Fiona.

Fiona's eyes widened. She had very much been planning to breathe. Usually the underwater jelly breaths and potions turned the water into air.

A second later, Fiona understood why. The heaviness of the air spores she had swallowed earlier lightened her body, and she found she didn't want to open her mouth. Didn't feel the need to take in a breath at all. Thinking about it made her uncomfortable, so she pushed it from her mind.

Didia motioned for them to swim toward the floating coral isle in the distance. The page of water's training pagemark for unread turners was a mass of dangling roots. Twisting, wet, tendril-like vines swung through the water, searching for anything to cling to.

A tickle brushed her hand. One, two—a school of shimmering fish swam around her, making their way to the darker areas of water. The weight of their movement pulled her along with them. She swung her arms, trying to stay near Didia and watch for Nic and Spine. Being underwater would have to slow them down.

Her heart beat loudly in her chest as the water surrendered nothing. A swell brushed up against them, pushing them toward a darker area. Warmth turned to cold. Trying to get to the floating reef was proving more difficult than it should have been. Her arms were already feeling worn out from the push through the flows. Her hair floated into her face, thoroughly escaped from its pins. The current shouldn't have been this strong. It hadn't been when she first came to this pagemark.

Fiona reached out to the floating colorful rocky coral reef, her fingers disturbing nesting fish within the crooks and crannies. She grasped the rock tighter, preparing to pull herself up, when the rock gave away. Gritty mud covered her hand. Confused, she grabbed the reef again, only for it to turn from purple scratchy coral to thick handfuls of rich earth. No, no. Was she not in control of this memory?

Light broke through the deep water, casting patches of sunlight into the darkness of the Depths. As the water disappeared, so too did the swimming fish, transformed into birds mid-flight. A robin, its red-throated warble loud in Fiona's face, jumped from the blossoming garden before her onto her shoulder.

"Move, Fiona!" Didia shouted from behind her. She was already up in the air, ornithopter spinning madly.

Fiona ducked as a vine pummeled past her face, hitting the now dirt-packed earth with a thud. She ran as the dregs of saltwater evaporated from her body. Tiny tufts of pollen from the garden poofed out, showering the ground where she had been in lavender-scented motes. Fiona leapt in the air, jerking the rip cord of her ornithopter. It caught, the only remnant of her memory thin strings of algae sloughing off into the distance as the blades rotated.

Didia weaved toward her. "We're in a bind," she shouted, leaning on turner slang. "Format is they have cloud cover."

If her memory wasn't strong enough to overtake them, what could they do? Spine and Nic's mind together was clearly too powerful. "They aren't going to stop till they get what they want."

"We might have to hurt them to help them," Didia muttered as Fiona flew up beside her. "I don't want to, as much as you don't."

"They think they are fighting for the end of the world. Their literal roles this entire time." How did you fight against someone like that? The page of mind seemed to give people what they wanted most, even if they didn't know it. It had given her a moment of home, reminding her of another time when her world had been rocky and she felt lost. It had reached into Mac's mind and gave her a moment of peace in a place she must've missed terribly. She would've expected Nic or Spine to be given much the same, but perhaps combined, this was what they wanted. Not to fight per se, but to fulfill their roles together. Perhaps to be done with it once and for all. "I think we need to let them win."

"What?" Didia exclaimed. She ducked, pulling away from Fiona as wild mushrooms flew through the air, pelting them.

Fiona grimaced against the stings. It was clear they were trying to push them toward the ground of the illusionary forest. "If they win the fight, they'll have done their duty. There's a chance that their being given what they want will soothe them." And if not, well, at least they'd be closer. Maybe they could smuggle them through a page turn.

"Sometimes you have to go along to get along." Didia nodded. "Seems sound."

"Follow my lead." Fiona surged toward the forest, hoping for Larrakane's sake she was right. As they entered the trees a rush of birds surrounded them as if funneling them toward a specific spot. Fiona didn't fight it and flew toward a clearing. Here the warm, rich earth was peppered with flowering bulbs. As she and Didia touched down, the bulbs flowered, covering their boots. Crisscrossing vines overlapped against their ankles and calves, locking them in place.

Nic and Spine flew over them until they were hovering up above, just out of reach.

"We surrender. You've won," Fiona yelled.

Nic narrowed their eyes, watching the two. They tossed their pine-green hair back across their shoulder in the wind. "You shall stay here until we can find your compatriots and subdue them. Don't try to escape."

Fiona tensed. Nic and Spine couldn't leave and continue scouting. No, they needed to be brought out of this combined mindscape right now. "We're the last of us."

"Yes," Didia chimed in quickly. "I suspect you want to interrogate us about why we were fighting and what our big plan was. Well, you won't get anything out of us."

Spine snorted, swirls of green smoke rising from her nostrils. "It is your quarry, Nicolosia. What would you like to do?"

Nic leaned against Spine. "I feel we are not out of danger yet, friend. We must keep working until everyone is safe."

Of course. They just wanted everyone to be protected.

Fiona's heart warmed. Well, there was only one way to guarantee it.

"Larrakane lives," Fiona said. She licked her lips and looked downcast. "And the Guardians are in control." If Nic's job was to look after the Guardians, perhaps this is what would make them believe it.

"What did you say?" Nic's voice lowered. The vines tightened around Fiona's and Didia's calves, causing them to sway to keep balance. The druid and the dragon landed on the ground before the women. "Say that again."

"You have won, druid. The Guardians of the pages are free to do as they wish," Fiona said.

"The city of Spine is still standing," Didia said, glancing toward the dragon.

Fiona hoped their argument was convincing. She had worded it carefully so as to not completely lie. But would even these buds of truth break them free?

Nicolosia patted Spine on the neck and leaned in. "Is it really over?" They sighed as Spine met their forehead with her own. "For so long this weight of responsibility has overtaken us."

They needed proof. Turning back to the city of Spine wouldn't give them that. But perhaps the desire to see the fight over would let them manifest it for themselves. "Despite everything, I can still feel the tug of the Book. Don't you?" Fiona said.

Nicolosia's drawn face tightened. But then they sagged against Spine. "I do."

Clouds shifted around them, billowing in to replace the rapidly disappearing forest. Fiona fell to her knees with the sudden release of the vines and flowers. Didia grabbed on to her shoulder for balance. The swirling gray clouds roiled in around them as if softening their landing.

Spine jerked back and looked around with wide eyes. "Where are we?" She wrapped her wing around Nicolosia as if seeing them for the first time. "Nicolosia! You're here."

"Spine?" Nic said in a drowsy voice. They rubbed the dragon's nose. "You're so small. What happened?" Nic blinked rapidly at Fiona and then Didia. "Dear Fiona. And Didia?" The druid stumbled off Spine toward them, but Didia met them halfway.

She wrapped her arms around the druid, each pulling the other in a tight hug. "You stubborn old thing," Didia muttered into their chest.

"You were trapped here," Fiona said, getting up and stretching her legs. "Dani seems to have left you and Mac in the page of mind."

"Where are they? Are they alright?" Nic glanced around before pulling their hands back in from the clouds slowly circling.

"Mac has gone back to the city with Gaili. We haven't seen Dani or the Binder." Fiona waved out toward the obscured landscape. "We're searching for him, but it could take forever in this page."

Nic shook their head. "You won't find Arc here. This page wouldn't work on him."

Fiona frowned. "Why?"

"Arc's knowledge of the Book is rivaled by none except Larrakane herself. This is the sort of place where ignorance is a trap all unto its own."

Didia and Fiona did have a much easier time not falling for the landscape of the forest or Nic's ways after already encountering Mac's mindscape. Plus, the Binder was quite stubborn when push came to shove.

"I wish he had confided more in us." Nic slumped, all remaining energy seeming to escape them.

Fiona put her hand on their arm and squeezed gently. "I'm sure by now he wishes it too. Do you know the way to the next page? It would be something that might align with time."

"Yes, and no." Nic swiped hair back from their face. "I have a vague recollection of metal off in the distance. But we are not the only creatures who wandered in here and are trapped. It could be anything."

"The other page had an arch, decorative and whatnot. Did it resemble that?" Fiona said.

Nic nodded. "It was rectangular and see-through. It felt out of place." They rubbed their chest. "Does your mark pain you, Fiona?"

She shook her head. "Not right now. It must be the metal Dani poisoned you with."

"Oh, I thought..." Nic trailed off. "That moment, when I felt connected to the Book, seemed so real."

"I know. I'm sorry. But it's what I needed you to feel to break this page's hold on you. We need to get you back. Removing the Seasons is not only destroying the city but has weakened Larrakane, I think."

"That's not all that's weakening her. We shouldn't be in these pages. They don't want us here and it's a distraction for her." Nic grimaced. "The sooner we're all out, the better. We'll see you to the metal door. Spine?" Nic leaned against the dragon.

Spine lowered her neck. "Climb on. Once we get there and know you can safely cross, I'll take Nicolosia back to the city."

Fiona had learned better than to argue with the druid. She helped Didia onto Spine and joined her. Though the dragon was about the size of the Keeper now, there was still plenty of room upon her back, though not at all comfortable with the small shrubs and trees.

As if Spine could read her mind, vines and branches braided themselves together, making sturdy, safe seats. They murmured surprise and thanks as Spine took off into the air.

"Nic, did you know these pages were connected to Larrakane's sisters?" Fiona asked, digging her hands among the vines.

"No. Not at all. I tried to keep the sum of what I knew to very little. To focus on my own role." Nic jerked back their pine-green hair, beginning to braid it together. "For all the good that did."

"It's not your fault Dani turned against everyone," Didia whispered.

Nic shook their head. "I won't pretend that I didn't have a hand in that. Even though I thought I was being a good sibling, supportive, pushing her to stand up to Arc, I didn't question *how* she was doing it. What was beginning to light a fire in her." Nic straightened up, chin high, "But I won't wallow around in regret. I will go back to Spine and keep it from breaking. I'll connect with all the Guardians. We will not lose our home."

"Or the Book," Spine said loudly. "She may try and release the Forgotten One, but we will prevail."

"She's—!" Nic rubbed their face. "Of course. It makes sense. He must've gotten in somehow. Found a gap in her defenses. Supported her when we had not."

Was that what it had been? It most certainly was one way to weasel into power. How many people had this Forgotten One deceived? Is that how he had convinced Larrakane to give him more magic than any other human in the first place? "I have seen them fighting. Larrakane and this creature. In the dark edge. I have heard her call out for help…" Fiona bit her lip, not sure whether to voice what she wanted to say. For she didn't really know if anyone could actually help the deity.

Nic's eyes grew wide. "You have certainly been through it. Arc will know what to do. He was the closest to her out of all of us, being the first inked and the Binder."

"We have to get to him first." Fiona sighed. She rubbed her temples and feeling the loose pins in her hair scrambled to set her hair back to right. She could at least control that.

"I see it," Didia said, spyglass to her eye. "It's almost like a warehouse door in the middle of clouds."

Nic squinted. "Yes, that was it. The clouds don't move toward it but away from it."

Spine circled down and landed in front of the odd scene. Small metal stairs led from the gray circling clouds up to a dark black metal door with a large handle and bolts bordering its frame every few inches. A square glass window sat in the top half.

Fiona and Didia clambered off the dragon's neck. "Turn the page as soon as you can. If we don't come back through, then we got there safely."

Didia snorted. "Whatever *safe* means in the page of time."

Spine pressed her snout to each of them. "Be well, friends. And keep your hands to yourself perhaps." She chuckled, deep and rumbling.

"As soon as you have Arc, you should all return. He'll know exactly what to do." Nic winced and clutched their chest. Slumping against Spine, they said, "And if you see Dani—"

They shook their head. "Go on."

It must have been difficult to want to convince Dani to turn back but know it may be too late. If Mac's sentiment was right, Dani had no choice but to keep moving forward, whether she wanted to or not. Fiona wrapped her scarf more securely around her throat. No, it was foolish to think like that. There was always a choice in this world. She clambered up the metal steps with Didia right behind her.

Now that she was closer she could see blocky letters painted in gold and black beneath the window: *Larrakane.*

"Now that's a bit unexpected," Fiona said, pointing it out. There were no inscriptions or remembrance like with the other doors. Perhaps for herself, she didn't want one.

"Can you see anything through the window?" Didia asked, standing on her tiptoes.

"It's all foggy."

Didia shrugged. "Well, suppose there's nothing to it but to do it."

Fiona clasped the handle tightly and pushed through the metal door.

COMPLETE DARKNESS. IT WASN'T a void in essence, but it was as if they couldn't see past the edges of the door. Fiona looked around the small structure, but it continued on with gray cloudy masses on either side. Hesitantly, for she felt as if she had literally been warned by Spine not to do this, she stuck her hand through the door into the blackness.

A warm tugging sensation gripped her hand. Without any grace she was pulled abruptly through the door into the darkness. She heard the yell of Didia very far behind her.

Smack.

The older woman, propelled by the same unknown force, knocked into her back. Fiona whirled around to grab her before she could move any farther. If this was anything like the dark edge, then—

Bold lights burst around them in a cacophony of explosions. Fiona shielded her eyes, but that did nothing for the noise, nor the smell of dust and scorched metal that filled the air.

"What's happening?" Didia shouted.

"I don't know," Fiona yelled back. She covered her ears, trying to block the riveting vibrations undulating around her. "But I think we're in the middle of something dangerous."

As if the world was acknowledging her words, the noise moved away from her, like it was pushed by a soft hand.

Darkness soothed the back of Fiona's closed eyes. She hazarded a peek to see that they were no longer surrounded by blurring flashes. But the view was still quite confusing.

Gray ebbing lights dimmed off and on in the distance. Some were much larger than the others. They brightened to a degree that was almost painful for Fiona to watch until they fizzled out in a puff, a boom, of bright smoke. Swirls and eddies of light twirled together, forming some sort of shape. Or was it more of a feeling? Emptiness pervaded her body and she felt bereft. But as the swirls came together, she felt filled. Whole.

In front of her lay the beginnings of a burgeoning world.

Didia shouted in her ear, "It seems all too much. I can't take this."

"Surely mere humans were never meant to. I think we're in Larrakane's laboratory. Or her workshop. I don't know, but things are being made. Unmade and remade." Fiona winced as the sphere in front of her rotated, quicker than her eyes could view.

"What do you mean?"

Fiona rubbed her mark. "It feels like—"

"No, no, never mind. How can we move forward? How can we get through this and find Arc?"

If this was time and Larrakane's domain, where worlds were being created and disassembled, then they needed to find a way to navigate it. "Let's try to put some meaning to it so that we can exist here. Sort of like we did with the page of magic."

"Even though we did that unknowingly and without any control?" Didia frowned.

"Yes. But if we think about it..." Fiona focused on the overwhelming cycle that was all around her. The essence of light growing and blossoming and then exploding and destroying the vastness of the darkness that curved around every edge of her senses. She thought of what she'd seen when she was in the dark edge of the pages beneath Larrakane, somewhat safe in her light. The pages, the Book *was* Larrakane. Through the symmetry of the categorized system, there was harmony. Wonder through design.

The saturating shade began to recede into rectangular structures. Wood grain etched itself into the space between lights. Shelves drew themselves together and deepened. Stacked symmetrically and spaced equally above each other. Rows and rows of bookcases appeared in front of them like a well-read corridor.

The stars, gray blinking lights, swirled and pulled themselves together, slotting themselves one by one, side by side, onto the shelves as books. Short, thin, fat, tall, the many different volumes took their places. Warm wood floor ran beneath their feet, unraveling itself from the greater creation. Light stone walls, the kind Fiona had a big fondness for in Richard's archive, shot up from the darkness, surrounding them like protection. And above, solid beamed ceilings clacked together with candlelit chandeliers.

Tick. The sound of a clock rang out as Larrakane's realm shifted for the women. Fiona blinked, unsure of what exactly had happened, but the inky soothing feeling of Larrakane's mark hummed in tune with the flickering of the candles, the settling of the shelves, and the scraping sounds of wooden chairs being pushed underneath tables.

"Larrakane, be kind." Didia blinked and pushed up her glasses. She grinned. "It's time. I really made it."

"You certainly did," Fiona said, unable not to smile herself. She exhaled roughly. "Let's see if we can find someone, the

Binder preferably, and get home."

"Well, it's a library, isn't it? Or what did you make?"

"*I* make?"

"I certainly didn't know what you were talking about. If it wasn't you, then who?"

Fiona supposed that it *had* been her thoughts that reorganized the world for them. "I was thinking about Larrakane's organization of the pages and how we always likened it to a book. So, yes, I suppose this is a library."

"Good. At least I know how to traverse one." Didia hefted her satchel on her back and motioned for Fiona to follow.

The ladies walked by shelves and shelves of books. It was odd how many there were in truth.

"Do you think all these are like our world?" Fiona asked.

Didia peered at some of the books and tilted her head. "I think these books *are* our world. Look." She pointed to a title. "*The Trouble with Pixies. Hags of Exile. An Era of Peace.* Sounds like the Court of Copper to me."

"I think you're right." Fiona ran her finger across a different shelf of titles. "*War of the Dragons. How an Ocean Flies.* Clearly related to Spine's page."

Tock. The familiar clang echoed across the chamber.

"Well, hello there. New patrons. How wonderful." A portly fair man in a loose-fitting cream robe had sauntered quietly up behind them. Over his heart lay the concentric black circles of Larrakane. He shifted his own golden spectacles on his face and smiled. "We do welcome you in. If you simply show me your entry pass, you may peruse at your leisure."

Fiona glanced at Didia, who seemed just as befuddled. Shaking her head at the oddity of it all, she said cautiously, "Er, I have it somewhere."

"I can't let you roam without it." The man leaned back on his soft sandals and clasped his hands together. "No one in or out without a pass."

He blocked their path forward between the bookcases, though he hadn't moved to do so. It reminded Fiona faintly of the door attendant Jacopo at the Pavilion of the Study of Seven in Copper all those months ago. Gaili had been able to talk their way around that situation. Perhaps she could do something of the like.

"We're expected. Indeed we are already running late. Our companion, Archae, has our entry pass with him."

The portly man raised an eyebrow. "He has *your* pass?"

Fiona didn't know whether to stay the course or try another route. He seemed surprised but not negatively so. Sometimes confidence was all that mattered. She stood up straighter. "Yes, and as you know, people like him are not accustomed to having to wait. I would hate to see what he says to any of us should we tarry longer."

The man licked his lips and glanced down the hall. He muttered, "I have my orders, unfortunately. I don't care if either of you do know the Librarian. If anyone else is allowed to roam, it will throw the whole balance of the structure off even more, and she'll be out of sorts about that!" He took off his glasses and cleaned them aggressively with his robe.

Unsure of whether that was confirmation that the Binder was here or that Dani had come through, Fiona turned to Didia and lowered her voice. "What do you suppose?"

"Sounds like he doesn't even want the Binder in this place." Didia glanced around the man as best she could. "Suppose we tell him the truth?" She grinned.

It was an odd gamble, but seeing as things were already

peculiar... "We've actually come to get Archae, so if you let us through, we'll be taking him when we leave."

The man's eyes narrowed. "To go where?"

"Home, away from here," Didia said.

Tick.

He cocked his ear at the noise and then nodded. "Alright, alright. But please have your pass ready when I come to check. I'd hate to have to throw you out." He stepped back and waved them forward. "You'll find your friend in the Reading Rooms."

Fiona smiled brightly, hoping the confidence would continue to work, and sauntered up the aisle. Didia's boots echoed behind her, albeit more slowly.

Fiona wasted no more time looking at the books they passed by. Not even when they turned from paper to stone tablets and tapestries. Time was of the essence. At least, she hoped there was still a chance to stop things. "I wish we could know what was going on in the wider Book from within these pages."

"I think you should look down this way then," Didia said in a strained voice. She had stopped at a row of bookcases that came up no farther than her waist, as if they had been ripped.

Fiona joined her and gasped. Dark black chains swirled in diffused blue light within the shelf. Books lay haphazardly, damaged. Some were torn in half, matching the ripped bookcases. Others were burnt or sodden. Fiona moved closer to see what the titles were, but one of the chains whipped out at her. She stumbled back into another bookcase, but its solidness kept it steady. Fiona pushed away from the shelving, back onto the path, as the chains receded. "The pages are splintering. We need to find the Binder."

They ran then through the narrow aisles toward a glass door at the end. Fiona could see into it another room much like this one with stacks of books. She tried to turn the handle but it didn't budge. She jammed her fingers gripping and threw her shoulder into it. It rattled, loosened, and finally, frustrated, she swung it open.

Coldness swept in from the void around them. She had thought the other library area was directly connected, but there was a circular metal staircase that went up. What happened if she stepped through the door and tried to make it up the stairs? "I'm not sure this is the best way forward."

"It's the only way," Didia said, adjusting her glasses. She pulled from her pack a tightly bound rope and handed one end to Fiona. "Here. You hold on to one loop and I to the other. We'll walk up and I'll be right behind you."

Fiona nodded, pulling the loop over her arm. She pressed it tight against her body. Once Didia seemed secure, she took a step onto the metal landing.

Wind whipped against her, pulling her curls from their pinned home to all sorts of angles. Fiona grabbed for the stair railing to keep from falling. Why was there wind here? And better yet, did it knowingly slow them down? Fiona felt the warmth of Didia behind her and tightened her hold on the rope. "Hold on, mistress. This thing seems to be fragile."

"The sooner we're on the next floor, the better," Didia yelled.

The piercing wind took snatches of her words, so all Fiona heard was "We're the better." Reading through the lines, Fiona nodded in agreement and took more steps up the winding stairs. On the next level, another glass door sat in the middle of nothing. She pressed her back against the door and held out a hand to Didia.

Didia scrunched up her nose, pushing her glasses up her face, and scrambled up the remaining stairs with Fiona's support. Fiona wrapped her arms around her as the wind pounded at them.

Fiona thrust open the door and they staggered inside the library. She sighed with relief, closing the door behind them. The room looked almost exactly the same as before with the rows and rows of books, but instead of wooden chairs at wooden tables, plush velvet seats were dotted sporadically around the area. Was it her imagination? "Are we truly somewhere different?"

"Perhaps it's different but there's only so many books to display." Didia shook her head. "I suppose there's some logic only Larrakane knows." She leaned against the side of a velvet seat. "And Larrakane can keep it."

Fiona rubbed the older woman's back before continuing on through the aisle. A scratching sound pricked at her ears from somewhere ahead. Was someone writing? Were they already in the so-called Reading Rooms?

A quick pace following the noise took them to a room devoid of bookshelves. Though there were the same upholstered chairs as the other area, this second one had small affixed writing tables before each seat with neat stacks of parchment.

And writing quills that wrote upon the parchment with unseen hands, the sound a steady grating in the otherwise silent room.

Each one scratched across paper as if vigorous writers were hurriedly recounting tales before inspiration dried. They moved in their own rhythm. Some dipped themselves back in ink pots perched delicately on the desks. Others sent pieces of parchment flying with a grand flourish toward the ground. Only one near the lone glass door at the end of the room seemed still.

"What do you think they are writing?" Didia said, taking tentative steps toward a table.

With an ounce of shameful curiosity Fiona also moved toward a table. "It's best to find out, I think. Better to be prepared than surprised." Standing beside Didia, she craned her neck to read:

Fiona helped Didia up from the floor, supporting the older woman gently. While they discussed the layout of Larrakane's library and its mirrorlike resemblance in sections, they shut the door. After ignoring some of the greatest current moments in Larrakane's domain, they came upon the recording room. In the quiet space they noticed the scratching of the quills upon the parchment sheets on each desk. Surprised, they walked to the desk and began reading an account of their current movements.

With a flourish the quill struck the last sentence on the page and pushed it to the ground. It floated gently onto a pristine stack of parchment.

"What in the Book is this?" Fiona exclaimed. Indeed, her thoughts were once again being summarized on the paper.

"It stands to reason that this section of the library has something to do with the present."

Mistress Humbledraft quickly realized that the section they were in was connected to the present. She smirked at her cleverness.

Didia smiled and nodded toward the desk at Fiona. "I am the smirking type."

Fiona stalked to another table, but this one was different. The sloping lines of the previous quill were replaced with tight lines cramming many words on to the page. While she could translate some of the writing, the faekin language was harder to decipher without getting very near. "This one's being written in faekin. I can make out some bits about nymphs swarming a village." Could that be an account of what was currently passing somewhere in Copper? She quickly peered over at the next one, and her breath caught in her throat. Rise!

All was quiet in the halls of the palace. The Queen sat perturbed but enclosed in her small hideaway with the principal secretary. Knights edged around them, with their sergeant making plans to retake the throne room from the ruffians.

It seemed as if Richard wasn't on the top of this invisible writer's mind. Perhaps he was safe alongside the Queen. But why wasn't he mentioned? The ache in her stomach grew as she fought the urge to continue watching the quill hoping for a mention of the stubborn man.

"This one is about Cobbles: Painted Edge are attacking the gnomes. One of them is trying to flee with something important," Didia said.

"Unfortunately, there's nowhere to flee to at the moment." Fiona moved toward the exit. There were scratches on the wooden floor below her feet. Some ran from one table to the table across from it. The others from one side of the room to the other. Were these tables rearranged? "Let's continue looking for the Binder."

Ignoring the other desks, she glanced through the exit door window to see another library section. But matching velvet drapes hung from floor to ceiling, blocking off sight of the bookcases on each side of the aisle. She pulled on the door, but it didn't open. Fiona twisted the handle up and down, throwing herself into it like last time, but still it wouldn't budge. She let out a frustrated breath and took a step back, assessing it. "I can't get through."

"Uh-huh," came Didia's distracted reply. She was back by the door reading the pages that had contained herself and

Fiona.

Fiona turned toward the woman. "Don't get distracted reading those. We need to find a way out of here."

"I'm not. I'm not!" Didia said as if she had been told not to do something such as this for a lifetime. "But this one speaks of Dani and the Binder."

"What does it say?" Fiona rushed toward her.

"The Binder just laid down. Dani is shivering and standing in front of a fire." She adjusted her glasses and inched inward as the paper leapt off the desk and onto the stack below. "Oop, now it's just the Binder. He's resting. Do you think that means Dani has gone?"

Fiona tilted her head, caressing the edge of her scarf. "I don't know. I don't even know how these quills pick what to be writing about."

"Well, think about it. This page represents Larrakane. There's an undercurrent of her pulling all this together." Didia glanced about. "Perhaps they are writing the things she most cares about?"

It was a credible theory. Fiona pushed back her frustration at the deity to think clearly. "There are twelve tables in here." Twelve invisible writers. Twelve pages in the Book, apparently. Twelve tables to twelve pages. It didn't seem a far-off possibility. And Larrakane loved her logic. Each one was noting current happenings in the pages. Except one. Fiona pointed to the table near the blocked exit. "Why isn't that one writing?"

"Possibly because there is nothing happening in one of the pages." Didia ambled toward the table.

But which page was it? And was that why the door refused to budge? "If we've got the elemental chapter in the first four tables. And the mortal chapter in the next five tables. Then these three at the end are the abstract. Which would make this one the page of magic." Fiona waved her hand toward the table. She frowned. "The quill is missing."

"It must've been taken out on purpose," Didia said, squinting through the small window into the next room.

"How in the dark edge—Dani." She must've whipped it through the door once she had figured her own way through. Possibly there had been a different sort of barrier to get through. "Do you have another?"

Didia nodded and produced a shiny black quill from her pack.

Fiona twirled the tool in her fingers. She hoped this would work and gently set it in the ink stopper on the table. She took a quick step back with Didia behind her. Nothing moved.

"Do you think we have to get it started?" Didia said in a light voice.

"I can certainly try." Fiona wiped her hands on her velvet doublet and tapped the now-filled quill against the inside of the ink bottle. "But what do I say?"

"Start with something like *The hall was filled with magic.* It's general but it's true, and maybe the quill will take it from there."

Fiona began writing. There was no paper on the floor stacked neatly. How long had nothing been written here? She finished the sentence but no thought or magic flowed forward from her. She bit her lip. What were they missing? Did these pieces of parchment and ink act like Richard's journal to her? If so, did the quill provided with the parchment have to be used for it? Or was it simply her that was the outlier? "It's not working."

"Well, I don't mind giving it a go," Didia said excitedly. She pushed Fiona delicately out of the way and grabbed the instrument. "It is my quill and all." Nib touched parchment, and Didia began writing in her steady-handed fashion. Ink slid across parchment matching the other sounds in the chamber.

The chatter died down as the hall remained empty. Magic bidden from one sister to another's home swirled continuously now through the Copper gate.

She hummed a little as she wrote.

With a click the door to the next section shifted in its frame.

"Brilliant, Didia!" Fiona patted the older woman on the shoulder. "Let's go."

Didia shook her head. "I can feel there's far too much to write. If I stop, we'll be stuck." She lifted the quill from the paper. There was a click, like a lock, and the door shifted again. "See?"

Fiona tried the door but it wouldn't budge. She swallowed. "You simply start writing, I'll open the door, and then we'll both run out."

"It won't work like that, dear." Didia sighed. "You have to go on without me." She dipped her quill back into the ink and continued hovering over the parchment.

It was too much. "Please, we have to try." Her chest hitched and she took a steadying breath. "I don't want to leave you."

"You need to get to Dani quickly, and we know she was just in this page. I believe you can talk to her. Convince her." The older woman adjusted her glasses and patted Fiona's hand. "I've spent a good deal of my life trying to get to this page. To explore it and try my hand at all those rumors. I'm not unread, dear. I know some adventures can't last forever. But I know when a moment is bigger than myself. I *need* to stay here so that you can continue." Putting quill to parchment again, Didia began to write. "Now go."

"As soon as I leave, you'll turn yourself to Spine. Yes?"

Didia hunched over the table, already writing again in smooth motion. "Not as soon, but I will."

Fiona wouldn't be able to simply come retrieve her. She knew that and understood Didia did too. But it was her choice, and she wasn't wrong. Slightly dazed, Fiona opened the door; the loudness of the wind whipped through the room like a cracked whip. Fiona took one look back at Didia before jumping to the first step of the metal staircase leading up, the door slamming closed behind her. She ran up the winding staircase two steps at a time to the glass door at the top. She tried it and it swung open easily.

Before she could dive inside, however, the portly man in loose-fitting robes with their circular symbol appeared at the door and held out his hand to her. "Entry pass?"

Fiona grasped on to the railing, her foot slipping against the metal platform in the battering wind. "I haven't gotten to Archae yet to get it."

The man shook his head. "All worlds must have their laws." He sighed and closed the door in front of Fiona.

She pounded the door, but the man walked away, ignoring her. What was she to do now? Race back down the stairs and try to figure out a plan with Didia? What if he appeared at that door as well?

Vivid colors signaled at the edge of her vision and the darkness exploded into a rapid succession of quick colors until a bright-blue storm eclipsed the entire field of view. Fiona clung to the railing and closed her eyes as the warmth of it washed over her. Pain racked her chest. She clutched where the mark was.

"*I see you again,*" the deep voice of The Forgotten One echoed in her mind. "*I have you.*"

Fiona lurched in panic, her foot sliding against the slippery metal. Eyes wide, she saw the blue had dimmed almost all but a small circle of darkness, like Larrakane's symbol prevailing where it could.

Of course. Her mark. Fiona pulled aside her doublet and pressed Larrakane's mark to the glass door. She jerked on the handle and it swung open again. But this time, only the dark edge was on the other side. The familiarness of it etched into Fiona's being. As much as she hated it, it was surely a safer place than in the blue eclipse of the Forgotten One's grasp. With a momentary thought as to the why of the prevailing dark edge in the between sections, Fiona took a quick step forward and jumped into the void.

14

"YOU CIRCUMVENTED THE BARRIER," a perky voice said from above her.

"We have tried to push past these walls many times," another more familiar voice intoned.

"Clever woman, but not as clever as you think," a slower, tired voice said close to her.

Fiona sat up from the thick, fluffy, narrow bed she had been lying in and winced at the light from the flickering fire in the fireplace. The heady smell of wood smoke lingered pleasantly in the air. At the foot of the bed sat an almost ethereal brown-skinned woman knitting. The ball of yarn balanced precariously in her lap was dull in color but still more solid than her. Her lace sleeves twitched with every pull and tuck. Her face was familiar, but from where?

A giggle drew Fiona's attention. Slimmer, with an unlined brown face resting on her hands, a woman slightly younger than Fiona leaned on the bed gazing at her. She had large curly black hair piled high on her head. Escaped tendrils brushed her bare shoulders and skimmed the top of a cream dress that only the nobles of Copper would dare wear, even in private.

Fiona frowned and straightened up, concern now coming to the forefront of her mind. Where was she? And who was she surrounded by? Movement out of the shadows, however, stole her words.

Larrakane, dowdily dressed like a tired matron from centuries bygone, walked into the light. A plethora of gray strands wove through her coiled afro. The lines around her eyes and mouth were much deeper than when they last spoke. Her brown skin radiated warmth, even at a distance.

Could Larrakane truly be here with her now? Had she always been in her own page?

"Where have you been?" Fiona threw back the quilts, untangling herself from the thick fabric. "And where is Didia? Did you trap her?"

The three women looked at each other with an amusement that further stoked Fiona's fire. But the younger woman spoke quickly. "We didn't do anything. She's writing."

"And she will be writing for some time," the woman at the foot of the bed said.

"It's not often we have visitors," the younger said, pouting.

"And now many in such a short time. Perhaps she is testing us," Larrakane said, looking at Fiona curiously.

Fiona ignored the other women and snapped at Larrakane, "Perhaps it is you who is testing me. For you're certainly trying my patience. The Book is falling apart. We need you. Find the Binder or Dani and pull them back to Spine."

Larrakane's brow wrinkled. "What's done is done. I have no sway in how it goes."

Beyond ridiculous. Fiona glared at the deity. "You must. So many people believe in you, and you would let them down, as if this was some silly game? What are you doing here? Why have you left us all to fight for you?"

The younger one behind her giggled. "You have it wrong, Lady Thornbeard. I am the one you should treat with, for I can still be swayed."

Fiona swiveled around, head throbbing at the movement. What was going on? "And who are you?"

Moving up from leaning on the bed, the younger one bowed. "I'm Future. Though you may call me many things." She pointed to the woman at the end of the bed who was silently knitting. "This is Present." Future narrowed her eyes at Larrakane. "And that is Past. Though you seem to know this human well?"

"I have not treated with this woman, I assure you. Perhaps she sees in me someone she knows?" Larrakane leaned in. "But don't believe all that she says, Mistress Thorne. I do have some power, if there is a deal to be made."

Fiona pressed closer to Larrakane, assessing her. Ever the inspector, she grabbed the woman's hands, eliciting another round of laughter from Future. They were rough but also solid. And free from any fading black chains. This truly wasn't Larrakane. But then why so much the likeness of her human visage?

For the first time since she awoke, Fiona took in the entire scene before her. The shifting light from the burning logs highlighted parts of the room just as it obscured others. It was a large space, more so than she had first thought on waking. Yes, she was in a single bed of cheerfully colored blankets. A big pillowed chair took up most of the area across from the fireplace. Left askew on the chair was a painter's palette dotted with every pigment in the world, it seemed. And an open doorway led into another room. Was she still in the so-called library?

"This is your room, or section, yes?" Fiona said to the young one.

Future's eyes widened and she nodded. "You're quick. Shall I give you the tour?" She bounced off the bed and tugged Fiona's hands until she was up. Fiona moved with all the grace of a stumbling giraffe toward the door. Why did it feel as if her legs no longer properly worked? "How long have I been here?"

"Ages," Future said pertly.

"Stop that," Present tutted and shook her knitting needle. "She's not going to treat with you if you behave so impertinently."

"Show some respect, sister." Past shook her head.

Future flopped back on the bed with a dramatic sigh. "Fine." She snapped her fingers.

Fiona felt strength return to her legs. What had the woman done to her? She bit back her frustration at being toyed with and ignored them. She would be on guard, for if they would play with her out of boredom, then they were powerful indeed. Powerful and yet needy. What kept them here?

Tantrum over, Future bounced up again and led a wary Fiona through the open doorway. A small wooden-walled vestibule covered the area between the chambers, but there was still the smell of fresh parchment like the other library rooms. Talking rapidly with nary a breath between words, she pointed out the particulars of the next room.

Wooden paneled walls sloped down into a carved headboard and a large, ornate bed filled out the chamber, leaving very little room for walking on either side. Each post on the bed was heavily detailed with leaves, figures, and fruit but in subtly varying styles. Beyond the decorative wood, it was the absence of material, unnoted by Future, that raised Fiona's brow. There was quite a stark difference between the two rooms, but before Fiona could wonder any further, Future tugged her arm forward, impatient, toward the next room.

Wine velvet drapes clung to the walls. To the ceiling, and even hung from the simple wooden poles of the four-poster bed in this chamber. The heavy material swallowed the room save for one corner. A small wooden table with bench seats sat in the notched space, welcoming. Various tints of embroidery thread lined up neatly before swathes of well-folded fabric.

Fiona pulled away from Future, trying to glimpse behind the drawn curtains of the bed, but the young woman was not to be ignored. Future clasped her wrist gently but forcibly pulled her through another open doorway into a large sitting room. Three chairs sat around another fire. Yellow and red leaves with dark-brown veins hung from vines across the mantel. A wide table held a bowl of ripe berries and cherries. And begging for attention was a large leather-bound book laid closed on an easel toward the end of the room. Despite the fireplace, a crisp chill cooled the air, making Fiona shiver.

There was no door.

There were no windows.

Past and Present had wandered behind the two at a leisurely pace, catching up when Future threw open her arms and bowed at the conclusion of her tour and asked, "Well, what do you think?"

Fiona pressed her lips together, trying to focus on the best way to get the specific information she needed, not on *all* her questions. She smiled wide to match Future's grin and took another roving glance around the room. A theory began to take place in Fiona's head. Their facial features and deep-brown skin were all reminiscent of each other. They all looked like versions of the deity, but as Past said, that may simply be her interpretation of their abstract forms. It was clear, however, they had their differences. Perhaps they were the same but split.

"Are you one person or a family?"

Future waved her hand impatiently. "Yes, yes. Surely, she has heard of us?" She quirked an eyebrow to Past. "I know she will know of us."

"We tell her now," Present said, lowering her knitting needles. Her ethereal plump cheeks jiggled as she smiled wide and said softly, "We are the Fates, dear. Family bound through time. We compose the destiny of all." She seemed to stop herself from saying more and focused on her knitting again.

Fiona wrinkled her brow and tried to let her whirring mind catch up. She had heard of the Fates as a child. One of the many stories about mythical creatures who held power to see into the past, tell the future, or change the present. She had also heard about unicorns, and she'd yet to encounter any of those! But she had to admit, the myths about hags had proven true. An itch of a memory that wanted to be scratched played at the edge of her mind.

A sigh escaped Future's lips. "There we go. In place. Now, have you come to make a deal?"

If these were creatures bound to time, what sort of deal were they looking for? Making a deal with a Fate felt worse than making a promise with a faekin. She had enough time with them to know that any creature who could command even a hint of magic was someone to be very careful with. Were they even part of the Book or from outside of it? Fiona rubbed the edge of her scarf and took a small breath. She needed to be clever and in control. Her confusion and curiosity were getting the better of her. "Perhaps a deal can be made. First I need to know if the Binder is here. Otherwise, there's no point in discussing deals."

The women looked toward each other, saying much with their eyes and gestures. Past—Fiona tried hard to remember she wasn't actually Larrakane but how Fiona was interpreting her—gestured to the velvet-draped bed in the previous room.

Quickly, Fiona pulled back the velvet curtains on what she had guessed by now was Past's bed. There lying within the linen was the Binder, fast asleep. Foggy exhales as his chest rose and fell rhythmically. His long silvery hair was disarrayed with sweat and dirt, flat against a pillow, and his long downy-furred ear flopped over his eyes. His gray doublet had lost its luster. His cream lace collar, askew. He looked as Fiona felt, having been dragged up and down the Book from page to page. Which, she supposed, he had. She shook him, his body ice cold.

And then the room fell away.

Dim light surrounded her. Fireplace flames had been replaced by the flickering light of torches. Packed earth and clay-bricked walls surrounded her. And a heaping of blankets, pillows, and what looked like the remnants of a sumptuous feast sat before her. She took a step forward to find the floor solid beneath, though covered in dust. Placing her hand over a torch, the heat stole the chill from her fingers. Faded drawings lined the wall, reminiscent of the Kerus pyramids she had skulked through not long ago. She was in a real place, it seemed, but had she been sent there, or were the Fates playing with her again?

A longing sigh roused her from her thoughts, and she crouched down, looking for something to hide behind. If this was a memory like Queen Eleanor Pompania's, she may be the Binder. But a quick glance at her hands and attire told her she was herself. Was this something more then?

The Binder entered the room, a conflicted scowl on his clear alabaster face. He was followed along by a creature, or person perhaps. Fiona couldn't be quite sure.

The being was tall, like a fae, but their smooth heart-shaped face was not as symmetrical as one. Their elongated, statuesque body didn't match any known specific creature. Soft gray light radiated from their dark obsidian skin.

Fiona's mark ached, telling her what she was slow to ascertain: Larrakane was before her, but more celestial than in any way she had ever seen her before.

The Binder rubbed his face roughly. "I truly don't want to have this conversation again."

"But we've never had it, Archae," Larrakane said, voice echoing confusion in a multitude of melodies like a chorus. "I mean to continue with my plans. I need to finish my designs."

"I don't see why that means you have to leave, Harmony."

"I don't see why that means you can't come with me! You may enjoy walking among the humans, understanding them. There are other Seasons to lead in your absence."

"You could be one of those Seasons! You could be anything you wanted." The Binder stopped, covering his mouth. "I don't want to do this again."

Fiona cleared her throat, feeling awkward at watching so personal a discussion. She didn't know who was more startled: the apparent lovebirds who immediately clasped into each other's arms, one pointing a rather familiar cane and the other her outstretched hand in the direction of Fiona, or herself for how quickly they had come together to defend themselves.

Squinting in the flickering torchlight, the Binder lowered his cane. "Investigator Thorne?"

Fiona slowly rose, gazing from the fae to the deity. "Binder."

As if reading her thoughts, Larrakane twinkled and in the blink of an eye was the familiar brown-skinned, dark-afro human Fiona had always seen. "Who is this child?" Larrakane said, lowering her hand, "and why does she call you such a strange name?"

He shook his head, his entire attention floating back to Larrakane. "She is a woman out of time, my love."

"But how? She's human." Larrakane moved closer to Fiona, but the Binder held her back. She glanced between them both. "She feels like she belongs."

"I do. I—"

The Binder stepped between them, "She's not the same Larrakane, Fiona. This is my past. My own personal...purgatory. Before I pushed her away and before she was swindled by that...that human. But the past can't be changed. It can only be remembered."

Larrakane frowned. "I am the same, though I thought I was clear about using my name."

"I'm sorry." He brought her hand to his mouth and brushed her knuckles against his lips. "And, too, for this: I must leave, Harmony."

"Nonsense. Why would you have to leave because of her?" She glanced at Fiona, frowning, and pulled her hand away from him. "Unless you want to go?"

He sighed, grasping her hand again. "Believe me, I don't."

"Then simply don't." Larrakane pulled him closer.

He swayed, clasping his arms around the deity tight, eyes for no one but her.

"Spine needs you." Fiona took a step forward. "The other Seasons need you so the city won't collapse and take the Book with it."

No response.

Fiona cleared her throat, stomach heavy with her next words. "The real Larrakane needs you too."

The Binder jerked away from the deity's embrace. He dragged his hand through his short silvery locks. "That version doesn't need anyone. She makes her own choices. Or haven't you noticed?"

"I have." Fiona shrugged. "But even I'm not so stubborn as to think she wouldn't change this, change it all, knowing how terrible it has gone."

"It would mean having to forgive me. She's not the only one to blame. And yet she's the one who put up walls and walls between us." Coldness permeated the air.

It was so unlike him, as far as she knew. Was this the Binder being vulnerable, or had he already wallowed too much in his past? Fiona lifted her chin and said loudly, "No. No bleeding-heart act from you. You *know* you didn't make her choices for her. You didn't convince her to wrap everyone into her fight."

"Didn't I? If I hadn't argued with her on her plans..." He motioned to the quietly watching Larrakane. "If I had listened to what she wanted and supported her instead of asking her to conform for me, perhaps she wouldn't have fallen for his honeyed words."

Fiona rubbed her face. "The real Larrakane is out there, struggling. She's literally calling out for help to anyone who can understand her!" Fiona repeated the words, in the language of the deity she had heard in the temple.

The Binder swayed. He glanced at the still, portrait-like version of Larrakane and then at Fiona. Eyes wide, he whispered, "I don't know what to do."

His past clearly consumed more of him than he knew if he was uttering those words to her, of all people. Fiona toyed with the edges of her scarf. "I understand. But no wall is truly invulnerable from a sundering by the heart. You can't sit here and let yourself be imprisoned this way."

His skin paled but he nodded. "I didn't expect there to be anyone left who could get here."

"Luckily for you I'm as stubborn as a smilodon and as chaotic as a fae. Now Mac and Nic are back in Spine. If it hasn't already splintered, it will soon, and the rest of the Book with it. We need to act now so the Fates can put you back."

He leaned heavily on his walking stick taking strides toward her. "You haven't made a deal with those creatures, have you?"

"Not yet, no. I asked to see you first."

"You cannot make a deal with them. Not without leverage. If you do, one will trap you in their place and leave."

Fiona sighed. She had hoped it would be somewhat more straightforward. She never found herself wishing for a contract with someone like Stella more than now. "How are you still here with those three then? Did Dani not make a deal?"

The Binder huffed. "She made a deal, alright. To pass through their prison walls. Unfortunately for us, she had a spare person and decades of planning. I am stuck in my own past for now, but the sisters have a new companion to do what they like with. Past, Future. They can move me where they like. They won't make that exact deal again."

Decades of planning, but for what? Not even a Season could force their way past more powerful creatures like the Fates, or else the Binder wouldn't be stuck here. She must have traded something else. If only Fiona had time to figure out what that had been. "Why are they making deals at all?"

"Those three are the last defense we have preventing that pestilence's escape. I assume you know the one I speak of." He glanced at Larrakane with worried eyes before saying, "They serve as a barred gate for the rest of the Book, but they won't be able to hold him for much longer if Dani succeeds."

Were they another group Larrakane wrapped into her world to fight against her mistakes? Of course the deity would have additional plans, but what had those three done to gain her ire and be trapped here? At least now she understood why they were so eager to make a deal with her. Fiona bit her lip; she needed a plan to retrieve the Binder from the Fates and turn the page with him back to Spine. But what's more, she needed to stop Dani before she reached her end goal. "Is there still time to stop Dani?"

"If the Fates are still asking for deals, there's a possibility available. You must make it into his realm. Think of it as the back cover to our Book. Even if I am not freed, you have to stop her from releasing that creature." He ran his hand through his hair again. "She's lying to herself. He won't give her the freedom she wants. It is my fault she took the initiative in the first place." He stopped and pinched the bridge of his nose. "That doesn't matter. She won't listen to me or the other Seasons. I'm not sure there's a person in the Book she will listen to."

Perhaps not in the Book. But maybe outside of it. "I'll see what I can come up with."

"Remember, 'things connected create harmony.'" He clasped Larrakane's hand and squeezed it. The deity looked up at him with wide eyes and cupped his face. "Sometimes, though, there needs to be a bit of chaos and heart to truly bring it all together."

Larrakane grinned. "I knew you were listening to me."

Grasping her hand, the Binder bent and placed a kiss on Larrakane's forehead. "Of course, my love. I always am."

Fiona turned away. How in Larrakane's name was she to get out of this and back to the Fates? Almost imperceptibly the room brightened, and she found herself lying beside the Binder, back to back. The room was empty, but a flickering light came from the open doorway. She sat up. She had fallen for one of their tricks again. They thought they were toying with her, but she had gotten far more out of that than they probably bargained for.

She carefully strode into the sitting room, listening for their whispers, but beyond the crackling of the fireplace and the sighing wind emanating from somewhere distant, it was silent.

The three sisters were grinning, sitting at the large book in the corner, though they had moved it so they could face the doorway.

"She's different." Present breathed out mistily, writing sloping lines with a quill. "More things than one."

"From cover to cover she's been. Almost," Past said, dipping a vibrant quill in an ink jar. "It makes a difference."

"She'll get there. She has a deal to be made," Future said, tearing parchment sheets in half. She slipped it into the book somehow, sliding it under Present's moving hand.

Thinking her question over carefully, as if she was trying to get information out of the likes of Stella, Fiona said, "How does he wake up?"

Past raised an eyebrow, looking much more like the

Larrakane Fiona was used to. "I can wake him."

"But are you the only sister who can?" Fiona said, dropping her arms.

The three women grinned widely. Their eyes brightened and they nodded at each other. Yes, the humanness about them was wearing off. Perhaps it had been the empathy in her that had painted it on.

Future ripped another sheet of parchment. "No, we can all wake him."

With that understood, Fiona clasped her hands behind her back and watched the trio work. If there was anything as annoying to people like the faekin, it was a bit of silence and lack of doing something. Time was precious, but the Binder had made it seem as if there still was some left to get to Dani. She would need to play this next hand very well if she was going to get to the back cover and have the Binder released. No matter what he said, she couldn't leave him to loop forever in his brokenhearted past. Mac would simply never forgive her.

She meandered around the sitting room, inspecting every inch of it. With a lack of windows, this room could've been anywhere, or any time. Eyes watched her move but the sisters said nothing. Fiona stood in front of the fire, hands outstretched to the flames. Real warmth exuded from them, and she bent, taking a closer look at the empty dark space behind the flames. There was no wall behind the fireplace. Interesting. Was that a twinkle she spied or a trick of her imagination? She let out a small, pleasurable sigh to attract the Fates' attention.

"Are you not ready to leave?" Present said, writing tight lines on a fresh sheet of paper.

"With what's happening out there? Why should I go?" Fiona

said.

"The other woman was quite in a hurry and ready to make a deal." Future pouted. She tore another piece of parchment roughly.

Fiona inclined her head, hiding her eagerness to hear more. With the Binder basically asleep she was the only real source of new entertainment. She simply had to remain disinterested. Then she could make a deal when she had them thoroughly roused. After another few minutes in which Fiona lingered near Future, thinking she was the most susceptible to the ruse, she traipsed to a chair by the fire.

In a showy flourish she pulled out her journal and quill from her scarf. She wanted to make sure they were paying attention when she revealed—what she suspected would be—the spark of negotiations. As she planned, the sisters stopped what they were doing when the journal appeared.

"I've not seen this before," Past said, setting down a new quill she had been sharpening.

Fiona didn't have to feign surprise, for she thought if anyone knew about the scarf it would be Past. "This? It was a gift. It has pockets to all the pages, see?" Fiona pulled it out toward the trio, showing them the different ones. "This one is for Blaze, these two are for Kerus, and, oh, these are for Rise." She stroked the small lace pockets lovingly. "It's where I keep my most prized possessions."

"May we see some?" Present stood from the book, closing it gently.

They all gathered around as Fiona began pulling out small things from her pockets. They seemed somewhat unimpressed with the small wooden spoon from Rise. The slingshot elicited gasps as it quite clearly was bigger than the pocket and therefore proved this wasn't a trick. Fiona thought about the pearl-handled dagger Stella had given to her. It appeared before her fingers and with slow movements she drew it out of her scarf. She presented it to the sisters still sheathed so they didn't think she would attack them.

"It's quite astonishing what one finds throughout the pages of the Book."

Past's face dropped and she glowered at Future. Present tutted and clasped her hands in front of her matronly bosom. Future's eyes widened and she gave out a squeal. "You stole it!"

"I did nothing of the sort," Fiona said, pulling her hand in. "I was given this and therefore it is rightfully mine."

Future glanced frightfully back at her sisters. "It was stolen. I promise."

"Oh, fess up that you lost it," Past said, waving her hand.

Present nodded and patted her shoulder gently. "We suspected for some time after that first debacle with the deity."

"But you never said anything," Future said.

"Well, what would be the point in that, sister?" Present said.

"You can't use it," Future said, rounding on Fiona as if remembering she was there. "It would be best if you gave it to me."

Curiosity got the better of Fiona and she said, "Tearing the parchment seems to work well enough. Why do you need it?"

"A clean cut is the best way forward." Future stood up taller. "Very well. I will release your Binder for my knife. Deal?"

Fiona stood up and tucked the dagger back into her scarf quickly, "No, that won't quite be enough I'm afraid. For a tool of the Fates, I'll require two things. The Binder awake, back in present day Spine, and a doorway to the back cover."

Future's brown eyes narrowed, and she dropped her arms. "You ask for too much. A doorway to the back cover is out of the question."

"Unless"—Past waved her hand toward her sisters—"you would be willing to trade with one of us. I could take the Binder through to the back cover and you become Past."

There it was. The real desire of the trio finally presented. Fiona wrapped an errant curl back into the mess of her once-tidy hair and remained silent as if contemplating. Dani hadn't gotten a doorway by simply giving the Binder as a plaything. She had decades of planning for this moment and probably a precise method of extracting what she needed without getting caught in the net. There was only one person who could give Fiona insight into what that *something* was and possibly talk some final sense into Dani. But she needed to get her here first.

No, Fiona didn't have planning, but she did know how to build to an opportunity. "Perhaps we could make a deal, but"—Fiona raised her hands as Past began to speak—"not with me. I must get through and I cannot stay here."

"Who would be more fitting than you?" Future asked, arms crossed.

Fiona glanced at Present and inclined her head. "You control the destiny of the now, correct?"

Present nodded, sitting down in her chair. She picked up her knitting and began working the needles. "She'll come now if you call."

"Excellent." Fiona cleared her throat and said clearly, "Stella. Stella. Stella!" As she suspected, the fireplace grew darker, the embers dimming as the flames began to die out and be overcome by inky black void.

From the darkened space trotted a coughing, furry Stella covered in soot. "Well, it's nice to know when I'm wanted."

SURPRISINGLY THE HAG'S APPEARANCE elicited a gasp from all the Fates. Fiona raised an eyebrow at this. Was it her natural hag visage or something more?

"Stella, may I introduce you to the Fates of the Book? Fates, this is Stella, she who gifted me Future's knife." She smiled to the hag, gazing at her turquoise eyes without breaking contact as she spoke. Would Stella understand what was happening?

With merely a small breath Stella inclined her head in introduction, and her form shimmered. Though it was hard to focus on her appearance, it settled quite rapidly once more. She was still Stella, big eyes and light copper fur, but appropriately attired in a cream bodice and skirt that would've made even Gaili jealous. "How do you do?" she said politely to the Fates.

"Entertained, to say the least." Past bowed.

"Now then." Fiona gestured for Stella to sit in one of the chairs by the fire. "Are you caught up with what is going on, or shall I advise you?"

Stella shook her head. "I couldn't follow along once you made it past the page of dragons, but as you're alive and in the page of time, I can make some assumptions." She glanced about the room, her eyes settling on the doorway to the velvet-draped bed. "I didn't think she'd have it in her to leave them," she said softly.

"I think of the three, Dani chose the one that would hurt the least." Indeed, leaving Nicolosia and Mac in the page of mind was probably her way of not taking them further into harm's way. Three Fates for three Seasons would've caused more chaos than probably even Dani wanted to deal with. "Listen, there's not too much time and Dani has already found her mark, I believe. She seems determined to see this through, regardless of what the true ending may be."

Stella stiffened. "Have you not gotten to talk to her at all?"

Fiona shook her head.

Before she could say anything else, however, Future interrupted, "It's all well and good that she's here, but what of our deal?"

"You've been here how long, and you can't wait a few moments more?" Fiona said

"Some of us do have work to do." Future motioned to the book.

"There won't be any work to do if the Book is broken," Fiona said.

"There will be even more, not less. There will still be this cosmology, even if it no longer resembles your Book. We still have to control what we oversee," Past said.

"My, you have been busy." Stella said, eyes pinging back and forth between them all.

Fiona tugged Stella closer. "What was Dani's plan to get them to open the back cover without swapping herself for one of them?"

Stella's thin lips pressed together. "Well, I don't rightly know."

"You don't?" Fiona despaired. She had hoped Stella would

be able to give her the information she needed to succeed in the same manner as the fae.

"Despite how it may seem, Dani and I didn't agree on every aspect of this plan. Everything she knew about the Fates she learned from *him*. She was to give them a gift they couldn't get themselves, one of the Seasons or something as valuable. And they would let her through. It's unfortunate for Larrakane that she left bribable jailers." Stella rolled her eyes.

"Is that why you had the knife?" Fiona said.

Stella shrugged, seeming to fall into her familiar pattern. She waved her hand. "It was an easy bind from Travel Guild HQ. I thought of all the places it might be searched for, and no one would think to look at you. With your curious nature I doubted you'd give it up. I was right." Stella smirked. "But seeing as you still have it, I guess Dani decided to use something else." Her smirk fell and she rubbed her arm. "I wish I could've gotten through to her."

Fiona glanced around again. What else could Dani have possibly given them? A rustle of wind lifted through the cool air emanating from the hanging leaves and she shivered. For a fire-touched windowless room, it was far too cold. Too crisp. Too—

That was it though, wasn't it? She had given away her magic.

Yes, it was everywhere. The bowl of ripe cherries on the table. The leaves and thick vines above the fireplaces. Dani had given away her very essence in order to succeed.

Fiona shook her head. "She used the one thing no one else would have."

Stella's eyes crinkled in confusion, but following Fiona's sight she gave a small gasp. Quickly she strode to the wall. Her fingers grazed the crunchy autumn leaves. "How could you?"

she whispered hotly. Her hand shook as she clasped it tight to her chest. "Fiona, without this she's powerless. You have to save her. That's what you do-gooders do, right? You have to help her see that releasing him won't get her home."

The urge to comfort Stella was not ignored and Fiona squeezed her shoulder. "She always has a backup plan, remember. We're not completely without hope." She turned the hag to face her. "We don't have power like that to give away. I have the knife to bargain with, and perhaps getting the Binder to Spine will stabilize the Book until we can get to her."

But Stella shook her head vehemently. "No, we do have something." She strode away from Fiona and addressed the Fates: "In exchange for what Fiona has requested and a moment to myself, I will take the place of one of you."

"No!" Fiona pulled Stella back. "I have no intention of letting you sacrifice yourself. That is not why I brought you here."

"You did me a good turn, getting me out of the dark. If you can move someone as mutable as me, you can get through to Dani."

"She won't listen to me. You're the only one in the Book she'll hear from!"

"Sometimes we don't listen to those closest to us for shame or stubbornness. Sometimes we need a breath of fresh air to cool our minds and shift our thoughts." She clasped her hand around Fiona's and stared into her eyes. "Trust me on this. I am best suited to stay here and give us both the moments we need."

Locked in her gaze, Fiona dared not look away, unsure of what Stella meant to do and trying desperately to think of an alternate plan.

Stella winked conspiratorially, breaking the focus, and pushed away from Fiona. She turned with a flourish to the Fates. "Now, who shall stay and who shall go?"

Silence ambled along before the sisters began to talk all at once. Future talked of the merits of tying people's hopes and dreams to the paths ahead of them. Past discussed how beneficial it was to see what had been done and ink lessons learned into people.

Present knitted, humming to herself, and simply waited, seemingly content. When the other two had taken a breath, she said, "If you are me, you are always there. And there is where you want to be."

Fiona pressed her lips together at the riddle-like nature of the Fate, but Stella simply nodded. "Precisely. Alright then." Stella clapped her hands, mirth seeming to return to her. She bowed toward Present and dipped her head. "I, Stella of the Wilds, agree to take your post, Present."

The robust Fate set down her knitting needles and clambered up. She hugged a pouting Future tight, her ethereal arms almost swallowing the young woman. "Take care, dear, and try to remember your manners. Your time will come, I'm sure."

Future sniffled before hugging the Fate back without words.

Present pulled away from her and straightened up. "Past."

"Present," the dowdy Fate said and stuck out her hand.

"Oh, don't be such a ridged fuddy-duddy," Present said and pulled her into a hug as well.

Past leaned forward, her composed face breaking as tears ran down her cheeks. "You were always my favorite."

Present sighed. "I know." She rubbed Past's back, and they pulled apart.

"Fiona, if you would be so kind as to give Future her knife," Stella said serenely.

Fiona reached into her scarf and pulled out the pearl-handled dagger. The suspicious part of her held it close, saying, "The Binder back in present day Spine first, please."

"Of course." Present sat down, dipping a piercing white quill produced from thin air into ink, and scrawled across the large open book. In a blink, the Binder was gone from the bed.

Fiona's shoulders sagged with relief. With the Binder back in the city of Spine, she hoped some order would be brought to the chaos. But she still had to do her part.

"Fiona," Stella hissed and whirled her hand animatedly toward Future.

With no more time wasted, Fiona handed the dagger toward the Fate, who whispered a thank-you before clutching it tightly to her chest.

"Excellent. Now..." Stella clasped the arm of Present.

Present clasped the arm of Stella with her other. "Be seeing you." With little fanfare, Present vanished.

Stella, who appeared unchanged from the outside, stumbled forward but regained footing quickly. She opened her mouth, tasting the air like a gaping fish, before swinging wide to the fireplace. Running her fingers across it, the embers died away and the inky dark edge stole what little light remained. She flung her hand out to Fiona. "Well, no time like the present. I know it seems odd, but truly you saw the end in the beginning. Now let's get you there before the moment's over."

Things were afoot, of that Fiona was sure. But if Stella had a plan, she could spend no more time here deciphering it. The hag seemed more trustworthy and real than she had ever been before. If she was to truly stay here, this would be the last time Fiona would ever see the clever woman. For a moment it was hard to swallow. It would be difficult to reconcile for more than simply her. "What would you like me to say to your sisters?"

Stella's eyes widened but she smiled. "Tell them the truth. I like to think they'll understand without too many questions. And forgive me for what I did." She rubbed the folds of her skirt between her fingers. "Tell them that I love them."

Fiona nodded. Appeased, she pressed her hand to the arched doorway now opened in the fireplace. If this led to the back cover, why did the Fates not simply take themselves? Perhaps it was their nature, like the hags, that didn't give them the ability to cross. "Thank you, Stella. I won't forget what you've done for everyone today."

The hag nodded slowly, her eyes seemingly far away. Her attention snapped back to Fiona and she held up a finger. "If I can ask one thing. Please help Daniele see that she will not be free as promised." She grabbed Fiona's hand, closing her own two around it. "Tell her what I did here. Make her understand, if you can."

Fiona's hand grew heavy as a cool metal object appeared in it. Before Fiona could see what it was though, Stella shook her head and kept her fist tight around it. "Remember what I told you. They need to destroy the very essence of Larrakane to fully release him. I hope by now you know what that is."

With more confidence than she felt, Fiona said, "More than when I started this journey anyways." She brought her hand to her chest, slipping whatever the ridged item was into her pocket as Stella leaned into her.

As soon as it was done, Stella stepped away. She sat at the book in the corner of the room, picked up the quill and twirled it in her fingers. Her attention diverted entirely away from Fiona.

With one last glance around the prison of the Fates, Fiona gave them a small wave, and walked through the archway out of time.

16

THE THICK IRON-BANDED WOODEN gate Fiona found herself at was surprisingly crowded. Tunic-bedecked men with a goat, minstrels with all manner of instruments, and several horses were waiting to pass through. The drawbridge they stood on was rather wide, but the stench from the murky water that buffeted each side made it feel confined. Red flags, adorned with a large gold lion, flapped in the whistling wind high above the towers on either side of the gate. She took a step back, surprised that she was now wearing a long violet gown that dragged slightly across the dirt ground. She patted the silken material, but it was as solid and real as herself.

Guards, vaguely reminiscent of the ones who stood at every entry at the palace in Rise, stopped their speech mid-sentence as Fiona moved. The guards quickly drew to attention and bowed deeply. "Milady."

Fiona pressed dry lips together, assessing the people in front of her. How had they gotten here? Did they arrive with Dani? Unlikely, otherwise a few more Fates would've certainly traded places. *Unexpected* was the name of the game, and she needed to not be thrown off. She would focus, find Dani, or Larrakane help her, stop Richard's brother from being released. She winced at the thought of him. But there was no vehement whisper in hear head. Was it only in the margins and the pages that he could reach her that way?

The guard cleared his throat. Fiona realized she had been too wrapped in thought. With all the presumption she had learned to wield in such situations, Fiona stood taller and inclined her head. "Lady Oatfellow arrived for His Majesty."

The shorter guard hesitated but bowed once again and waved her through the curtain wall. "This way, milady."

Fiona sauntered past him, mind whirring on what to do next. As she passed through, a deep icy spike in her chest stole her breath. Her hand flew to Larrakane's mark, but she forced it down to avoid drawing attention to the spot.

"Milady, are you unwell?" a guard said, rushing to her side.

Fiona waved him off. "A moment." She took a deep breath, inhaling the musky smell of horses and sweat that permeated the air this close to the guard. As the cold withdrew from her chest and became a low, dull throb, she gritted her teeth, pushing down the lingering discomfort. Was Larrakane protecting her in this place? Or was the deity being attacked? Fiona swallowed and continued on as if she didn't have anything to fear.

The guard ushered her forward into a large courtyard. Horses neighed, moving restlessly. Their hoof beats against the ground rang out as an underscore to the stable hand's calm, measured words. Servants wearing belted tunics and clutching pots and stacks of firewood hurried from a long building to a smaller one with a short steeple.

Fiona narrowed her gaze at each person, looking for anything odd, but they seemed as alive as herself. Could it truly be possible there was another group of humans separate from her own?

Guards watched from above on the stone curtain wall

surrounding them all, weaponry on their side and backs. In the distance, a towering keep stood high upon a hill. Many stairs led up to its formidable entrance. What was this place? It was quite unlike the palace of Rise, in any case. Was this where Richard had grown up? Had tried to save his people, their people, as king?

She slowed her steps, looking for a place to stride off away from the guard. Perhaps the bakehouse near the entrance. Or what looked like a chapel in the short distance. She couldn't simply be presented to Richard's brother as if this were a normal world and a normal visit. What was to stop him from imprisoning her? His eyes had seen right to her in the dark edge because she had thought of him. Only her father's scarf seemed to have protected her. She clasped her hands around her neck and sighed with relief that it was still about her neck. It was more of a silken veil now, also covering her hair, but as long as it was there, she had much at hand. Though she was alone, she wasn't without ideas. "I would like to freshen up first, before meeting his majesty. Show me to my quarters."

"Milady, he prefers if visitors meet with him immediately," the guard said politely. "He's in the Great Hall, where there will be food and drink to sate you."

That he didn't grab her and pull her toward their destined area meant that certain rules were in play in this fake kingdom. For better or worse. And those rules probably hadn't counted on the likes of her. "I will not make a formal visit with mud on my boots and sleep in my eyes. You will escort me to my bedchamber so I may freshen up or take your leave."

The guard straightened up and quickly nodded. He led her away from the Great Hall building toward the towering keep. Up the stone stairs to the only entrance, the guard pushed back the large banded doors and ushered Fiona ahead of him. A discord of voices rang out from somewhere deeper within. She strained to find a familiar voice among them, but nothing.

In the entry chamber, candles flickered on side tables, though twin wall torches gifted much of the light. Between them, a resplendent tapestry hung as tall as the wall itself. Her eyes watered at the sight of a man who looked much like Richard, golden crowned and robed in deep-red with a scepter in one hand and closed book in the other.

Though the guard had slowed his step to allow her time to view, he quickened his pace up a set of stairs and into a narrow hallway. Swallowing a sigh of relief, Fiona paid attention to where they headed and how many steps it was from the front doors to these chambers. "Is there another lady from far away visiting the king right now?"

"Aye, ma'am," the guard said. "She may be in the Great Hall or her bedroom." He stopped and pushed open a wooden door. "This will be your chamber. Please make yourself at home. I will be here when you are ready to be escorted." The guard stood at the door.

Fiona thanked him and then closed it softly. She surveyed the room. A large bed, a chest, and a few tables took up most of the cold space. She pushed back the curtain of a window, eagerly leaning out. A sun lazed high in the sky. In the distance rolling green hills beckoned from beyond the stone wall. The moat was quite wide outside the wall. How was she so high to see so much? They had only climbed a few stairs up to this floor. And was that a real sun or like the light in Spine? Unnerved, Fiona pulled back from the window before anyone could spot her.

Did Richard's brother know everything that went on in

his domain? Larrakane wasn't omniscient, so why should he be? Fiona ventured to test her theory. She needed to change clothes so she didn't appear out of place. Then find a way to get to Dani privately to convince her to leave. Regardless of Dani's magic being gone, she was still a Leaf. She needed to be in Spine with the others and help balance the Book.

If Richard's brother could sense or know what was happening, she wouldn't get far. And if he couldn't, well, it wasn't her first time skulking around a castle. Fiona opened the door again and said quietly, "I must take a small rest. Please don't let me be disturbed." She closed the door quickly before the guard could offer his objection. She pulled the chest behind the door, giving herself a small barrier should anyone try to get in.

That done, she needed to change. She dug into a coarse-furred pocket of her scarf and tugged out a simple thin dress from Rise. She knew it wasn't exactly what the others wore, but it was better than nothing. Trading in her silken garments for the woolen one was a good start. She would find an apron or more to complete the look near the kitchens. Tucking the magically changed scarf into the top of the dress gave her the access she would need.

She slipped her hand into the blackened leather pocket of her scarf, knowing its location by feel above all else, and pulled out a length of fire-hardened chain. With haste she took out her grappling hook, unfolding it, and promptly hooked it to the stone ledge of the window. She pulled a few times. It would hold her weight, hopefully.

But would the chain last? From this perspective she was at least seven or eight floors up. But what was real: what she had walked or what she saw? She imagined Didia's words, *Don't assume unless you're a blotter.* Banishing the thought from her mind, she swung over the edge of the window, grasping the chain tight. Face to the wall, she hurriedly climbed down the length of the chain, reciting the pages in the Book to keep her mind on something else.

In short order she landed on solid ground. She pulled hard on the chain, swinging it with precision from the window. It fell with a loud thump. Fiona grimaced. There was no catching something that could harm her like that!

A voice raised in question a short distance from her.

With as much speed as she could manage, she bundled the chain up in her skirts. It would have to do for now. She took off running toward the smell of baking bread. There would have to be kitchens.

But did anyone follow? She glanced back to see if anyone was after her and ran directly into a broad chest.

Strong, rough hands grabbed her arms. "Bonnet of bees isn't in the hive?" His tone was urgent but curious.

"Richard?" Fiona stared at the man before her. Golden-reddish hair swirled out from under a soft green cap with small bells on it. A green-and-silver patchwork tunic covered his broad shoulders. A lute hung listlessly from his back. This couldn't be the real Richard. He had to be safe back in Rise. But his trimmed beard and familiar jaw told her otherwise. She took a deep breath, trying to ease the burn in her throat, and glanced over her shoulder. The earlier voice had fallen away and no one rounded the corner after her. Yet. "We have to go."

"Only the damned watch where they are going." Richard raised his eyebrows high and tugged at her arm. "Foxes trot."

Fiona kept a tight hand around her chains; the other she let

Richard's own hand swallow in his warm embrace. He felt real enough. As they hurried away from the keep she couldn't help feeling a wave of relief that almost made her giddy. He was here! He was alright and not besieged by the Painted Edge or cuffed in chains. She laced her fingers through his, gripping tight.

Richard pulled them into the courtyard, ducking into a low covered wooden building. Dry hay scattered across the floor, and the fluffy white sheep, uninterested in their new company, turned back toward their food and grazed loudly.

Drawing in a breath, Fiona hastily began tucking the chains back into her scarf. "You shouldn't be here. This place has to be dangerous for you. Unless you've come with a plan?"

Richard stroked her cheek and frowned. "Bees make the honey. But winter kills the bees."

She raised an eyebrow but didn't move away from his fingers. "What are you talking about?"

He sighed and dropped his hand. He pointed to himself and made a talking motion with his hands. "Fools make mortal words cheap."

What in the dark edge was he saying? He hadn't made sense since she— A sinking realization overcame her and she grabbed his face. "Say my name."

"Bonnet." He tilted his head forward till his forehead touched hers. His eyes closed and he whispered again, "Bonnet."

Her face flushed as the sudden anger within her ignited. "He took away your words, didn't he?"

"To the wind," he said quietly.

Without the means to speak, his power would be gone as well. Richard wasn't here with a plan. He had been captured.

She gripped his arm, leaning in. "I will get you away from here. I promise."

Richard shook his head. He pulled away from her and began making a motion with his hands in the shape of a book. "Nest in the flower."

Was he telling her to open their journal? She placed her hand into the lace pocket of her scarf, but he grabbed it and thrust it away. Shaking his head he made the book motion again and then waved at her. "Nest in the flower!"

"Absolutely not." If he thought she was running away from the situation, he had no idea what it had taken for her to get here. She had little time to explain it to him. Clearly he could understand her, however. "I've been through magic, mind, and talked my way out of time to get here. I will not leave until I've solved this and gotten you away from here."

He opened his mouth to speak, but Fiona threw her arms around him. She pulled him close, kissing him softly and then urgently.

Richard responded in kind, hands clasped around her face. As if she was the oasis he had been searching the desert for all this time. In this moment neither of them seemed to need words to discuss how they felt.

Long before she wanted to but with rational thought prevailing, Fiona pulled tenderly away from him. She took his hand again, unwilling to let him go completely. "No arguments. Agreed? Now, how does this place work? Does he know everything that happens?"

Richard shook his head, bells jingling. He smashed his fists together. "Singing makes lovers dance between sheets." He sighed and then pointed toward the door. He raised one finger, then two and three. "The damned do much."

She pressed her lips together, trying to understand. Though his words sounded nonsensical there was a sort of poetry to them. "He's fighting? But there are others to be more wary of who can act in his stead?"

Richard nodded and flashed his roguish grin.

"Right." Fiona ran her finger across his rough jaw, warmth radiating through her that she could understand him even in this state. "Well, guards aren't the worst thing in the Book. At least not the ones I've come across. We need to get to Dani's room. She's a fae. Clay skin and copper hair. Do you know where her room is?"

He nodded aggressively.

The footsteps walking past the cabin made them both jump. Fiona gave Richard's warm hand a squeeze. Only the sounds of their breathing hung in the air between them. Once the footsteps disappeared she pulled him up from the floor with her. She tugged off his hat, the bells sounding a tiny alarm, and dropped it on the ground. Quietly she opened the door to see that the area was vacant. With small steps she led them both outside.

THERE WERE WATCHTOWERS ON the three corners inside the stone wall. Fiona shaded her eyes from the bright light of the sun to see if any of the several guards on the watchtower looked their way. But none did. No one knew she was here, besides the one she had talked to. Did he stand outside her room waiting patiently, or had he left while she slept? Hopefully the latter.

She looked around and saw that there was a bricked well farther off in the courtyard near a smaller building. The scent of bread and smoke from that direction singled it out as the bakehouse. Murmuring to Richard her plan, she dropped his hand for the moment and led him confidently in that direction, keeping close to the wall.

A few servants stood in the courtyard, washing vegetables and clothes in buckets nearest the well. Though a couple of women gave Richard a second glance, no one paid any attention to Fiona. Hurriedly she grabbed a bucket of water and mumbled under her breath, eyes drawn to the ground, about taking it inside.

The kitchen held no real deterrent for them. As servants they were unseen as any other. Fiona dropped the bucket of water in the prep area near the pots and bowls. Drying bundles of rosemary and lavender brushed down from the ceiling, plucking at her hair. She swiped a cap from the few on hooks by the door and tucked her hair in smoothly. Richard handed her an apron to tie around herself.

Taking his cue, she grabbed a platter, quickly moving food onto it, and a bottle of wine. If they were to skulk around the guest rooms, better to look as if they were going to feed someone. The few in the kitchen barely glanced their way, and wanting to waste no more time, they made their way out.

But as they trudged back to the keep, Richard leading the way, a guard crossing their path stopped them. "Where are you taking those?"

Richard shuffled and mumbled something under his breath.

"Speak up, minstrel," the guard said.

"We're taking a meal to Lady Oatfellow, who has just arrived," Fiona said, deepening her voice to match the man's accent as best she could.

"Another one?" He raised an eyebrow. "Surprised his Grace has had two visitors in the same day. But come, it doesn't take two. You." He pointed to Richard. "You're supposed to be playing for the king right now, aren't you?"

Fiona's stomach clenched but she muttered out, "She asked for some entertainment while she ate. He was coming to see to it."

The guard rolled his eyes. "Very well, but you be in and out quickly. Pigs shouldn't travel the halls."

Richard nodded his head, lips pressed tightly together, though his golden eyes flashed darkly for a moment.

Fiona prodded him in the back and they hurried up the stairs and through the front door of the keep. Richard took the tray gently from her as they went up the narrow servant stairs to the apartment above. To think she had already arrived here once as a lady and now as a maid.

Her previous guard was unfortunately still standing outside her room. She turned away before he could see her face and whispered, "Which room is Dani's?"

Richard strode to a door farther down the hall and rapped on it with his knuckles. There was no sound.

The guard glanced at them.

Fiona cocked her head and said, "Come in," working to mimic Dani's voice. She pressed forward, swinging the door open. Richard led into the room. Fiona glanced back at the guard to see if he watched them, but he was already turned away again.

They set the tray down in the empty room. Though it was furnished much like Fiona's, it was larger by far. Beyond the bedroom was a connected sitting room with a chair facing a fireplace. The curtains were drawn, the bed unmade. But a satchel, similar in its texture and drab color to a Travel Guild one, lay on the bed out of place.

She picked up the satchel. A wooden spoon, a copper coin, and a bundled cloak were all that was left inside. So little to show for how far the fae had come.

"Dani must be in the Great Hall," Fiona whispered.

"John," Richard said, frowning at the wall across from the bed.

In the darkness it was difficult to see. She pulled back the curtains, letting light cascade over the focus of his attention, a large woven tapestry. Dani, with braided and partially hidden copper hair, knelt beside a tall human man. Richard's brother, John. His reddish-gold hair was clear as day, as were the three lions on his rounded shield. He looked down on her as she poured a pitcher of water on his feet. Perhaps a stark reminder to wake up to every day of what John expected from her. It was troubling that Fiona couldn't tell what expression she had on her face. "I can't believe she'd allow this. Is this...? Are they...?"

"Bonnet," Richard said quietly. He gave a deep sigh and then waved for her to follow him out.

They exited the room, but before they could take another step, the guard called out to them, "Halt. Is the lady in?"

Fiona paused at the doorway, plucking at her apron, head cast down. Richard nodded but turned back the way they came.

"Maid, stay here and wait for the one in here to wake. She'll need to be seen by the King immediately."

She took a tentative step forward. If he went away, then it would buy her even more time before someone learned Lady Oatfellow was missing. But if she got too close he might recognize her. Or worse, notice her *and* Richard, drawing unwanted attention.

Seeming to understand her hesitancy, Richard continued down the servant stairs, his heavy footfalls fading away.

Fiona slid up next to the guard, keeping her head down. She clasped her hands together in front and bowed before straightening and pressing her back against the door.

He lingered, staring down at her.

She was determined not to be caught out and said, "Happy to oblige." She giggled and turning her head slightly away as if shy.

The guard sighed deeply before making his way down the main stairs.

After a few moments to make sure he wasn't coming back, Fiona darted away from her bedroom door to the servant stairwell.

Richard blended in with the shadows. His wide eyes closed,

shoulders dropping as she appeared. Instead of going back down the stairwell, Richard tugged her arm, leading her into a narrow passageway that went behind the guest apartments and deeper into the keep.

"Where are we going?" Fiona whispered.

Richard didn't reply but his lined and grimacing face told her he thought it was important.

A small wooden door put them outside at the back of the keep. Hurriedly he took her through the short distance to the chapel with its tower. It was a small building on the outside, but as she stepped over the threshold, it seemed to continue on for ages on the inside. Dozens of wooden pews lined the floor on either side of an aisle. Some with kneeling parishioners who didn't look up from their prayers. Flickering candles on the walls accentuated the sun and lit the room up in wavering light.

The stained glass windows toward the ceiling took up the bulk of the space. The colored glass, set and shaped into tiny pieces, would've put the Court of Copper's to shame. Fiona found herself at the first one, oblivious to her steps. John and Richard stood side by side, arms around each other. The next panel depicted them fighting, not against each other but against some larger enemy of men. The next, a crack of lightning from the sky, splitting the army in two. The lightning was replaced by a womanly figure in the next panel. She was bathed in silver light between the two men. Larrakane.

Fiona hurried her steps, taking in each panel of the story. Larrakane holding hands with John and Richard, her silver light bathing them both. In this one a small group of humans appeared over John's shoulder, also in Larrakane's light.

The remainder of the panels told a story unfamiliar to her eyes. Richard and John now at odds with each other. John, larger than his brother, pushing him into the shadows. Larrakane kneeling before John, the light around him now blue. A crowned Larrakane and John, sitting on thrones, clasping hands side by side, as silvery-blue light bathed the small groups of humans around them. John's throne diminished hers.

Fiona squinted up at this last panel, trying to ascertain the look on Larrakane's face. It was inscrutable. But the stitched lines of black chains from her seat linked to similar ones from John's own throne shifted as the sunlight poured through the stained glass.

Richard pressed a hand to her waist and glowered. "Lovers are true."

She sighed, rubbing her temple. Richard's words were hard to interpret, but knowing they were not what they appeared on purpose gave her small clues. John and Larrakane had clearly been lovers, but that love had not been true. John's interpretation of his story was not surprising in the least. "I understand." She rubbed his arm. "Now let's find Dani and make her understand as well."

The Great Hall was an immense open space with vaulted ceilings making it feel taller than any she had ever seen before. Scores of heavy dark wooden tables littered the hall with grazing nobles at each. Banners of red and gold hung from the wooden walls. Rushes crunched beneath servant boots that moved up and down the aisles. Music drifted down from the balcony. The minstrels' gallery. A seat was clearly vacant in front of the other musicians. At the end of the hall, a raised dais stood with two wooden thrones, one smaller than the other, and several seats before them.

Dani sat on the dais in the smaller throne. She looked outward, disinterested. The once-vibrant Autumn Monarch was clouded and mute.

Fiona ducked back out of the Great Hall before she was seen. "Is there another entrance?"

Richard crooked his finger toward the back of the building and strode around.

They entered through another servant door. Food and drink carriers tarried here, crammed together. Many turned to the newcomers, but Richard's scowl had them quickly looking away.

Fiona darted in. She grabbed a serving tray and, before anyone could ask questions of her, followed after Richard back into the Great Hall. This time from a more approachable entrance beside the dais.

Fiona took a breath before traipsing lightly, half bowing to the throne. She hid her face from Dani and said in a deepened voice, "Milady, a new guest would like a word with you."

"Would they? And what would this dangerous guest like to say?" Dani said sharply.

"In private," Fiona said.

Dani stood abruptly, not bothering to say more, and walked to the back of the dais. She pushed open the wall showing a small alcove and hurried into it.

It could be a trap, Fiona knew. But she couldn't hesitate to wonder or inspect the surroundings. Her intuition told her to follow. So she did.

Richard slid from the shadows right behind her. He closed the hidden door, setting his back against it.

It was a small meeting room, with a table in the center. Maps of the pages of the Book were laid on it like a war table. Dani stood behind it, hands splayed on the wood as if she was using it to hold herself up. Up close, her reddish face was lined from years of laughter and many frowns. Faded copper hair lay limp against her neck, hiding her ears. The only ornament that gave any indication of the fae's usual style was an intricately woven small iron and obsidian ring. Narrowed crinkled eyes widened at seeing Fiona. "I thought it was you. You don't belong here."

"Neither do you." Fiona set down the tray, using the motion to cover her other hand resting near her scarf. "We have to put a stop to this, Dani. Together."

A look of disgust crossed the fae's face. She pushed back from the table. "He's what we *need* to be free. For so long he has been chained, but look around! He has the power to create like she does. And he has the power to tear us from her grasp."

Fiona shook her head. "He won't. Dani. He has to destroy all of us to be fully in control of his power." She had had enough time to truly parse the words of Stella. That he needed to destroy the very essence of Larrakane to be fully released. But everything, everyone, was Larrakane. "The Book can't remain for him to be free."

"No. You don't know what you're talking about. I've been conversing with him since I was inked. Doing the research. Asking and learning. We have brought him the keys. He is released. He'll destroy Larrakane soon and we'll all be home."

Richard started to speak, but Fiona held up her hand. "That's not true. Stella told me, Dani. She told me, after seeing what he truly was." She leaned in and said quietly, "I pulled her from of the dark edge."

Dani frowned. "You're lying."

"Why would I lie? I know you care for her. As she loves you.

She sacrificed seeing you again to make sure I could get here. To convince you there is no freedom with him." Fiona pulled out the metal object Stella had given from her veiled scarf. It was a well-sculpted small bronze fox.

"Stella is free?" Dani's fingers plucked the fox from Fiona's grasp, rubbing her thumb across it. Her cheeks darkened as she stared at the small creature.

"She is in the page of time, waiting for you. But there will be no time and no Stella if you don't help us stop this." Fiona held out her hand. "Come home so that we can save Spine. Save the Book. Everyone. I promised I would get her out of the dark, and I did. I make the same promise to you."

Dani blinked slowly, eyes on Fiona's hand. Then she straightened her dress, forcing herself to be taller. "You have no proof that's he's planning to destroy the Book. No. He wouldn't do that to me. Our bond is *unbreakable*."

"Dreary leaves float on the mound. Bonnet in the nest!" Richard muttered in Fiona's ear.

"No, I won't leave without her," Fiona said. Dani was bound to him. Breaking that bond was difficult, but was it impossible? Fiona felt she hadn't been aware of the right question to ask until now. Beyond the weariness of being mortal, there was something off about Dani. But what was it? "Your family is waiting for you, Dani. Your real family. There has to be something that will *help* you understand this will not end the way you planned."

Dani licked her lips. She shut her eyes, as if by removing her sight she was removing Fiona. "There is a room in the keep I cannot enter," she said in a small voice. She pointed up before thrusting the small bronze fox into her gown. It disappeared from sight. "Be gone from my sight before I call the guards," she said in a louder voice.

Fiona stared into Dani's eyes but she could read between the lines. With haste she exited the room, pulling on Richard. She didn't know how long they had before Dani lost her resolve or Richard's brother returned. She would find what would help Dani break away from this all and take her home.

THEY FLED FROM THE Great Hall, Fiona only stopping to walk normally once they were halfway toward the keep again. They bypassed servants and the main door. She preferred the small entrance Richard had shown her earlier now that she knew about it. She glanced at the chapel as they walked past, frowning at the lying stained glass windows. John thought himself bigger than Larrakane. There was no way he wasn't simply using Dani. But what would they find in the room the fae wasn't allowed to enter? And was it that she was forbidden to go in or physically couldn't?

Richard tugged at her arm, pulling her toward the wall of the keep and out of her reverie. He held her face tenderly for a moment before kissing her.

Confused, Fiona melted into the kiss. The sounds of guards running past them broke into the moment but also provided clarity.

He ended it, leaning back from her. He glanced at where the guards had gone before giving her a raised eyebrow.

"I was going to question your timing, but I see it was on point as ever," Fiona whispered.

"Damned watch," Richard said before sighing and leading her the rest of the distance into the keep. The hidden door was impossible to see from the outside, but he pressed his hand against the wall, pushing with confidence.

Quietly they plucked their way up the dusty narrow stairwell and back to the empty passageway. The only things that seemed to have disturbed the cobwebs in the corners must've been themselves earlier. The understanding that this truly had been Richard's home before sank into Fiona's mind. No one else knew of the passage and stairs. Just him. And probably his brother.

"Do you know the room Dani spoke of?"

Richard shook his head but waved for her to follow him. He turned sideways as the wooden hallway narrowed. Fiona did likewise, trying not to sneeze as dust flew in the air from their steps. After what felt entirely too long in the dark, cramped space, Richard pushed on the wall in front of him. It swung open noisily. She winced but there were no exclamations or footsteps to be heard. Nothing beyond their breath.

They stepped through into what looked like half museum, half storeroom. Cloth-covered paintings, wooden crates, busts, figurines and bulky furniture cluttered the room. Uncovered paintings, mostly of John in various poses—on horses, on a throne—crowded the wall. A large wooden chair sat next to a small table with a bottle of something brown in the middle of it all.

Richard picked up a metal helmet and rubbed his arm against it, shining it. "Light that meandered and lost." He brought it up to his head, apparently tempted to put it on, but stopped. His shoulders slumped and he placed it back on a crate.

"It seems your brother lives in the past. Let him wallow there. You are for the future." Fiona squeezed his hand and continued around the room, searching for a door.

There, with its own place under candlelight, was a statue of Larrakane. Fiona's version of Larrakane with a human face, coiled afro, and voluminous robes. She was sunk on the ground, arms wrapped around the legs of John. He was unmistakable in the marble. Her face was a mask of longing, gazing upon him. His, something akin to adoration.

Fiona jerked back from the statue, covering her mouth. She did not think Richard's brother could be more delusional, but here yet again was more evidence. In the chapel they were equals. Here his true feelings showed. Did he sit here and look upon this version of Larrakane? Plotting?

Richard's hands brought her back to the present, caressing her shoulder.

She leaned into him, breaking away from the appalling view to the tall ceiling. In the dim light of the candles Fiona noticed a trapdoor above. She pointed it out to Richard, but the confusion on his face told her it hadn't existed before. There was no ladder to be seen.

In short order, with hand direction and like mind, Richard had settled crates below the door in minutes. With one hand to help her up and another to hold the crates steady, he availed himself to her.

Fiona climbed up the crates and stood on the tips of her toes. Her fingers brushed against the door ring. She yanked hard and it swung down before her. Grasping the edges of the opened ceiling, she pulled herself inside.

Towering trellises of sweet-scented ripe blackberries surrounded her. The ground was cool and moist beneath her hands. Fiona dug her fingers into it. The soil crumbled beneath her.

"Bonnet?" Richard called from the storeroom below.

She pulled out her sturdy chain and lowered it down. Looking for somewhere to anchor it, she pushed the tongs of the grappling hook into the squares of a trellis.

Richard tried to pull through the trapdoor, but he hit an invisible barrier. It rippled from his impact. "Ducks skim the pond!"

"It must be a ward to this place." Possibly why Dani herself couldn't come in either. But then why could she? "Stay there. I'll be as quick as I can. Keep your thoughts to yourself, Mourninghide." Fiona gave him a quick smile and then walked away from the trapdoor.

The sky was amber, deepening out in the horizon. Beyond the berries were rows of trees, most without leaves, leading off in the distance. Fallen leaves swirled in cool wind, drifting to and fro like children with the whole of an afternoon in front of them. And not a care in the world.

Soft humming was the only sound that broke the stillness of the area.

Fiona frowned, uncomfortable with what she might find in this oasis. But she tugged on her scarf—in this place it was back to its original multi-colored form—and thrust her chin high before walking toward the sound.

Daniele sat among a pile of fading flower blossoms, staring up into the sky. Her copper hair splayed out behind her like waves of silken water, only interrupted by her long downy ears. Her red clay skin was draped in satin robes of bright bronze and gold that shimmered against the amber sky. Light copper tattoos danced across her smooth face. She looked up as Fiona approached and smiled wide. "Hello there, friend. Do you need a place to rest?"

Fiona shook her head. "No, but thank you, Daniele." Would

her name spark recognition or any effect? Was this like the page of mind or how the Binder had been trapped?

Hopping up from the pile of flowers, the fae dusted off her dress. "I'd hoped not to see you again, Fiona, but I see that was foolish."

"You know me?"

"Of course." Daniele sighed. "But I wanted you to save yourself. Save Spine."

"We need you to do that."

"Perhaps. But unless you're very obtuse, you'll realize I'm stuck here. Fae pacts aren't easy to break."

"But you made a pact with a creature that is bent on destroying everything."

Daniele flinched. "I was foolish, but I can't change the past."

When Fiona had made her own bond to Mac, it could only be removed if Mac released her, one of them perished, or it was broken. Though she hadn't worried at the time, she wished she had asked more questions about that third option. "Surely you built in a means of escape."

"What sort of fae would I be if I didn't?" She wrapped her copper hair around her hand and then let it fall back across her shoulders, almost hiding the sadness of her face. "But he was smarter than me. And separated what was chaos from Dani. She had already given up so much to get to him. I wasn't hard to take away."

Fiona's chest ached at her quiet words. She pushed past the feeling. There had to be some way to help. "What if I can reunite you again?"

Daniele shook her head. "She can't step foot in here. And I can't exist alone out there."

Fiona wouldn't see Dani perish. And convincing John to

release her was implausible. But what if she could carry the chaos? "What is it that you said once? I'm a little bit fae."

Amber eyes widened. "I suppose that explains your presence at all in this place. My, you do slip through the cracks. You're like a flaw."

"Well, I've been called worse things," Fiona huffed. "How would this work?"

"You have to carry me in your heart. If we harmonize, then I'll disappear." Daniele squished up her face in embarrassment. "Don't ever tell Arc I said that. He'll know I was paying attention." In this form she seemed more like the young woman of two hundred years ago than the tired Dani down below.

Wrapping her arms around Fiona, Daniele pulled her into a deep hug. With only a moment of hesitation, Fiona hugged her back. The tall fae was warm. Solid. The mix of scents from her skin was somewhat intoxicating. Fiona hugged her tighter, hoping this would save Dani.

Only the absence of cloth announced that it had worked. Daniele had vanished.

Fiona blinked. "That was uncomfortably close to what happened with Stella and Present." She skipped through the pile of fading blossoms back to the trapdoor. Before reaching it, she stopped, as the brilliant copper sky's rays warmed her through.

Wasn't it a beautiful, bright day?

"Bonnet!" a frantic Richard whispered up at the trapdoor.

She tilted her head. He was awfully close to falling from the chain. Had he been holding on all this time? Sense kicked into Fiona and she hurriedly leaned over the trapdoor. "I got distracted."

He frowned but made his way down the chain, giving Fiona room. She climbed down, removed the chain and closed the trapdoor. But on stepping off the crates, her body moved much faster than she had expected. The chain fell to the floor in a loud clatter. Fiona winced. They hadn't prepared for that eventuality.

"It's a good thing that he can't see or hear everything all at once." Fiona pulled the chain closer to her to put back into her scarf.

"What, have I to be omniscient when I have loyal servants who have eyes?" a deep voice said as a hidden wall door swung open.

John. Silken wine tunic and mantle hung from his broad shoulders. His golden strawberry hair waved almost imperceptibly as if there was an ongoing wind buffeting around him. The wild eyes and unkempt beard of his visage in the dark edge was nowhere to be seen. Only cold, beady pinpricks of amber focused on the scene in front of him. He snapped his fingers, the sound a whip crack in the impenetrable silence. Guards scurried around, flanking him on all sides, but he barely acknowledged them. His golden eyes were on Fiona and Fiona alone.

"Lady Thorne. How good of you to visit us. I will say that I didn't expect you to make it all this way, but now that you're here, I congratulate you."

"You're too kind." With a tilt of her head, she stood taller and lowered her arms from Richard, though she didn't move away. Larrakane's mark on her chest throbbed in beat with her pounding heart. She resisted the urge to rub it. It was oddly tempting to push this man until he was disoriented. Muddled. To crack his bravado. She could think of a dozen lyrical things to say that would have him questioning whether he was coming or going. What was this? Was it the newly harmonized chaos within her? She took a breath, focusing. "I would like to see Dani." If she could get herself back to Dani, surely she could reunite her with Daniele.

John grinned, making his mirrorlike appearance to Richard all too evident. "Are you sure you haven't already seen her?" He glanced about the room in exaggerated gestures as if searching for something. He pointed up toward the ceiling where the crates sat beneath the closed trapdoor. "Your friend seems to have forgotten whose castle this is." He winked at Fiona, smirking. The trapdoor disappeared. The ceiling was smooth as if it had never been there. "Temptation unveils us all, doesn't it?"

She was sure he didn't know they had already been through. But she wouldn't give him any answers. Instead of acknowledging his words, she focused her mind and her mouth on one thing only. "There is nothing here that could tempt me."

He chuckled. "I doubt that very much, but we shall see, shan't we?" With barely any movement, the scene around them changed. Crates and paintings were replaced with tables and flickering candlelight. The noise of chatter and thumps of mugs hitting wood encapsulated them. They were within the Great Hall again. And John was unnervingly close.

From the great dais at the end of the chamber, Dani's eyes widened at the sight of them. But her face quickly became disinterested in Fiona. She swept from the dais gracefully and bowed deep to John. "I am glad to see you returned, King John."

"I found a rat or two lurking in the storage room." He raised an eyebrow and called out, "But perhaps there is one more to find at my feet?"

Dani's drawn face paled, and she shuffled back into her chair without word.

Fiona had to get close to her. She subtly tried to grab Richard's hand so that she had them both in reach, but he was nowhere to be seen. She whirled around, panic clawing at her. When had he disappeared?

"Fear not." John leaned in, inches from Fiona. "He is in his place. See?" He pointed to the minstrel gallery.

Richard sat in the empty seat, lute in his arms. Though he seemed in control, shimmering light reflected around his body. Subtle dark chains wrapped around him. Had those been there before, or had John added them? If so, it showed an inkling of concern from him. She would work with the wariness. It was all she had besides herself at the moment. She remained silent.

Done with his tricks, John sauntered among the eating nobles, who greeted him enthusiastically at each table, to his own seat. He sat, patting the wooden arm of the throne where it took on a golden sheen. Guards quickly filled in around Fiona before she could move closer to Richard or Dani.

"You see Dani. She is well." John waved his hand toward the woman. "Though confused. But I have time to help her. It is what a good king does, of course."

Ah yes. A king. How far could she go in this pretend court game? She took tentative steps forward. "I request an audience with her," Fiona said, barely lowering her head in a tilt.

"So speak!" John banged his fist on the throne.

"In private." Fiona continued closer to Dani.

"Bah," John said. "You are entertaining but not enough for

this." He waved his hand. "Drop her in the void."

Guards grabbed Fiona, making her stumble back away from the dais.

"Cut!" Richard struggled to rise from his seat. "Turn the fire to the fool. Bonnets should flutter in the wind."

John barked a laugh, watching his brother. "You always were a gibbering simpleton. Quite better this way. I only wish Mother could see you now."

"She would be disappointed," Fiona said, struggling to pull her arms from the guards. "Queen Eleanor was a kind and gracious woman. She would never approve of what you've become."

"Become. Become? I am the most powerful creature who has ever walked this shambles of a cosmology. The Book. Pages. Bah, juvenile. This is a place of promise. Not some creator's experiment to give and take what she likes." He sat up straighter, chest heaving.

It was silent in the hall except for the subtle breaths of Richard, Dani, and herself. Like Larrakane, John didn't necessarily need to breathe. So then why was he full of exertion? There was something here, she simply needed more time.

"If this is such a place of promise, why this castle? This land? You have had a few hundred years to make your world. But all I see is a remnant of a past lost."

Dani rose quickly. "You have no idea what you're saying, Fiona. Think—"

John waved a hand, and Dani fell silent. "The investigator is bold." He nodded to Richard, still struggling to leave his seat in the gallery. "I can see why you find her so appealing." He crooked a finger at Fiona.

A subtle pull washed over her. Her mark throbbed but eased away quickly. And she found herself in the throne seated to the right of John. Where had Dani gone?

"You're right." He sat back on his throne and grinned at her. "I have wasted my talents on something beneath me. A memory of what should've been, had this fool not engaged our ally in his plans to ruin me. *But you are right, dear Fiona.* All that is over now. I have won. I should show you what winning looks like. For this is the last time you'll see what a true deity can actually do."

The stone walls wobbled as if drunken after a long night. Shifting and undulating, they didn't break or crack as an earthquake might rend them. They melted away.

The nobles and guests who lined the tables in the Great Hall screamed, as surprised as Fiona by the oozing gray stone. Many clambered up from the tables, trying to escape. Others sat stupefied, mouths open wide. But before anyone could flee properly, they abruptly disappeared one by one. It was no act. They had been as real as herself. And now they were gone.

The wooden tables splintered and shattered. The raining bits were sharper than she expected. Fiona dropped from the throne and ducked behind it as they came flinging directly at her.

John's gleeful laughter echoed over the sounds of the chaos he had started.

The throne turned to glass. Cool and see-through under Fiona's fingers. She backed away from it hurriedly, before it could have an effect on her, and frantically looked around for Richard and Dani. Fiona called out for them.

Richard's answering yell as the minstrel gallery disappeared under him beckoned her. She rushed to him, tugging at his arm from within the ethereal chains. She couldn't release him. He moaned painfully but muttered, "The nest."

Above them, the unmoored ceiling crumbled like cascading sand against the obscenely sunny blue sky.

Richard threw himself at Fiona, trying to cover her. Grains sifted across them, piling up around them as the sand packed up. They would be buried alive if they didn't get away. Shielding her eyes, Fiona looked for somewhere safe. Anywhere she could take a moment to either come up with a plan or turn, defeated, to Spine.

Sand stopped falling. It might be the only chance they had. She darted forward, pulling Richard struggling along, his invisible chains slowing their progress. Would the ground hold out beneath them? Or would that disappear too? With more steps than she desired they were out in the fading courtyard. The grass melding into nothing. The animals and servants had vanished. The stone walls were breaking down around them. Stone blocks fell directly over them. She cried out at the sharp pain. This was a pointed attack meant to hurt but not kill. He was toying with them.

"Does spring come too early?" Richard moved closer, eyes grazing over Fiona's arm.

"Don't worry about me. If you are. We need to get you out of those chains." She wished she could do something for his speech. If only she could get him out of this place and back to Spine. But would the chains allow it? The place had become a tinted blue void in mere moments. "Dani! Where are you?"

Across the boundless landscape John's strong voice reverberated: "Ah, still so concerned for your friend. You should be more worried for yourself. You are in my world. Though I created what I could in this *prison*"—he spit the word like bitter sap from his mouth—"I have also mastered her so-called Word. Do you want to see, dear Fiona? You might appreciate it." Buildings shot up around them. A stone keep, a small yurt, a two-story manor, and a small hut. Cobblestone streets shot from nothingness in front of the buildings fading into the unknown. The sky became a tranquil blue and the air filled with the sound of rushing aqueducts. Rapidly more buildings surrounded Fiona and Richard. Fresh blades of grass swayed beneath them and the smells of fresh-baked meat pies wafted under their noses. Spine.

"You love this city, yes? I have seen it in Dani's mind and in the countless dreams of my army. A piece of your precious Larrakane, nestled, connecting every page."

A sharp burst of lightning struck down at the wooden hut, and it went up in flames. Fist-sized ice pelted from the darkening sky at the stone keep. Fire sparked in the grass and smoke filled the air.

Before her eyes, Spine was sundered. Fiona gasped. Though she knew in her heart it wasn't her Spine, that did nothing to ease her fear. She couldn't let this happen truly.

"Did that hurt?" The sneer was evident in his echoing voice. "It'll hurt much more when she comes to ruin. When I destroy her very being and break free of her at last." Buildings rebuilt themselves once again. This time, the rounded top of the stone temple in the center of the city appeared before them. "Want to see it again?" A large flaming rock sailed out of the bright-blue sky and smashed into Larrakane's temple.

Was she to be forced to watch her city be destroyed again and again before her eyes? "Dani, please," Fiona called out to the fae.

Dani rushed out of the void. Her eyes were averted from the

display of Spine falling to ruin again. "I can't. You have to go without me. Run."

"Take my hand," Fiona hissed as Spine reformed around them again. They were in the Copper district with its narrow lanes and verdant vines creeping sinisterly around them. "Now. I won't leave you. It's not too late."

Vibrations rumbled around them as Spine, dear, blessed Spine, rebuilt itself slat by slat. The cacophonous market was alive with the smell of grilled meats and overpriced perfumes. A familiar carriage rolled to a stop at the stand, but the curtains were drawn. Fiona's chest throb increased beat by beat, her body beginning to cool. She gripped Richard's hand harder and inched toward Dani. "No one deserves this as punishment. Come home."

With a quick lick of her lips, Dani shook her head. But at the same time she darted out her hand and clasped it to Fiona's. Warmth and cold. Rain and sunshine flew from Fiona and into Dani.

Daniele's cream-and-gold tattoos surfaced, drawing themselves along her face as if she was being inked for the first time. She gasped, eyes fluttering as the lines of her face smoothed over. Her gaze focused on Fiona, amber eyes piercing hers. "Thank you." She gripped Fiona's hand tight and grasped on to Richard as well.

Something small and metal dug into Fiona's hand, but she didn't dare drop Daniele's to look at it. Fiona hurriedly thought of Spine, her Spine, and the cozy nook of her home. Dripping coldness swept over her from head to toe as the familiar tug of the page turn centered in her. Then her hand erupted in pain.

Daniele jerked back from Fiona with the force of a cleaving axe.

Fiona's eyes snapped to hers. They were wide. Pleading.

With another yank, Daniele gasped and then disappeared.

Screaming blocked Fiona's ears as frustrated tears poured freely from her. "You coward!" The stabbing pain that had eclipsed her hand was soothed in a rush by the familiar cold, dripping throb of Larrakane's protection throughout her body. She barely noticed the iciness of her fingers or that Richard held her closer in his arms.

"Now where did that chaotic little mouse go?" John's brow furrowed as he appeared before Fiona. "I've never removed someone she created from existence before. It felt like nothing." He smiled. "I'd like to try it again. Perhaps with you it would be more moving."

Richard threw Fiona behind his back but not before John could touch her. The cold from her body took over to her notice this time. Even Richard had a sharp intake of breath. But he didn't let her go.

John pulled back quickly. "I see Larrakane's got her devilish claws in you." He bared his teeth but swallowed and straightened, growing taller to tower over them. He spit on the ground. The surrounding Spine shifted from peaceful and vibrant to a flame-ridden city. "Because she couldn't handle the passion and imagination I brought to her, she chose to go back to ice, is that it? It is like a woman, to be so easily distracted by the sweet nothings of a charmer."

"Larrakane chose love when you proved to be not what you displayed," Fiona shouted.

"And you think he'll stay the same and love you all your days?" John pointed at Richard.

Richard stiffened, the chains pulling tighter. "Fools drown by the river of mad—"

"Let her hear your mistakes," John said, waving at Richard and shaking his head. "Before I throw her into the void. I am sick of her." He took a step toward Fiona and sneered. "*That* her precious deity cannot stop me from doing. When I have sundered your creator, maybe I'll save you."

"Enough. Your fight is with me." Richard pushed Fiona behind his back once again. He said loudly, "Let no one else suffer for our rivalry."

John ran a shaking hand through his golden-red hair. "Your mistakes. Suffer for your mistakes. If you hadn't made my mother side with you like a child, I would be king and you would be dead!"

"You let your ambition and the gift of magic overrule you. Even now you are too blind to see that you still have no control," Richard shouted at him. He squeezed Fiona's hand behind his back, pumping it twice.

Fiona tried to understand the dangerous game Richard was playing. He was trying to convey something to her, but what?

"You can make and break Spine here, of course. This is your cell. I am your warden. And while I have no doubt in my mind that you will enjoy torturing me to the end of time, you will *never* be able to topple what Larrakane has built." Richard took a step in front of her.

"I already have." The flames of Spine grew higher around them. "Even now my army invades each and every page and conquers in my name."

Richard squeezed Fiona's hand. "But not her realm. Not Spine."

Of course. If he was brought into Larrakane's realm, she should have more power there to overcome him. "You can't master everything without having control of Spine. Larrakane has more power than you," Fiona said. She gripped Richard's hand tighter, refusing to let go.

John made a face of disgust. "It is nothing to take what I want." With a sickening tear, the world ripped apart in front of them. Shreds of John's blue void draped into the view of Spine. John rubbed his hands together. "Absence does make the heart grow fonder." As if they were nothing more than puppets, John pulled Richard through the torn opening between the back cover and Spine.

Fiona and Richard's tightly gripped hands were wedged apart by the force of the pull.

"No!" Fiona stumbled forward after them, but a swinging black chain careened into her, knocking her back. Where had it come from? Had his chains still clung to him, invisible to them all?

A resounding snap. The torn entrance to her home disappeared. Along with Richard.

19

"ABSOLUTELY NOT." WITHOUT A moment's hesitation, Fiona connected to Spine. Her city. Her home. The connection was immediate. Stronger than before. Fiona took a step forward as the scenery around her peeled back, giving her a glimpse of the city. A riot of colors drew her eye upward to row after row of pages, revealed all at once.

Fiona stared open-mouthed at the twelve slices emerging from the center of the city. The horizon of the torn sky pressed so closely in that she could feel the vibration of the cacophony of mixing sounds from the now-visible pages. Each one a sliver pressed directly into Spine. The Book was far more open than it had ever been before.

Blaze with a molten woman, Soots, burning brightly against an unseen barrier.

Jets of water from the Depths as the merfolk built their own defensive wall.

Silken blue vortexes of air from Mistral throwing themselves toward the opening.

Rock golems from Cobbles, that could rival a small mountain, pounding their fists against their prison.

An airship pressed against the binding in Rise with humans shouting to be heard.

An army poised to march at the opaque wall stopping Kerus.

Nymphs and fae swallowed by a roiling copper sea as they broke down piece by piece their locked Copper door.

Brass swords and shields moving like blurs against their own combatants from the window into Phyta.

And a lone rocky dragon sitting at the entrance to the dragon page.

The abstract pages were the only ones silent. But still they shone.

Their connections revealed. Their citizens trapped.

Swallowing, Fiona took another step onto a worn and familiar road. Jackets swarmed the area, ladened with gear and weapons. She was outside the Hinge. But that was all of her Spine that truly seemed to remain. Pale and tepid, like pulped paper laid flat to dry, was the surroundings of her beloved city. This building stood, but the homes, the vibrancy, were gone.

"It's me. Investigator Thorne." She held up her hands to the approaching jackets, surprised to see the cuffs of her normal doublet on her. She shook her head. "Where is the Binder?"

An echoing crack in the distance pulled her attention. John, a giant of a man overshadowing all around him, held up his hands as the now-visible black chains split and ruptured from him. The torn entrance from the back cover around him shuttered but did not close.

The vignettes shook as if they, too, had been broken. Jackets began running down the street toward him, Fiona completely forgotten. Other page turners, those not prepared for the sight, stood ground watching with trepidation.

Why hadn't she come through to the same place as John took Richard? Was it her thoughts or— The cold metal digging into her palm throbbed. Opening her hand revealed the intricately woven ring Dani had worn earlier. But now it was amber and iron, wound together. Why had the fae given it to her? Whatever it was, it was so linked to Spine that it had brought her here. To the Hinge.

The blue void of the back cover closed with a sigh behind her. And a heavy weight fell on her shoulders from the scene around her. How was she to get to Richard and the Seasons? What could she do?

"Move, Fiona," she admonished herself. Slipping the ring on finger, Fiona ran, following the jackets, from the Hinge toward the center of the city. Toward John.

Her eyes frantically roved what was left of the area. Broken walls and collapsed buildings trailed out into the road, making for a hazardous path. Empty carriages and shattered chariots lay scattered. More than a few people had fled from here.

She faltered at familiar voices that rang out from everywhere all at once.

John's acerbic laugh bore through the air. "A trick, brother? Have you not learned your lesson?"

Richard's steady voice answered, "No trick of mine. I wouldn't waste cleverness on a coward."

The antagonistic words surprised Fiona. Why was he still baiting him? No. She had to focus on getting to them. The Seasons had come back. The city center would surely be where they all were.

Her anxiety proved useful as she stuttered to a stop a few feet away from a group of people fighting. Painted Edge, cloaked in blue, brawled with the Travel Guild jackets. Even without John the fight had already begun in Spine.

She took quick steps back, hoping they hadn't spotted her. Darting down an alleyway, Fiona let her intuition guide her. Her familiarity brought her without thought to the market.

Ripped tents of stalls fluttered in the air as if panicked themselves. Fiona picked her way through barrels and crates, rushing around trying to keep a bead on her surroundings. Closer now to the center, she saw the round stone temple on its grassy mound. She urged herself forward, bargaining with her wobbling legs that she would be there soon and could collapse then.

The massive rip John had made through to Spine stitched itself up, gray thread flowing back and forth.

As it closed, comforting coolness flowed over Fiona. Her hand flew to her chest.

Larrakane rose on a shimmering bridge of crystal-clear ice from the temple. The curls and coils of her black hair flowed around her, a protective veil. Streams of radiant light pulsated from her. Where they reached, calm confidence radiated.

Turners spun their faces toward the deity, heads held high as they basked her in light.

Not far behind, the bright, snowy face of the Binder streamed out of the temple in a freezing frenzy. Showers of snowflakes trailed behind him as he flew beside the deity.

The radiating power from the two was enough to knock Fiona to her knees. Tears pricked Fiona's eyes as relief washed over her. The temple had been obscuring her presence and that of the others. Thank the Book.

"You are a fool," Larrakane said, taking measured steps toward John's larger form. "Do you think to make me cower?"

"I think to make you irrelevant," John said dismissively. He smirked and a fountain of fire struck the entrance to the page of water, wreathing it in flames. Bubbles burst in the rapidly heating water.

Larrakane tossed her hand toward the page, dangling black

chains clashing against her robe. The bubbling subsided as the fire was redirected to Blaze. "Why don't you deal with me directly for once?"

"Oh dear, have you not heard? I make the rules now." With a snap of his fingers, Kerus's barrier fell.

Armor-clad smilodons leapt from the opening onto the parchment ground. Shields raised and weapons poised, they broke apart with righteous roars, darting off and around the jackets.

The Roma soldiers had finally invaded into Spine.

Fiona ducked behind an overturned cart, sounds of metal crashing into metal in her ears. The sharp smell of crisp ice had her pop back up to look.

The Binder thrashed out his hands toward Kerus. A wall of ice blocked most of it now, but it only seemed to delay the Roma soldiers as they hacked their way around it.

Taking the reprieve, Fiona jumped up and ran around the edge of the market, skirting the attacking soldiers and the defending jackets. She turned the corner, making her way around a crumbled building. She couldn't see the temple anymore, but Larrakane in the sky couldn't be missed.

Eyes on the deity as she ran, Fiona missed the cluster of enemies that spotted her. She stopped too late as a mixture of Roma and Painted Edge circled her. Swords drawn, they pressed in, eyes on her. Focused.

"He said to capture you," a lightly golden fairy said, a forefinger tapping on the side of her bald head. "Seems easy enough." She lunged at her.

Fiona dodged back, but hands grazed her from behind as well. They were too close. An opening between them? No. There were no gaps. If she dropped to the ground to scurry beneath any legs, they'd be on her and she'd be defenseless. She reached for her scarf, desperately trying to think of a useful tool in this situation.

A callused hand jerked her arm painfully back behind her. "Get the turn stoppers."

Fiona struggled, her lack of might no match for this many. Would an impromptu and likely dangerous page turn be her only option?

The man holding her dropped her arm, shouting a pained noise as a red marble whizzed by and struck him. Another one whistled through the air, hitting the back of the fairy and pushing her down. She cursed, angry burning welts appearing on her golden skin.

"Hail, Lady Thorne!" Henrietta's charming gravel voice shouted above her. "Grab on, lass, and hold tight."

A rope barely missed Fiona's head, but she happily seized the end of it.

The fairy, not one to be daunted, flew up beside her and tugged on Fiona's torn doublet, trying to pull her back down. With a rip the jacket pulled completely away from Fiona. The fairy careened back at the sudden lack of tension.

Fiona hurriedly climbed the rope, flying much closer than desired over the heads of those fighting below.

The golden hand of Gaili grabbed her wrist and hoisted her over the edge of the *Nimble Nymph*. Fiona had never been so glad to see stolen property in her life.

"Gaili!"

"Fi!" Gaili crushed her in a hug. "She's on, Captain!"

"Aye." Henrietta brushed her wild strawberry-gray curls from her face. She shouted, turning the ship's wheel, "Let's see if I can fly around a giant bugger now, mistress."

"To the temple, please, Henrietta." Fiona squinted; now aboveground she could see much easier.

Ice clashed with metal as the Binder continued to throw up walls. He seemed to be blocking off the entrance to the temple as best as possible and funneling as many Painted Edge members as he could around it.

Shadow cast over the airship but departed just as quickly. The emerald-scaled belly of Spine flew overhead. Nic, plaited pine-green hair swaying in the wind, clung to Spine's neck as they barricaded the other end of the Binder's funnel. A trap.

Netting whipped out from the Spring fae and their dragon toward the mass of surprised Roma soldiers. The trees on Spine burst to life as lithe druids rappelled down from them, swinging into the crush of the blockade. With their own vine whips, they snagged and grappled soldiers, subduing more than fighting.

Henrietta whistled as she turned the wheel hurriedly away from the ice and flocking trees. "I can't land this on the temple, but I can swing you above."

"Understood." Fiona grabbed the rope, preparing to drop down. "There are others, by the Hinge."

"We'll go back for them. Don't you worry," Gaili said. "The temple's the only safe spot in the area."

But for how long? Fiona swallowed thickly. She swung her legs over the bow of the ship, gripping the coarse rope tight in her hands. She clambered down, slipping on the rope but catching herself.

Strong hands grabbed her legs, supporting her weight. "I've got you," Richard grunted from below.

She let go of the rope, dropping into his arms in the center of the madness on the tiled roof. The noise of the Book was loudest here. The revealed pages were thin, pulled taut at the peak of the round dome high above them.

"Fiona, get into the temple." Richard pushed her toward the stairwell. "He won't kill me. Go!"

From the stairway door, Priestess Raina shouted, "You must come inside. The Seasons will handle the Painted Edge. We must put our thoughts to Larrakane so she can win."

"No! I'm not going to leave you again," Fiona said, holding to Richard tightly. "I knew the Leaves would have a plan."

He tugged at his beard, exasperated. "Of course you did. Blasted woman."

"They'll finish it," Fiona said leaning into him. "That's what they're here for."

Richard shook his head. "He's simply toying with us, Fiona."

The amber sky of the Court of Copper darkened rapidly as a shadow befell it. The faekin's loud gasps and panic reverberated through the barrier, echoing on the temple roof.

Fiona winced, the ring on her finger tightening. She reached out her hand toward the page, but Richard pulled her back.

Nymphs and fae scattered from view as a plunging molten rock broke free from Blaze and hurtled into their page.

Larrakane thrust her hands toward the page and barely succeeded in slowing the meteorite down. Her chest heaved as she crooked a finger, pulling the fiery orb out of Copper. She flung it at John, arching it with bludgeoning globs of ink for an attack.

But they melted away into the parchment of the broken city before they even came close to reaching him.

John merely smiled, unmoving. Unrelenting.

"I don't understand. He should be doing worse here, not better," Fiona whispered. This was Larrakane's realm, her slice from her own. What was wrong? Was it because Dani wasn't here?

"This is her realm, but it is attached to his." Richard grimaced but then shouted toward his brother, "She gave that ownership to him. And here, in this place, the coward is still in *control*."

"This is the difference between you and I, Richard." John smirked. "You think it's about the land. I know it is the people who matter."

"We won't let you into our hearts as easily as you may think," Fiona shouted at him.

"You will be humbled when your peers fall to their knees in worship of me. Perhaps then you will see what you have failed to grasp. That is, before I remove them from existence too." John grabbed at Fiona.

A flurry of parchment scattered into his view, each piece cutting him. He swung his arms at the daggers of paper, momentarily distracted.

"Richard, it has to be now." Larrakane's voice echoed, a multitude of sounds harmonizing into one—the language she had so desperately called out for help in. *"I will make it painless as promised."*

Fiona's eyes snapped to Richard. Did he understand Larrakane's language?

Richard said nothing in return. He simply stepped away from Fiona toward John. "Fiona. Go inside. Please."

With a sickening drop in her stomach, she reacted before she could contemplate further and threw her arms around him. "Absolutely not. Who cares if it's painless. It is a preposterous plan. What are you thinking?"

His eyes widened. "This is our last thread to pull. And we've come to that," Richard whispered to her. He pulled her close and pressed his forehead to hers. "I have to die so that he can be weakened. We are the same blood. The only ones." She shook her head, but he continued, "I am the warden. He is the prisoner. But in this mortal space he can be destroyed if I am destroyed."

"That's why you wanted to come to Spine." Her heartbeat throbbed in her ears. Richard wouldn't have been able to leave Rise unless the page was broken. He had let himself be captured so that he could get to John. Get to Larrakane. Of course Richard was willing to make the sacrifice. He always had been. All those goodbyes and unwillingness to think of a future with her. "You knew all along."

Richard simply nodded. "It was my charge for fighting. For asking our mother to choose sides that beget this entire mess. Don't you see I have to do this? There's no one else who can bear the burden." He placed his hand on her cheek, then pushed her toward the temple stairway.

"Come, Richard. I can only hold on to this power for a moment more," Larrakane urged with a trembling voice.

"No!" Fiona shouted out toward the deity. "You can't ask this of him. It's not right." His life versus that of everyone in the Book was an unfair request.

"What else can I do? You of all people know I am only what is made of me. The Book's faith in me isn't strong enough to defeat John any other way. If I sacrifice myself alone, it will not be enough." Larrakane stumbled on the melting water of the ice bridge, falling to one knee. She threw a hand toward the door of the fae page, gritting her teeth. "I'm so sorry. To all of you. I'm trying but—"

The Copper page's barrier burst open. A crashing wave of

amber sea washed into the fray. Nymphs and fae floated out, hurriedly running toward the temple.

Radiant white sunbeams encircled the chaotic creatures, throwing them off balance. They tugged at the offending magic but a boisterous Mac shouted at them, encouraging them to enjoy the sunshine. Some of the fae began to slump over, falling asleep, but not all.

While Larrakane regained her footing, the Binder became her shield, pelting ice and darkness toward John. More melted than not, barely striking the giant of a man.

They were fighting still, but even with as much ground as they took from the Painted Edge, it was John who stood victorious. He called out, "You are the inheritors of a new age, my allies. Cut quick, for to us go the spoils of this infantile war."

Even now he was lying to them. Soothing them all. They both, Larrakane and John, had been lying and soothing people for hundreds of years. One out of fear, and the other for control over a life he felt owed. Oh yes, a deity had to be defeated. But sacrificing Richard wasn't the only way. Fixing Spine. Empowering Larrakane. There were other avenues.

Fiona dashed toward the temple doorway, but instead of going down with Priestess Raina, she ran up the temple stairs toward the peak. Had it truly been almost a year since she had been here last? Her booted feet pounded the stone stairs, and she pushed herself through the last arch and scrambled up the slim bell tower.

She could see clearly the twelve pages slicing through at their thinnest point. Could she interact with them all at once? The ring pulsed on her finger.

With the same curiosity that had carried her through life,

she dived toward the slices, standing in the merging point in the tower of every single page. Sounds of crashing waves, snapping timber, and shouting voices echoed in her ears and mind. Hot, sweaty skin flushed against rocky, itchy sand and cooling wind. She connected with all of them. As if she no longer wanted to turn one page, but flip through them endlessly. Pulled toward them, she felt herself being stretched thin.

The ring vibrated again. She steadied. Centered. Rooted in place.

"Listen to me!" Fiona called out across the Book. Her words scattered and echoed among the margins of the worlds, seeking their targets. She rushed on as the icy bridge below Larrakane began to crack. "They are lying to you. He has to wipe everything connected to Larrakane away to be in power. And that includes you. All of you. Even if you fight for him, he will get rid of you like you're nothing more than a speck of dust. Don't believe me? Ask yourself, Where is Dani? Where is the Autumn fae? Where is your leader of the Painted Edge? He removed her from existence. He'll do it to you." Fiona wet her lips and carried on speaking as the sounds from the pages quieted down. "But Larrakane won't. Yes, she's lied to us too. Made us believe she's a deity with vast power to do and be everything and everyone to us. But she's not. She's not all-knowing. She's just like me. Like you. All of you. She has experienced loss. Her sisters are gone from her, and she mourns them. Who among you hasn't felt the loss of someone you love? And done things you regret?"

A fiery bolt shot toward her. She flinched. A foggy wall of light surrounded her before the bolt could make impact. She had to keep going. That he turned his attacks on her meant she was onto something. There were those who were listening, just as there were those who were still fighting around her.

"Larrakane's not mortal, no. But what's more mortal than looking for love? Finding it, losing it, and when it feels like all hope is gone, seizing the chance when you find it again? Larrakane is not faekin or beastfolk, but she's also not unchangeable. She shifts and conforms to be what she thinks we want. Who among us hasn't changed who we are for someone else's notice or affection? Who hasn't made a mistake? Or tried the wrong thing for what you think is the right reason?" Fiona took a steadying breath. "I am far from perfect. My friends know my stubbornness and tendency to talk before I think. But I put in the work to make things better. Larrakane is not perfect, by any means. But she has been putting in the work, fighting for centuries to fix her mistakes. To make sure the futures we wanted can even be attempted. She is a part of us as we are a part of her. Bound even. I believe in her ability to make amends to us. I have faith in her. Can you keep faith in her too? Because that is what will end this fight once and for all. Give her that chance, here and now."

Voices echoed her thoughts, ringing throughout the diminished Book. Some loudly, others whispering. Many simply said the name of the deity, but with more voices joining, the tempo and volume increased.

"You she-devil," John screamed out. Disregarding all else, he pushed his way through his allies and fighters at his heels toward the temple, scattering them about. He smashed his hand down into the building, swiping at Fiona.

Wind swept against her face as the sky darkened, and she involuntarily closed her eyes. But cold, hard ice against her back made her open them, surprised. Gray robes billowed around her as she lay beside Larrakane's relaxed form.

"Enough," the deity said quietly. She tilted her head, regarding John.

He began to diminish, his form shrinking away from the bridge and Larrakane. With this sudden change, John shrieked. Flinging his hands about, waves of sharpened quills sprung from him toward Larrakane.

She effortlessly parried his attacks with a wave her finger. "Enough," she said again.

The voices of the Book increased, her name rising louder than the sounds of the pages.

The blackened chains on Larrakane broke. Their bits and pieces showered the bridge around her and faded away. "I will not bind you again in the hopes you can be persuaded. I have learned that lesson. But the powers that I gave you, I can now remove. And with them, a befitting ending."

From the edges of Mistral, azure poured in above them, bringing back Spine's familiar sky.

An arc of fire burst from Blaze, bouncing from phoenix wing and lava to layer and blend itself with the sky, turning into a deep sunset.

Rock and dirt tumbled from Cobbles onto the pale parchment landscape of Spine.

With barely a nod, Larrakane drew water from the Depths to wash over the new ground, painting the city like a watercolor. Green blades of grass shot up, brightening the land around them.

Fiona sat up, bewildered, and scanned warily for John's retaliation, but she saw no sign of the man remaining.

WORDS OF ENCOURAGEMENT AND belief turned into surprised murmuring from the many surrounding the temple. The pages' cacophony harmonized in wonder at Larrakane's power. Only Fiona and Larrakane, it seemed, remained silent for a moment more.

"So I am a liar, eh?" Larrakane raised an eyebrow, but her softened face showed mirth at the question.

"Sometimes the truth is a bit cleverer than a lie." Fiona took a shaky breath. "This kind of power works for people like you, if I remember correctly."

"That you do." Larrakane held out her hand toward Fiona and helped her up on her feet. "Thank you for trusting me."

Fiona withdrew her hand gently and stared at the deity. Her power could hurt her, but there was more truth to give and only a moment to do it in a way she thought she would understand. "I chose to believe in you because I believe things can be different. I saw you. You asked for help. So let us help you this time."

Staring at Fiona, Larrakane said nothing, her smooth brown face a mask hiding her thoughts.

She met eye to eye with the deity. Not as a challenge, but as an equal. But before Fiona could say more, Larrakane turned abruptly away.

The bridge flowed like a rapid waterfall under Larrakane's feet as the deity strode down to the gathering crowd. Fiona hesitated before following. Instead of settling near the deity, she turned away, jogging back to where she left Richard. It wasn't long before she saw him running toward her.

He grabbed Fiona's hand as if she would disappear again. "What in the devil made you think to do that? And how on earth do I get you to never do it again?"

Fiona pressed her hands across his chest without shame or fake reluctance and leaned into him. "You could kiss me quite a bit to start."

His eyes widened. "Fiona, I'm-."

She shook her head. "Sir Mourninghide, I do believe a request has been made."

"Well, you certainly deserve any request I'm able to fulfill." Richard kissed her softly.

"Keep that in mind," Fiona said. She tugged his hand, drawing him after her.

Druids, jackets, and page turners in between gathered around Larrakane, talking to her all at once. She seemed to be able to carry on multiple conversations, though Fiona couldn't hear her speaking at all. Priestess Raina and Fali flanked either side of the deity. His elephas bulk gave Larrakane a small amount of breathing room from the crowd, but not by much. Raina seemed to glow at being so near to Larrakane. She waved to other page turners who had taken tentative steps, encouraging them to come closer.

The Binder—his long white hair in disarray, his dirty and torn clothing untouched, forgotten perhaps—stood off to the side. Snow piled beneath his bare feet on the ground as he watched the gathering carefully. He seemed almost wild, reminiscent of his younger self. Mac stood beside him, golden tattooed hand on his arm as if steadying him.

Nic sprung from the edge of the crowd over to the duo. The druid patted the Winter fae's shoulder, smiled at Fiona as she approached them, then said, "The druids are seeing to anyone wounded."

"That's good," the Binder said distractedly.

"And the jackets are…?" Nic raised an eyebrow.

The Binder ran his pale hand through white hair and glanced about as if realizing that was a question he should be able to answer. "Marcius and Marcia have it in hand."

"Of course." Nic frowned at him but turned their full attention to Fiona. "That was quite the speech, friend."

"I slightly made it up as I went along."

"Couldn't tell a bit." Mac winked at her.

Fiona shook her head. "Thanks." She swallowed hard and said, "I'm sorry. About Daniele. I tried to help her, but I think I was too late."

The Seasons glanced at each other. Only Nic seemed to have the power for immediate words. "It's not your fault, Fiona. We know you did everything you could."

"It'll be hard to exist without her." Mac lowered her head.

The Binder rubbed his throat, closing his eyes. "No one can replace her. That is a fact."

"In the end she helped as much as she could. With this." Fiona showed them the ring that allowed her to withstand being in all the pages at once. "She made sure to give it to me."

"It's her binding to Larrakane. She must've separated it from herself," the Binder said, handing it back to Fiona. "A symbol of her hope in you."

"Received by none other than one who could use it most to

move forward." Mac gave a small smile. "I'm not surprised."

Fiona was. That Dani had said she had high hopes for her played at the edges of her memory. The Autumn fae truly did always have another path forward prepared. Fiona glanced at Richard, wondering his thoughts.

He nodded, silent, and squeezed her hand.

Dodger and Marcia jogged up, only sharing the barest of surprised faces at the gathered group. They both saluted the Binder.

"Jackets have secured most of the dangerous forces." Marcia's natural hag form shimmered slightly, but she remained herself.

"The Hinge is still standing, so we've instructed teams to fortify and put them there," Dodger said.

"Good. Good," the Binder said, staring off.

Fiona followed his gaze to Larrakane still talking to Raina. Ah, yes. He probably hadn't seen the deity in person in some time. "Perhaps you should speak with her."

He shook his head, seeming to realize he was staring. "There is much to be done."

Marcia nodded. "Now we get to the hard work of rebuilding."

Fiona sighed glancing out at the ruined structures and the still-visible pages. "I don't even know where we start with moving forward and rebuilding."

"I could use a drink. Can probably get a quick version of the Thread up shortly. If you all ignore what you're about to see." Mac clapped her hands together. The atmosphere changed into a warm, cozy interior. Sketches of paneled wooden walls flew up around them with wide windows letting in a waning summer light. Wooden tables, bar stools, and a few kegs appeared in the space. Mac sighed. "I may not be able to rein myself in again now that I've let loose. But hopefully this will do."

"I trust that if anyone can tend to the spirit of recovery it would be you, Marcela," Larrakane's smooth voice said lightly. The deity stood at the threshold of the temporary Thread. Though she seemed at ease, her shoulders were high and her hand clenched her robe. "May I join you?"

They murmured yeses and *of course* as they made room for her. Mac, at ease in her element, gathered mugs and began pouring drinks for everyone around her. Most sat on stools or leaned into the cushioned pillows with some relief. Fiona sat next to the deity with Richard next to her. Laughter threatened to overcome her at the quick change of scenery, but it was clear the deity was trying to ease a word in with the group without commanding them.

"Thank you all for what you have done. For your sacrifices and your strength." She glanced at Fiona before saying, "I truly don't know how to ever make it up to you, but I would like to know. I have talked to many people so far but would like to hear from you."

Confused, eager, and careful glances met each other around the room.

Fiona leaned toward the deity. "Daniele's actions were mistaken, but her motivation was not. Do not simply say you have given us freedom. Give us freedom." She waved her hand toward the windows, looking out to the still-visible pages. "The people will accept you or deny you again, but you will still be you regardless."

Larrakane inclined her head, looking at them all in turn. Fiona hadn't realized that she couldn't hear the others when they spoke until she stared at Richard, his face taut but mouth moving. A moment of private given to everyone. How enigmatic.

"You are my steadfast generals. I gave you nothing but responsibility, and as has been suggested, I can start with freedom from that responsibility." She raised her hands, and with a small wave, the thin line of the dark edge receded from between the pages. Each merged into each other, their borders suffusing with a mixture of the page on either side of them.

Astonished cries floated out from the sliver of pages as each disappeared from view within Spine.

The tug Fiona always felt to Spine pulled her forward. She lurched across the table before the pull snapped. The homey, warm connection spread throughout her body. Restful. Peaceful. Instead of an absence or a pull, she felt solid. Her eyes flew up to Larrakane's. "What did you do?"

"I removed the barriers. Traverse through the pages however you please, wherever you like. No one is bound to me or this place anymore." The deity tilted her head. "The city will remain though. A connected pathway, but perhaps we build it for newer days."

"Simply like that?" Fiona said with a raised eyebrow. Others around her seemed to be as flustered. Page turners rubbed their arms, stepped out into the grass. Took steps and exclaimed to themselves.

"A new chord for a better melody." Larrakane's human form shimmered into her natural abstract shape. Though her aura was dimmed, her ebbing gray light was still vibrant enough to fade out everything behind her. "A truth instead of a lie."

"You should rest." The Binder had settled some distance away from the deity and the group in a darkened corner of the makeshift bar, perhaps subconsciously.

Larrakane's form diminished. "Of course. There is much to do." She stood gracefully and inclined her head to all.

Fiona shook her head. "You two are absolutely draining. You think the world of her, and she adores you. If we're doing second chances, why not began with you two?"

The Binder jumped to his feet. "Investigator Thorne-"

Mac cut him off: "She's not wrong, Arc." She grinned over the rim of her mug. "You're not getting any younger."

Nic nodded. "Why continue to waste time pretending?"

"Mac. Nic. Not you too." The Binder pushed a hand through his hair. His shoulders sagged and he muttered to himself, "This isn't how I saw this conversation going."

Larrakane floated toward him. "Perhaps you would take a tour with me, to assess the rest of the pages. Help me put things to right?"

"In an official capacity, of course." The Binder tilted his head and stood taller. More like his old self. But his hand shimmied around Larrakane and he grasped her close. He murmured to her. Her aura brightened.

Fiona thought she heard a hint of exchanged apologies. Fiona assumed the Seasons' hearing was far better than hers, for, with unspoken words, Nic and Mac sprung from their areas toward the Binder.

They each hugged the blushing Winter fae and then pulled away. With no more than a backward glance, Larrakane and the Binder took two steps out of the makeshift building and were gone from view.

Page turners who had finally noticed the temporary bar piled in, sitting on the floor, leaning up against crates, and generally packing themselves in. Mac quickly got into her routine of giving drinks and welcoming people, though a touch faster and brighter than previously.

Turners exclaimed about the change to themselves and Spine. Throughout the city reports came in of vibrant and unyielding paths that seemed to run like roads within Spine to each of the pages. Many were already testing them out, walking from one to the other and exploring the connection. Other reports came of the druids helping allies and previous enemies alike remove to a sturdy building of vines on the dragon Spine to recover as the Hinge bustled with activity.

"I can't believe Arc left," Mac said, making her way back to the weary group. "Good on him."

"Who is going to keep this lot in shape now?" Raina said. "It can't all be on you, Marcia."

"An open council might be nice." Fiona gestured to the group around the table. "With the changes, perhaps we should follow an example from Copper—though don't tell them I said that." She grinned. "There's no reason for the Leaves anymore. Nor the Guardians, though they might react differently to that knowledge." Fiona pulled away, looking at Richard. "I'm sure we can get an able council going with all the pages and Guardians involved."

"All the ones that remain as Guardians, yes," Richard said gruffly. "Clearly I'm willing to be involved, though I don't know if I consider myself a Guardian of anything anymore." He patted his heart. "I no longer have the connection to Rise."

Had he asked for that from the deity or had she simply given it to him? Fiona leaned into him and stroked the rough beard of his jaw with her thumb. "Would you consider puttering around for a bite while we rebuild Spine?"

"Are you asking me to stay with you?" Richard made a

humming noise and tilted his head. "Isn't that moving a bit fast for you?"

A lightness drew itself over her exhaustion and she laughed. "I think it's better to keep you in sight."

"I think the same of you," Richard said before kissing her softly.

Fiona smiled into the kiss before humming a harmony of her own making.

Epilogue

THE SAILS SLAPPED AGAINST the hoist as the wind picked up from the dancing gray-white swirls near the front of the ship. Fiona leaned over the railing, hand gripping the wood as if she might be blown overboard at any moment. And she very well might, with all the rocking and lurching. She sighed and rubbed her face. She had promised him a calm trip. A nice, easy trip. But it was just like the emperalis of Mistral to decide to start their festivities a bit early.

"Are we coming up on the connection?" Didia stood on her tiptoes, peering over the rail with her spyglass. She whistled. "Look at those sparks! I've never seen anything like it." She dropped the spyglass, letting it swing down her chest, and scribbled in her notebook.

"Yes, well with nine pages left and a blend of neighbors between each one, there was bound to be something new to show you." Fiona grinned at her old neighbor. "Worth letting go of the page of time for?"

Didia tilted her head. "Almost. I'll let you know when we get to that mushroom page you're always talking about. Or when I retire in Copper."

"I don't think I've ever heard about you seriously retiring before," Fiona said.

"Well, there's a first time for everything." Didia winked at her. "No one thought the Roma would fall, either, but even the oldest of us have our declines."

"Oh, stop that, Mistress Humbledraft."

Richard's deep voice surprised Fiona. She prided herself on not jumping as he came up behind her.

"You and I both know who is older out of the two of us. If I'm not falling to pieces, neither are you." He wrapped his hands around Fiona's waist and pulled her toward him.

Fiona leaned back against Richard, smiling. Though there had to be some adjustments to sharing a life, they seemed well worth it. For one, visits with her mother had never been easier. Fiona tipped her head up to look at him. She tugged on his single curl of graying locks. Every time a new gray strand appeared, she grinned. For some, aging would be a rough ride. For them, another day. "And what are you doing that you so sneakily appear to scare me?"

He snuggled into her neck and whispered, "Simply keeping you on your toes, Lady Thorne."

"Toes kept, Lord Thorne." She turned to tease him, but the ship tilted aggressively, and she gripped the railing instead. Sparks of light drew closer in the distance. They had safely bypassed the air elemental party and gotten to their main destination: the new Lightning Edge.

"I thought you said this would be an easy ride." Richard scowled.

"And so it should continue to be! If anyone knows how to skirt around an emperalis party and hold us on the edge of a lightning storm, it's Henrietta." Fiona waved to the captain.

Henrietta's face was squished, squinting in the distance as she held the wheel steady. Matteo sat at Henrietta's elbow, sketching quickly on parchment as they sailed. Gaili stood on the other side of her, pointing in the distance, mouth moving a mile a minute. She noticed Fiona first and waved back before prodding Henrietta to do the same. The captain diverted her attention long enough to give a nod before pulling Gaili closer and whispering something to her. Gaili laughed, pink curls bouncing with whatever they shared between them.

Richard laughed. "If anyone knows how to be distracted by two fawning fauns, it's Henrietta."

"Didia, what do you—"

But the older lady was nowhere near them. Already slipping away toward the steering and Captain Henrietta. No doubt to gossip about Fiona and Richard.

The ship lurched again. Fiona held on to the sides as it rocked, deftly darting away from the lightening. "I should think you like an adventure now and then."

"An adventure, yes. But only with you, my love." Richard gripped her hand, rubbing his thumb over it lovingly. His gray-touched golden-red hair whipped into a frenzy in the wind.

* * *

Glossary of The Planar Pages series

Find expanded lore, world information and more at
go.dhalerambo.com/tpp

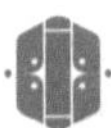

Spine: A realm connected to every page in the Book. All page turners live here and can suffer ill effects for being gone too long. Split into over a dozen districts.

Seven Known Pages (as stacked in the Book)

Elemental Chapter

Blaze: page of fire, contains salamanders, flarions, ragnis, and other fire elementals

Depths: page of water, contains water elementals, merfolk, turtles, and more

Mistral: page of air, contains sylphs and other air elementals

Cobbles: page of earth, contains gnomes and other earth elementals

Mortal Chapter

Restless Rise (Rise): page of humans, contains a central mountain with floating islands all round it

Kerus: page of smilodon, elephas, and ursidon

Court of Copper (Court): page of faekin: fairies, fae, fauns, centaurs, and nymphs

Terms

Aer: language from page of air, Mistral
   Aguan: language from the Depths

the Binder: leader of the Guild

the Book of Larrakane (the Book): all the known pages of the universe

bookmark: token from a page, used to travel there by a page turner

the Card: a free leaflet by the Travel Guild

the Church of Larrakane: organization devoted to worship of Larrakane

Circle of Seasons (the Seasons): ruling group in Copper before the Order of Seven

Claire: a language from page of fire, Blaze

Depth's Door: a lake in Spine

diamonnette paper (papers): universal currency

dusty: used to described a page turner who's ready to retire

elephas: like elephants standing on their hind legs, from Kerus

faekin: fauns, fairies, pixies, centaurs, all from the Court of Copper

Fallen Bubble: a cocktail

flarion(s): fire elementals who live in pools of magma from page of fire, Blaze

the Followers: a subset of the Church of Larrakane

format: slang for rumor

the Gilded: six leaders in the Travel Guild, including the Binder

the Hinge: Travel Guild headquarters

inked: blessed by Larrakane with the ability to turn pages

the Inking: historic event that created page turners

jacket(s): slang for officers of the Guild

kora: fish with an oily excretion from page of water, Depths

Larrakane (she/her): bestows the ability to turn pages and creator of the Book

Order of Seven (the Seven): elected council overseeing Court of Copper

pagemark(s): safe places where turners can move between pages

page turners (turners): people who can move between pages

the Painted Edge: a group of rippers marked by blue tattoos on their chests

pulp: slang for creatures from various pages who are not page turners

ragnis: metallic-boned quasi-flame creatures from page of fire, Blaze

ripper(s): slang for thieves and smugglers across pages

Rock of the Nest: home of dragons

Schiflan: a language spoken from page of humans, Restless Rise

skimmer(s): slang for tourists visiting other pages

skips: slang for criminals on the run

smilodon(s): catlike people, from Kerus

Sod: language from page of earth, Cobbles

spotter(s): cartographers

sylph: stark white air creatures from page of air, Mistral

the Travel Guild, the Guild: organization that regulates all the comings and goings of page turners in the Book

unread turner: slang for someone new to being a page turner

ursidon: bearlike people, from Kerus

the Word: Richard's particular magic

About the Author

D. HALE RAMBO IS a fantasy author whose books transport readers to wondrous worlds filled with magic, mystery, and humor. With compelling and memorable characters at the heart of her stories, Hale Rambo weaves tales to entertain and enthrall.

A lifelong storyteller, she's been writing and creating other worlds since she was old enough to mark them on her bedroom wall.

When she's not writing, you can find her enjoying a stiff cosmopolitan while reading mysteries alongside her favorite pet companion.

Discover more about her wondrous worlds, the versatility of gnomes, and fun fae cocktails at www.dhalerambo.com

Also by D. Hale Rambo

A SERIES OF DECISIONS ON KAIRAS
A completed cozy high fantasy trilogy set in the world of Kairas
where the deities may be sealed away but their troubles are not.
Buy it now: teleport yourself to books2read.com/toat
Book 1, TOOLS OF A THIEF
Book 2, COMPONENTS OF A CASTER
Book 3, ROUTES OF A RANGER

THE PLANAR PAGES
A completed epic fantasy mystery series with investigator Fiona
Thorne and her motley crew of friends.
Book 0, HIDDEN WORDS (newsletter exclusive prequel)
Read it for FREE by signing up for my newsletter at
www.dhalerambo.com/freestory
Book 1, BETWEEN THE LINES
Book 2, HARD BOUND
Book 3, PRESSED
Book 4, FRAYED EDGES
Book 5, COVER TO COVER

If you enjoyed *Cover to Cover*, spread the word by writing a review! Reviews really help my books get into the right hands, so I'm super grateful for every single one.

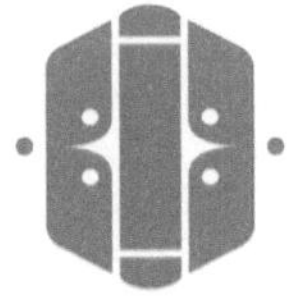

About *HIDDEN WORDS*

Life flourishes in the Book, a world of stacked realms spanning the ages. Those who can travel between them are page turners, blessed with the power to go from one page to the next.

For investigator Fiona Thorne, turning the page is normal life. Solving mysteries is where the excitement lives. No case is too small to ignite her curiosity, no page too familiar to explore.

Hired by her charming, gossipy neighbor to track down a shipment of rare books, Fiona thinks it'll be easy. She'll search for clues, sort out the issue, and be back in time for her nightly cup of coffee. And her reward? An introduction to one of the most reclusive leaders in Spine, the Druid Elder.

But that dream slips through her fingers as she realizes there's little evidence. She'll have to kick this investigation into high gear if she wants to impress her neighbor and earn her way into a privileged connection.

You can only read HIDDEN WORDS by signing up online for my newsletter at https://www.dhalerambo.com/freestory

9 781960 123312